She's Dangerous When She Sings

SHE'S DANGEROUS WHEN SHE SINGS

Patty,
In this world there are good friends & dear friends. The dear friends remain friends no matter the distance or circumstances. You, Patty are among the *very* dear friends in my life. I love you,
Kelly

Kelly Scott

P.S. Just because you are a very dear friend does not mean you can lie to me about these books. Whether you love them, hate them or are indifferent, I'd really like to know! Thanks!

To order additional copies of this book, contact:
Xlibris Corporation
1-888-795-4274
www.Xlibris.com
Orders@Xlibris.com
67899

CONTENTS

ACKNOWLEDGMENTS

Projects such as this one cannot be completed easily without much help and encouragement. So I would like to thank my good friend and teaching colleague Capri Helgeson, who volunteered to read this in manuscript and correct my errors. She kept watch to make sure my hero didn't lose his accent and my characters didn't misuse the English language too much. What she missed, the editors at Xlibris caught. Thank you everyone for helping to maintain my dignity.

I would also like to thank my brother-in-law, Charlie Scott, for his encouragement and enthusiasm when he read it. My ego is always in need of a good cheerleader! As always, thank you to my husband and my kids who always support my endeavors with patience and love

CHAPTER 1

Personality Conflicts

Colter Stecks was a six-year-old nightmare for Lacy DeMark. He had been enrolled in her first-grade class in Riverton Elementary right after Christmas break. Life in the classroom had not been the same since. He had transferred from one of the other eight elementary schools in the area due to personality conflicts. *Personality conflicts, my foot!* Lacy thought. *He is evil!*

She stood looking deeply into large blue eyes. They could be quite beautiful when he smiled. But he wasn't smiling now! He glared at her. She sat in front of him holding his legs down while someone else sat behind him and held his arms crossed securely over his chest in the chair. Still another person held his head so that he wouldn't fling it back into the person behind him. This unfortunate moment had come about as a result of today's rainy day recess. The children were kept inside for recess, and Lacy had turned on a cartoon to entertain them. Fifteen minutes later, when recess was over, Lacy turned off the cartoon and told the children to return to their computer work stations to begin class.

Colter was not pleased. He wanted to finish watching the cartoon and promptly said as much. Lacy tried to keep it peaceful when she explained to him that they would save the cartoon for the next time they had indoor recess and finish it then. Colter stood and walked defiantly over to the media station to turn it back on again. Lacy caught his arm, reversing his direction. As she took hold of him, he tried to twist his arm out of her grasp. He was unsuccessful. He heard the hummed familiar tune even as he turned, but he didn't heed the warning. He threw his foot at Lacy with all the force his little body could muster. She sidestepped it easily, but opted to restrain him until he calmed down.

Wrapping her arms around him as gently as possible, Lacy had him from behind and tried to sit down in a nearby chair to hold him as she calmly but loudly called for Jade, a sweet girl with green eyes and long straight dark hair, to go push the principal's call button. Jade did as she was instructed, and the children of the class then exited the classroom and lined up in the hallway per the usual drill whenever Colter flipped out.

The principal, Ms. Ferguson, was in the room in less than thirty seconds followed closely by Mr. Campbell, the behavioral specialist. Ms. Ferguson was a tall woman of stocky build. Both she and Mr. Campbell, as was Lacy, were fully certified ADDs, agents of defensive disablement, although judging from Ms. Ferguson's rather thick middle, Lacy supposed she had been neglectful of her workout duties. Attainment of the ADD qualification took a grueling full year and demanded a proficiency in negotiation, martial arts, arms training, defensive maneuvers, and pressure point anger diffusion. Of course, everyone in the school was trained these days. The schools had become the nation's battlegrounds. There wasn't a day that went by without an incident or two in one of the schools in the area. Usually you only heard about the high schools. They were the most dangerous, with shootings, knifings, and drug busts almost every day in one school or another. As a result, teachers were required to wear an armored body suit while working. It fit the body snuggly, like a wet suit from the thighs to the shoulders. It was sleeveless, lightweight, thin, and skin toned so it was almost invisible under clothing.

Teachers and administrators had become the social workers of the nation. They were required to teach and treat everything including manners, appropriate behavior, citizenship, ethics, and as of a month ago, defense classes. On top of that, they were required to discipline, teach, and defend students under a variety of very stringent stipulations.

They had to be trained to restrain, meaning that if a student flipped out in the classroom and threatened another student or a teacher, if the adult on hand wasn't trained to restrain the child yet did so anyway, the adult would be liable, not the parent, if the child hurt the adult, another student, or him or herself! All these laws were set in place to protect the errant student, but they neglected to protect the caregiver and other students. And for all the promise of a gentler society, it didn't do any good as far as Lacy DeMark was concerned. Things were getting worse and worse. The government had taken all ability to discipline children away from parents. They could no longer spank, ground, or deprive children to get them to behave appropriately. What had begun in the late 1900s as an effort to alleviate child abuse had ended up tying parents' hands completely, and without parental backing, students pretty much did as they pleased. Lacy often wondered just how long it was going to go on before teachers finally rebelled.

Teachers in Riverton Elementary were probably closer to that rebellion than most, solely as a result of Ms. Ferguson's poor administration of these incidents. Her position was that if they misbehaved, the errant student should be put in a cool-down room with pillows and soft music until they were back under control. This did not work because the students *liked* the room. It got them out of class! Thus, there were no consequences to poor behavior! Lacy was frustrated and angry about the whole mess. To top it off, there was Mr. Campbell. He was a tall, skinny man with a long hawklike nose, beady dark brown eyes, and long dark hair that he pulled back into a ratty-looking ponytail. That wasn't what bothered her though. What bothered her was the way he always made it look like it was Lacy's fault when Colter flew off the handle. He would talk down to Lacy despite the fact that both of them had gone through almost exactly the same training!

Lacy continued to struggle with the child as the principal entered. "Ms. DeMark, go ahead and let go of him."

"I can't do that, Ms. Ferguson."

"Yes, you can. He isn't going anywhere. Mr. Campbell and I will take it from here. You need to be out in the hall with your class now."

"Yes, but I still cannot do that right at this minute because he is biting my wrist!" Lacy said through gritted teeth.

"What?"

"He is biting my wrist!" she snapped back at the principal. Honestly the woman was so daft! She turned back to the boy with the death clamp on her arm. "Colter, let go, please." He didn't let go and clenched down harder. "You are hurting me!" There was still no move to release her. "Remember our discussion about hurting people? What would be a better way to handle your frustration?" She knew the negotiation technique would not work on him, but at least the principal would hear her making the effort.

At this point, Mr. Campbell knelt down in front of them, took Colter's cheeks between his thumb and forefinger, and squeezed hard to get him to unclench. Colter's response was to kick him soundly between his legs. Mr. Campbell dropped like a very ripe apple from a tree in a stiff breeze, rolling on the floor in pain. Lacy, not caring much for Mr. Campbell and enjoying the shocked expression on his face just before he dropped, would have laughed if her wrist had not been in such pain. She was also a little worried about diseases the boy could possibly pass on to her if he managed to break the skin. So instead, she held very still and hummed a familiar song in Colter's ear.

Colter began to relax with the song, but then the principal knelt down in front of him. Her intention was to grasp his legs and begin round two of negotiations. Colter tensed again and caught her off guard. He managed to kick her solidly in the lip. It split and began to bleed.

"Damn!" The expletive was out of her mouth before she even thought it.

"Hang on, I'll be right back," Ms. Ferguson said as she left the room.

Lacy had had enough of this. Her tension began to build as she thought of all the wasted teaching time! She began to sing the words to the song now, and her muscles tensed as she held Colter. The minute the words poured out of her mouth, Colter released her wrist.

He knew that when the words accompanied the music, Ms. DeMark was no longer in a negotiating mood. He also knew from experience that when she hit that point, he was in trouble. He liked Ms. DeMark, but he would never let her know that. He couldn't! He had a mission, he reminded himself. Like it or not, he had to finish it! He wished that he had Mr. Campbell for a teacher, which would make it easier. He didn't like Mr. Campbell; he had skinny legs, beady eyes, and he didn't smell as good as Ms. DeMark.

He had seen Ms. DeMark defend students from angry intruders in the school before. Once, he had watched as she had taken on an armed man at least twice her size. She had negotiated and hummed until the man threatened to shoot. At that point, she had added words to the song. It was as if she needed the music to concentrate. Colter had watched her disarm and disable the man in less time than it took to peel a banana. He remembered how she had grabbed hold of his shoulder and the man just . . . went to sleep. He wondered why she had not tried that on him at times when he was at his worst. But she never did. Even now, when he had drawn blood biting her wrist, she hadn't done that to him. Sometime he would ask her why, but now was definitely not that time!

Lacy pulled her wrist back and yanked Colter up under her arm. She carried him out of the classroom and down the hall. He had begun to scream and wiggle around like she was kidnapping or killing him, but she kept walking. No one even peeked out of the other classrooms to see what was happening. They had heard it all before. Lacy deposited him in the room with the pillows and locked him in. Colter spun around as soon as his feet hit the floor in an effort to escape, but he was a step too slow. His screaming and pounding could be heard as Lacy turned to leave him and headed to the nurse's office. She saw the principal in the hallway, on her way back to Lacy's room again.

"Where are you going? Where's Colter?" she asked Lacy.

"He's locked in the quiet room. I'm going to the nurse's office."

"You locked him in? You can't do that! It's against regulations!"

"So is biting a teacher, but that doesn't stop Colter, now, does it?"

"Ms. DeMark, your class is in the hallway, you can't just leave your class in the hallway!"

"So sit with them until I get back. I am also forbidden to bleed all over them!"

"I can't sit with them! You have Colter locked up in the quiet room. I have to go sit with *him*!"

"He's not going anywhere . . . so sit with my class until I'm bandaged up or the secretary can get a substitute in here! Then you can go see what the little monst—uh, sweetie is up to! Oh, and someone needs to make sure that Colter washes his mouth out once he calms down. At least I don't have any life-threatening diseases. Still, he probably got some of my blood in his mouth."

"Lacy DeMark, the students come first!"

"Ms. Ferguson, if you choose to reprimand me as my mother used to by using my whole name, you should include my middle name for the best effect and for your information, Mr. Campbell is still in the classroom. The children have never really been alone. Get him to watch my class! At least he isn't bleeding all over the hallway carpet!"

Lacy entered the nurse's office and sat down. "Colter have any diseases I should know about?"

The nurse turned to look at her and noticed the wrist at the same time. "Wow, that's a nasty one! You know you're going to have to go the hospital for this?" She sucked in a breath. "You're going to need stitches," she continued as she probed around the wound, assessing the damage. She began to clean it and bandage it. "I'll call the subsecretary and see if I can get a replacement for you for the afternoon. You can go have it looked at as soon as the sub gets here. Okay?"

"Anything that will get me out of the classroom where I don't have to work with the dynamic duo."

Margo, the nurse, was a good friend of Lacy's and laughed at the statement. "You get bitten by a little classroom terror and yet it is the principal and her sidekick that you wish not to see the rest of the day. Isn't that just a little weird?"

"Well, he's only six. I can understand that he might have issues that he is not capable of dealing with appropriately. But the Batwoman and Robin are adults and should be able to take control of a situation. He took them both out in the space of a minute!"

"No kidding? What happened?"

"He got Campbell in the 'netherlands' and then he got Ferguson quite appropriately in the mouth! As far as I'm concerned, he should get a metal! I just wish he wouldn't have bitten me. If I could, I'd sue the school for lack of action! They are probably not even going to send him home today . . . They never do."

"Well, at least you won't be here!"

"Yeah, but my class is suffering as a result. We have been interrupted by him at least once each day this week. Something needs to be done. I'm going over the principal's head. I'm going to request a hearing myself!"

"You may lose your job! Everyone hates a whistle-blower."

"Yeah, well, at this point, I'll take my chances!"

CHAPTER 2

The Chase

Chasing stupid, arrogant drug-dealing teenagers at twilight was not his idea of the perfect evening, but that didn't mean he didn't like it. As pastimes went, chasing anything or anyone that allowed him to pull his gun from its holster was a thrill too good to pass up. The fact that these particular targets could get him the recognition and subsequently the job he wanted was just icing on the cake. They had disappeared down the street as soon as they saw him throwing his briefcase in his car. He yelled for them to stop once, but their haste to get away from him was all the indication he needed to grab his gun from his holster, slam the door, beep-lock his car, and tear after them at a dead run.

It never failed to amaze him when these weak-ass kids thought they could outrun a fully trained ADD in top shape. But they always ran anyway. The chase only fired him up more. He loved to run, but running after a target was more arousing than a hot date. And catching them was satisfying enough to keep a smile on his face for a week! He saw them turn down an alley and barreled after them. He was catching up quickly. As soon as he turned the corner into what had looked at first like an alley but had turned out to be a dead-end dirt road leading into the forest that surrounded Riverton, his heart leaped in his chest. He almost had them! He saw them turn toward what looked like a shed and disappear in the combined darkness of the twilight and the tall trees of the forest boarder.

Running toward the shed, he took cover along an outside wall and held his gun, ready to fire in his right hand. He pointed the gun up and held it with both hands about three inches in front of his face as he crept toward the entrance of the shed. He peeked quickly around into the doorway. It was clear. He lowered his gun to chest level, pointed it forward, and carefully and quickly stepped into the entrance and to the side, allowing for minimal exposure with the light behind him. Nothing happened. He kept the front wall to his back as he waited for his eyes to adjust.

Where were those butt kicks? He was sure they had slipped in here. But if they were here, they were well hidden, and it was odd that they hadn't at least taken a shot at him in the fraction of a second when he was vulnerable in the back light at the door.

He wondered what this shed was. It was built into the mountain behind it. Perhaps it was a storage shed, or it could be an old mine shaft. He knew there were a few of those in the Riverton area. The town had originally been a gold mining town, but there hadn't been much and it had most likely all been mined out years ago.

His eyes were beginning to adjust a bit, but it was pretty doggone black in here. He listened intensely. He heard a noise! Holding completely still, he concentrated on the stillness waiting for the sound again. There it was! He stole into the blackness, feeling around the walls until he could get around to the back of the room and use the light from the doorway, limited as it was, to try and make out the lay of the area. Thank goodness, he was paranoid. He'd kept the walls to his back, and it was a good thing too! There in the middle of the floor about six feet into the shaft was a great hole. A ladder leaned against one side of it. Feeling certain that no one shared the room with him, he cautiously made his way forward to the ladder. As he leaned down to peer into the blackness, he heard again the sound he had heard earlier. It was voices! But there was no light down there. It probably led to another room. It must.

Taking hold of the side of the ladder, he swung his leg down onto the first rung. It seemed sturdy enough, so he made his way down the length of it one rung at a time. By the time he had reached the bottom, he found himself in complete blackness. He reached into his pocket to retrieve his penlight on his key chain. He pressed his fingers tightly around the keys to keep them quiet as he fumbled for the light and pressed the little button that turned it on. It wasn't much, but it was enough for this. He walked off in the direction from which he had heard the voices.

As he ambled down the tunnel, he noticed another hole in the floor just before he took the step that would have sent him falling into unknown blackness! It had surprised and scared him. He had been so close! The thought to turn around and go home almost sent him back toward the ladder when he heard it again. Yes, it was voices! They had to be in there. He leaned down and listened. There it was again! Well, it was definitely a good hiding place for a lab or storage place for drugs. It was cool, dark, and hard to get to! He had to hand it to them. How had they found this place anyway? There would be time to find out as soon as he had them in tow.

CHAPTER 3

Singing in the Dark

It only took two weeks before Lacy had managed to get what she wanted. She had gone to the superintendent of schools, explaining about the amount of restraint time and what went on during quiet room times. She explained how much time was being lost in the classroom to deal with Colter's issues. The superintendent was very understanding. Well, about as understanding as a two-year-old that is asked to sit in one place for more than a minute. He had ignored her and told the principal that one of her teachers was going over her head. Undaunted, Lacy had gone over his head also, appealing to the school board. Fortunately, Jade's father, a long-time board member and well-respected district attorney, took up her cause, albeit in his daughter's best interest if not Lacy's or Colter's. He pressed the school district to have a hearing to discuss other options for the further education of Colter Stecks. Ms. DeMark was given a summons to deliver to the Stecks' household by seven this evening.

A quick survey of the old house gave ADD Lacy DeMark the impression that the inhabitants didn't care much about their possessions, their property, or themselves. The yard was fenced in with old and rusting chicken wire. The wooden supports were silvered and cracking with age. A stiff breeze could probably take the entire thing down in under thirty seconds. There were old toys and tools scattered in the yard with a rusted old bike with two flat tires leaning up along one side. The lawn was nonexistent for the most part. The only evidence that it had ever existed was the few straggling tufts near the posts. An old barn could be seen barely standing in the back. Its roof sagged, and the paint had chipped off years before. She wondered what kept it standing.

Lacy might not have been so surprised at the look of the place except that Dan Stecks drove a brand-new black Excalibur pickup with all the frills and an ice blue flame running down the sides. She could also see an oversized big-screen high-definition 3-D TV tuned into World Wrestling in the living room as she approached the front door. She could see the wrestling match playing out in the center of the living room. The new high-definition 3-D gave the illusion that those in the room were watching the event ringside.

Oh yea! Wrestling fans! Lacy thought. No wonder little Colter Stecks was having so much trouble keeping his hands off his classmates in her first-grade class. He had been trouble since the first day he had attended Riverton Elementary. Colter's antics in school were out of control. He would kick, punch, pinch, bite, and push his fellow students usually without any more provocation than a glance in his direction.

Lacy was good at her job, one of the best actually, but she was tired of Colter's home issues manifesting in the classroom. Even with the martial arts, weapons, and defense training that all teachers were required to have in order to teach in public schools as of the year 2026, Lacy was having difficulty maintaining control in her classroom with Colter in attendance.

She was here now to deliver the summons to Colter's father requiring him to attend a parent/ADD hearing. If the hearing went in her favor, Colter would be taken from the home environment and placed in a special facility where twenty-four-hour care and correction would be administered with the most current medical, psychological, and educational attention to try to turn the child at risk from the path he was on in favor of a more socially acceptable direction. Dan Stecks wasn't going to like it.

Dan was a troublemaker. He was rumored to have been in a few scrapes himself, and word had it that he dealt in drugs for his living. He hadn't actually been caught yet, but Lacy didn't have any trouble believing it. He was also known to be a real hothead. That was why Jeremiah, the other first-grade teacher in her school, had offered to come with her as backup. She had declined the offer. No one in their right mind would attack an ADD. Even an elementary ADD was a formidable opponent, though elementary ADDs were trained more for negotiation rather than defensive disablement. It was also darn hard to get past an ADD's armor which protected against bullets and knife or puncture wounds.

The program for getting ADD and teaching certification was grueling. Most candidates washed out in the first six months. Today's school system required much of the same training as was given the military. The problem was that teachers were not considered to be at war. They were trained to negotiate, defend, and protect; but in reality, especially in the junior and senior highs across America, educators were most certainly at war. They were required to defend against outside intruders, maladjusted students, and disgruntled parents.

In order to attract the numbers of candidates that were needed to fill the positions across the country and successfully navigate the intensive training, salaries were formidable. Teachers were now better paid than most doctors or CEOs. That was definitely a nice perk, but Lacy longed for the days when teachers were only expected to teach. That had been her dream as a little girl.

She thought that by becoming a teacher herself, she might be able to make a difference. So she had stuck it out through that torturous training that seemed to go on forever. She had thought that she would never make it through at times. Her saving grace was having learned to keep her focus only on the task at hand in that particular moment. Keeping her head in the moment had been her motto.

Eventually she had made it. She had even graduated with top honors. In martial arts, she could take down almost anyone in her graduating class. Only John Finley could beat her. He had towered over her by about a foot and outweighed her by at least eighty to ninety pounds, and every last inch of him had been muscle. When she delivered a kick to his midsection that would drop most of their classmates on the first try, it felt tantamount to a rabbit taking a swipe at a bear. John would just smile and throw her on her backside with a flip of his wrist. She had wondered how he did that so easily until she finally talked him into sharing his tricks. He did, but after Lacy had nearly dropped him during their finals, John had blamed it on her infernal habit of singing as she fought. He tried to tell her that her beautiful voice had distracted him. Lacy wasn't sure she believed him since they sparred together regularly during practice and she always sang. He should have been used to her little quirk. As if to regain his superiority over her, the next day, he'd fallen on top of her and given her a hickey just to prove he was still the king of the hill. She'd have killed him in his sleep if he hadn't been heading to the high school arena! High school teachers were hard to find and harder to keep! Well, maybe she wouldn't have killed him. After all, besides being an Adonis, he did teach her how to take down guys bigger than he was; she just never quite managed to get the drop on *him*. Well, she did manage to inflict a beautifully colored black eye in payment for the hickey that forced him to admit that she was a formidable opponent!

She missed John though; once in a while, his attitude about teaching had left her feeling a little confused. He seemed to enjoy carrying the gun and commanding respect—or eliciting fear—more than he liked being in the classroom with the students. Lacy had toyed with the idea of dating him at one time. He had made it perfectly clear that he wanted her in more ways than one. But she couldn't get over the slightly uneasy feeling she sometimes got around him. The differences between them became impossible to entwine. Lacy thought that what children really needed was a good set of enforced rules interlocked with love and respect. What John thought children needed was a healthy fear of authority. Lacy rarely carried her gun with her. She kept it in a secret compartment in her classroom desk most of the time. John probably showered with his still strapped to his shoulder!

Ah well, it really didn't matter since she had concluded right after the hickey incident that he wasn't the man for her. Besides the obvious chasms between them, he had also been offered a teaching position in some inner-city high school in Detroit. Lacy preferred the small-town atmosphere and relative safety over the inner-city hubbub. She hadn't seen him since they graduated. She hadn't even written to him. She didn't feel bad about that though, because he was supposed to have written to her to give her his new address. The life of a teacher in this day and age left very little time for anything but physical training, lesson planning, and teaching so she figured he'd just gotten busy. Most nights Lacy came home tired and ready for her favorite pastime, a good book and a glass of wine before bed. Sometimes she took the book and the wine to the oversized tub in her spacious bathroom and soaked the day's troubles away before bed. Since Colter had been assigned to her classroom, those baths had become more and more frequent. In any case, John was probably just as busy as Lacy.

Thinking of Colter had brought Lacy back to the present, and she sluggishly tromped up the steps to the front door. The doorbell must not have worked or more likely was not loud enough to be heard over the TV. No one had answered the door after three tries. Lacy stopped ringing it and knocked loudly. She could hear a large dog bark, and the floor of the porch shook as someone approached the door. Lacy had never met Dan Stecks face-to-face, but she would have recognized him anyway. Little Colter looked just like his dad. Both of them had greasy strawberry blond hair that probably never got combed and a hateful glare. The only noticeable difference between the two—other than size, of course—was in the eyes. Colter's were a deep blue that could switch from sweetness to evil between blinks. Dan's eyes were a muddy brown that also switched moods quickly but never displayed a sincere sweetness. At the moment, his eyes were sort of glazed, and his pupils were almost as big as his irises. Lacy noted that even through the obvious haze in his vision, his leer projected pure lust.

Dan looked Lacy up and down before he spoke, enjoying what he was seeing. He noticed her long shapely legs. Her knee-length skirt was professional and smart looking. She was wearing a light blue sweater and a pair of comfortable loafers. Although the loafers downplayed the teacher's appeal, as far as Dan was concerned, he still could not hide a slow and slightly sinister smile of approval as he took in her dark brown eyes and long blond hair.

"Hello there! What can I do for you, beautiful?"

Ignoring his foolish attempt at flirtation, Lacy held up the summons as she introduced herself. The slimevat would have known her if he had bothered to come to any of the school's many parent-teacher conference nights.

"Hi, I'm Ms. DeMark, your son's teacher. You are hereby issued this summons to discuss your son's future educational placement."

"What the hell are you talking about? You can't just summon me without any warning!" Anger flared in Dan Stecks's eyes. His sinister smile changed abruptly to a stiff frown as he stared down into Lacy's eyes.

"Actually, Mr. Stecks, you have been warned on several occasions. You have chosen to ignore my calls, my notes, my e-mails, and those of my superiors. If you choose to ignore this summons, Colter will be taken into custody and removed from your household without a hearing. The hearing is scheduled for one week from today. It can be moved up, but not postponed, at your request. If you have any questions, you can reach me via the phone number enclosed within the summons. Good day!"

"Wait just a cotton-pickin' minute! You are not taking my son from me! I won't let you, so you can just go back to that school of yours and tell them that I won't be attending your little powwow and I will not allow anyone to take my son. I'll teach him here at home first!"

Lacy loved that threat. Most people did not realize just what hoops homeschoolers had to jump through these days. Gone were the days of being able to just pull a child from school, buy a curriculum, and teach on your own. The government had taken over even the homeschool aspect of education, now demanding that parents attain a homeschool teaching certificate. It wasn't as detailed as classroom teaching certificates since much of a public teacher's training included things that a homeschool teacher would not need, like classroom management and modifying lessons to include special-needs children, and of course, the ADD training.

Lacy looked into Dan's eyes and smiled sweetly.

"That is your decision, of course, but I must warn you that you have to pass the homeschool teacher certification process to be allowed the privilege of teaching your son. You must complete that certification by next Friday. If we do not have that certification in our possession by Friday, Colter will be picked up by child services immediately following the hearing. Good luck, sir!" She enjoyed the look on Dan's face and then turned to leave, happy that she had accomplished her goal and was ready to go home. Lacy caught movement out of the corner of her eye. She reacted as training dictated and turned in time to deflect a baseball bat that Dan Stecks was swinging toward her.

The bat grazed her forearm, thankfully sliding the length of her arm rather than making a direct hit. Somewhere in the back of her mind, she made the connection that Dan's sudden violent reaction had been triggered and acted upon as quickly as little Colter Stecks flipped out daily in school. At the same moment, she heard Colter yelling at his father.

"No, Dad, don't hurt her! Leave her alone!" The child's reaction surprised her since she still bore the scars of several of his tantrums from school. The most prominent being the bite mark on the inside of her right wrist that had sported ten stitches up until a couple of hours ago. She only had a moment to react and deflect the bat once more as Dan redirected the swing toward his son.

She wasn't as lucky this time and took the entire force on her left forearm. But she was quick enough to grab the screaming Colter and pull him out the door with her right hand. She shoved him behind her as she turned and swung her foot up to catch Dan in the neck. She was too close to him and it only stunned him, but it gave her enough time to grab Colter by the back of his pants belt and haul him away as she sprinted for her car.

Too late she realized that her keys were hopelessly lost in the bottom of her purse.

"Chits!" Lacy glanced behind them and was horrified to see Dan running toward them, bat held high, evil exuding from his eyes. He seemed to have lost all sanity. Colter looked back at the same time and began to scream more loudly. He scrambled to get his legs under him and break away from her grip. She let him go once again to defend herself.

The song that Lacy had been listening to in the car as she arrived at the house sprang from her lips. She sang as he approached. The song surprised him but did not slow him at all. Had anyone been watching, they'd have thought she had suddenly lost her mind, but the singing was not something Lacy even thought about. It just happened whenever she became overly agitated, excited, or was in fight mode as she was now. It had become a habit of hers as a little child, and it continued through her training, earning her the nickname Singer. She had always thought the name very unoriginal, but none of the names she had suggested had stuck, so Singer became her signature.

As Dan ran forward, the arduous training she'd had took over, seeming to cause her body to react without thinking. Dan crumpled to the ground in unconsciousness, and with the beat of her song, she noted with a smile. But Lacy's view of the front door didn't get any better.

There standing in the doorway was yet another man sporting the same muddy brown eyes with the same slightly glazed look. This one was pointing a rifle at her. She had just enough time to duck behind her car. Although she knew her armor would save her, it still hurt like a son of a gun to get hit. She frantically looked around for Colter. She caught sight of him hightailing it through the woods behind her car. She watched, horrified, as the man turned his aim toward Colter in response to movement in his peripheral vision. Lacy was up and running to get between Colter and the bullet in half a second, the man with the gun firing after her. Fortunately, the obviously drugged moron was trying to run after her while he shot, and his aim was atrocious.

Why hadn't she let Jeremiah come with her? For that matter, why had she come unarmed? The questions running through her mind were suddenly replaced by anger. How dare they attack a child or an ADD?! Just wait till she told her superiors! Mr. Stecks would lose this hearing and spend the rest of his days in prison if it was the last thing she did! The bullet whistling past her ear reminded her that she had to survive long enough to make her report. She was singing as she picked up her pace and caught up with Colter, his little face filled with fear and covered in sweat.

There was some sort of structure coming up on their right. Lacy reached out, took hold of Colter, and pushed him into the dark entrance. He began to yell, even as she realized that it would only take a couple of seconds for the man with the gun to catch up and find them in the only structure visible within the seclusion of the massive trees that made up the woods.

"No, not in here! Mama said this place is too dangerous! We can't hide in here!" Colter turned back around and ran right into Lacy. She grasped him and pulled him into her chest as she ran toward the back of what looked like an old storage shack. She thought to hide him and then face her attacker using the blackness to her advantage, but the thought didn't even have a chance to formulate into a real plan before she stepped into the blackness and realized that the floor she had assumed ran the length of the shed did not exist more than six feet beyond the entrance.

As soon as the two started to fall, Lacy's training kicked in again. She rolled her body around the child and landed hard on her back in the inky blackness. The breath had been knocked out of her, and she struggled to force her body to suck in a much-needed breath when she felt this floor give way also. They were falling again. It was all she could do to hold on to the child as he fought against her and screamed in terror.

Once again they landed hard. Lacy had managed to keep her body between the child and the newest floor under them, but she still had not managed to get a good breath before they were falling once more. The armor had kept anything from piercing her body, but it didn't cushion the concussion of each landing. This time they fell for several seconds, and the landing not only knocked the wind out of Lacy but it also knocked the consciousness from her.

When Lacy finally fought her way back to coherent thinking, her ears were assailed by Colter's wails. He sat beside her in the blackness pounding on her chest, trying to get her to wake up. His little fists hurt like hell, but she couldn't see an inch in front of her face and so couldn't quite get hold of his fists to stop the assault.

"Colter, stop!" she told him with firmness but without yelling because she didn't want to upset him more than he was already. When he didn't respond, she had to raise her voice to be heard over his. "Colter! Stop hitting me! I'm awake!" The intake of air necessary to bellow at Colter stretched her rib cage and sent a jolt of pain up through her body. She must have cracked a rib on her way down, she reasoned. She concentrated on Colter then to take her mind off the pain while it subsided.

"Ms. DeMark?"

"Yes, Colter, I'm awake. Calm down. Where is that man? Has he come inside the shed yet?"

"That was my uncle Tony and I don't know if he came in or not. I can't see anything. It's too dark!" he half yelled and half whimpered.

"Shhhh. Let me listen." She held her breath and listened, but she didn't hear anything except the boy's breathing. Pain exploded in her as she finally took a breath.

She felt around in the darkness, half afraid to move both to avoid aggravation of the pain that throbbed intensely within her chest and for fear that the floor was as fragile as the others they had fallen through. The floor wasn't wooden, she discovered, but dirt and rock. They must have finally hit the bottom of the shaft. Where were they? Her hand hit something soft and flexible, and upon further exploration, she was overjoyed to discover that it was her purse. She had thought she had lost it by the car, but here it was. That was a good thing because she had a little purse flashlight in it.

"Colter, how long have we been down here?"

The little boy sniffed and answered in a small frightened voice, "I don't know."

"Did I wake up right away, or have I been out for a while?"

"For a while. I was scared you wouldn't wake up and I would be all alone."

"Colter, your family will probably be calling someone to come get you out of here. They wouldn't just leave you down here."

"I don't think so."

"Why not?"

"Because wrestling is on. Daddy never misses his wrestling show."

"He would miss it for you."

"No, he wouldn't."

Lacy decided not to argue with him. She tried to sit up and almost passed out as the pain shot through her again. Chits! She probably had more than one cracked rib. She took a mental inventory and decided that her legs and arms were okay except for the spot where the baseball bat had hit her, but at least it didn't feel broken, just bruised. She was sporting quite a headache, probably from the final landing. She gingerly rolled to her side and pushed herself into a sitting position. The effort made her feel dizzy, but it passed after a moment. She felt around for the lump that was her purse and pulled it into her lap. She knew generally where the flashlight should be and felt her way into the little compartment within the purse. She found her keys first.

"Of course I would find you first now!" As soon as she wrapped her fingers around the light, she felt for the switch and turned it on. Since she rarely used the little thing, the batteries were strong. It actually lit up quite a bit of the area for such a little light.

Lacy began looking around them. When the light hit on Colter, she made him come closer so she could check him over for injuries. When she was satisfied that the boy was all right, she resumed her survey of the immediate area. She had almost made a full circle when she saw a pile of debris that on further inspection revealed that her car had been completely cleaned out and everything that wasn't bolted down had been thrown down here with them. That did not bode well, but at least she also caught sight of a familiar bag a few feet behind Colter.

"My gym bag!" Lacy stared at it in disbelief. "What is all this doing down here?"

"It fell down here a little while after we did," Colter said. He didn't elaborate, but Lacy saw the tears begin running down his cheeks again. The tears managed to remain in the same tracks that previous tears had clearly marked on his dirt-covered little face.

Chits! Lacy started to hum a favorite tune as she stared at the little pile with the gym bag perched haphazardly on top. If Stecks had thrown this stuff down on top of them, he sure as heck wasn't planning on coming down to get them any time soon. He was planning on leaving them there. The words to the song tumbled sweetly from her lips. She sang more confidently as she thought, the tune a haunting melody. It was a curious thing that she could sing the words to a song as she thought or fought through a situation, but she sometimes didn't even remember having sung anything at all.

As she sang, Colter listened. He wasn't sure if he could relax as she sang or if he should worry. He had heard her sing on many occasions, usually when he was causing trouble in the classroom. It had always soothed him no matter how hard he had struggled to hold on to the nasty attitude he needed to survive. He supposed that since they were alone and no one was watching, he could relax into the tune and let Ms. DeMark think. He knew she was thinking of a way out of the dark, just as she always used the music to think a way out of the messes he worked so hard to foist on her during school. He quieted and the tears stopped. He curled up next to her and just listened.

Lacy hadn't missed the movement of the boy and allowed him to snuggle into her as she thought through the situation. She wrapped her arm around him as she looked down into his upraised face.

He really was a beautiful little boy, she thought. His big eyes, when not overflowing with anger and hate, were a clear beautiful blue. And on the rare occasions when she had seen him smile, his face had lit up like the little angel he should be. He was small when compared to his classmates, but then he was also one of the younger ones. She supposed he would catch up to them sooner or later if he turned out to look anything like his father. Just the same, she had been thankful for his present small stature because she had been obliged to physically overpower him on more than one occasion in the last three months of school. And several times she had been required to pick him up and remove him from the classroom altogether. Having just seen his father display the same behavior, Lacy began to wonder just how deeply the behavior had been ingrained in Colter. She said a little prayer that it was simply a matter of time and discipline until Colter could learn to behave.

Lacy loved her students, all of them! Even this impossibly difficult one. She never blamed her students for inappropriate behavior. After all, they were all between the ages of six and seven. If there was a problem with one of her students, there had to be a reason. She believed that there were no bad children, only bad examples. That, she supposed, was why she had managed to stay so calm on the day Colter had taken a little "taste" of her arm. The only other time she had been bitten was when she was a teenager and her dog had bitten her. Out of reflex, the small ball of fluff had been thrown unceremoniously across the room. Good thing she hadn't thrown Colter across the room.

The beam of light was bright enough to illuminate enough of the shaft from which they had fallen to dash their hopes of ever climbing out. Even if Lacy's ribs weren't beyond hoisting herself out of the black hole, she would never be able to drag both her and Colter out, and she wasn't leaving him here. She wondered how long it would take someone to start looking for them. Jeremiah would call later tonight to hear the gory details of her summons delivery. But he might not suspect that anything was wrong until Monday. No one else would miss her either. She rarely went out socially. She was usually content to work at home on the weekends. It really was pathetic, she thought. Her life consisted of work and home. She didn't go out with friends, didn't have a love life. Her only hobby was developing lesson plans that might entertain her students while they learned. Happy and entertained students were learning students.

The longer she thought about it, the more sure she was that she and Colter were on their own. They would have to find their own way out or die here. Colter nudged her then.

"What do you need, Colter?" she asked as calmly as she could. He had calmed down, and she didn't wish to upset him again.

"You already sang that verse. Did you run out of song?"

Lacy smiled. "I guess I did. Shall we get up and try to find a way out of here?"

"Yes. Uh, . . . Ms. DeMark, I'm a pretty good climber, but I don't think I can climb that wall."

"Yeah, me neither. We'll have to look for another way out. Do you know what this place is? It looks like a mine shaft."

"Mama told me it was the place Grandpa used to get gold out of. When Grandpa was here, we had lots of money. He builded the house we live in. Mama said it was really pretty when she was little. Mama wanted to fix it up again, but Daddy said she couldn't go outside and work 'cause he don't trust her. But I think Daddy's wrong. He don't trust no one 'cept Tony."

"He doesn't trust anyone except Tony," Lacy corrected out of habit.

Oblivious to the correction, Colter just agreed with her. "No, he don't."

"I'm sorry, Colter. We'll try to get it all straightened out when we get out of here. Okay?"

"Ms. DeMark?"

"What, Colter?"

"Don't try to get my daddy to change."

"Why?"

"Because he's real mean. I don't want him to be mean to you again."

"Colter, I can take care of myself. I've been trained to take care of myself and the students under my care. I won't let him be mean to me again or to you." She almost laughed at her own promise. Wasn't it her wrist that sported the fresh red wound from a bite the six-year-old she was trying to comfort had given her? And weren't they even now in the bottom of a black hole, having been chased there by the very demon from whom she was trying to convince Colter she could protect him? Still, she couldn't stop herself as she continued, "And if everything goes the way I think it will, he won't be mean to your mother again either."

"Oh, he'll never be mean to my mother again."

"Why do you say that?"

"Because she left us last year."

"What?!"

"She and Daddy had a real bad fight one night and she said she was leaving and she was taking me with her. But Daddy said I couldn't go and if she tried to leave he'd help her out but she wasn't taking me. He made me go to my room. I heard a lot of yelling and then it stopped. The next morning, Mama was gone. Daddy said we were better off without her."

"Oh, Colter, I didn't know. I'm sorry." Lacy had a bad feeling about Mrs. Stecks. She was going to do a little checking into her whereabouts as soon as she got the two of them out of here. She wasn't sure how she was going to get out of this hole, but she knew once they did, she would never ever allow Colter to go back home.

The beam of light stuck on a darker section of the hole. Lacy stood up carefully and walked over to it, shining the light directly on it. It was a tunnel! Hallelujah! It was a tunnel!

"Colter, maybe we can get out this way. Let's get my gym bag and my purse and see how far we can get." Lacy stuffed the purse into the bag and took Colter's hand. She led him step by step down the dark tunnel. She had to duck several times when the ceiling was too low, but most of the time she could walk upright. That was a good thing because ducking required bending her midsection and her ribs complained loudly each time she bent down and her head would throb until she straightened again. The tunnel headed down in a steep descent. Lacy wondered how long they would have to walk before they found a dead end or a way out. She was trying to remember the area where Colter lived. How wide were the hills? How far would they have to walk to actually reach the other side of the hill? Or mountain or whatever they were in?

They had been walking for what seemed like hours when Colter finally refused to take another step. He was exhausted. Actually, so was Lacy. She checked her watch. It was 3:54 a.m. Colter was hungry and thirsty too. Thank heavens, that evil son of a—well, thank heavens, he had thrown her gym bag down on top of them. There were a couple of bottles of water in her bag and some sports bars. They tasted nasty, but they had lots of calories in them to keep them walking. She gave Colter a drink but didn't allow him to drink too much. She wasn't sure how long it was going to take them to get out. She would have to ration it. She expected him to throw a royal fit when she took the bottle back. That's how he would have reacted in class, so she was pleasantly surprised when he just said, "Thank you."

"That's it? Thank you? Colter, are you feeling all right? Why aren't you arguing with me or fighting me for the bottle? That's what you would have done in class."

"Yeah, I'm sorry, Ms. DeMark."

Lacy waited for him to explain. He relaxed against her but didn't speak again. "Well, . . . aren't you going to answer my question?"

She looked down into his face. He had drifted off to sleep. Lacy wasn't sure exactly what to do. She would either have to turn off the flashlight to save the battery and sleep with him, or carry him and keep going. Since she didn't relish the thought of waking up in this horrible place, she opted to carry him and keep going. She strapped her gym bag over her shoulder, picked him up, and put him right back down again, nearly dropping him. The pain in her ribs as she tried to lift him shot through her body like a lightning bolt.

Tears filled her eyes and dizziness nearly overwhelmed her, but she managed to stifle the yelp of pain before it escaped her lips and alarmed Colter. It seems that two hours each day in the gym to build a set of abs that were the envy of many men did nothing for her without a healthy bone structure. She sighed, staggered down beside Colter, and flipped off the flashlight. She gingerly pulled Colter closer and rested his head on her lap. She wrapped her arm around him and leaned up against the wall. She slept fitfully, never getting into a deep enough sleep for dreams, but that was probably a good thing, she thought. Colter slept for two or three hours before he woke them both, screaming in a panic. Lacy flipped the flashlight on and sang to him until he drifted off to sleep again. Turning the flashlight off again, she tried to doze for a while more.

It was eight thirty in the morning when Lacy woke Colter up, turned on the flashlight, and fed him another sports bar. They each took a drink of water and started on their way again. She wasn't sure just how long the flashlight was going to last, and they needed to get as far down the tunnel as they could before it ran out and they were forced to feel their way out. That's what really scared her. When they no longer had any light at all, how would they find their way out of this place? So far, there had been no other tunnels leading off in any direction, but who's to say the tunnel wouldn't fork out later? The path was still heading downhill, but the slope wasn't as steep as it had been last night.

They walked for another couple of hours before Lacy noticed the light was beginning to dim. Panic seemed to push in from the back recesses of her mind, or maybe it was the *black* recesses of the tunnel around them. Colter hadn't noticed the light until he heard Lacy begin to hum. He immediately began looking around for the source of her agitation. As she started the words of the first verse, Colter finally noticed that they could no longer see from one side wall to the other. It would not be long before they would be walking in complete darkness.

"Ms. DeMark?"

The song paused as Lacy answered him, "Yes?"

"Are you afraid of the dark?"

"Well,...no...yes...maybe. I'm just concerned about tripping or bumping my head." It was only a little lie. She was terrified. She was really worried about finding a way out before they ran out of water. Of course, she wouldn't even think about the possibility of being lost in this hole. She kept telling herself that there had to be a second way out. There just had to be. What miner in his right mind wouldn't have a second way out? There could be a cave-in . . . A good miner would have an escape route, . . . wouldn't he?

"Are you afraid of the dark, Colter?"

"No," he paused, "well . . . yes, but I'm just a kid."

"It'll be okay, Colter, I'll get you out of here. I promise."

"I know, Ms. DeMark. But you can go ahead and sing. I know it helps you think."

"Thanks, Colter." She smiled to herself. "Do you have a request?"

"Yes, could you sing a Christmas song?"

"Sure, which one?"

"Mama used to sing one about a 'sleigh ride together with you.' That's the one."

"I know that one! Let's see, how does it start . . ." As Lacy sang, it wasn't long before the light faded out, leaving the two to feel their way down the tunnel.

"Don't let go of me, Colter."

"I won't." With the death grip he had on her, she knew it would take a gale force wind to get him to lose his grip on her sweater. As that seemed an unlikely event in the confines of the tunnel, she relaxed a little.

The going was slow in the endless blackness. Lacy had to concentrate to keep from losing her orientation. She was amazed that Colter never once cried or even complained. He sniffed a couple of times and she worried that he might be crying, but he never let on to her.

They walked on for hours. Well, it felt like hours. Lacy wasn't really certain just how long it was. She was too worried about following the walls, making sure that there weren't any forks in the tunnel that might get them really lost if they had to backtrack, or any holes in the floor that would send them plummeting again.

They stopped to rest only a couple of times, feeling around in the gym bag for water bottles and sports bars each time. Lacy only ate half at a time, making sure that Colter ate a whole one each time. She needed him to have as much energy as possible so they could keep going. Her ribs ached, causing short bouts of nausea, and she wished she could take a look at them or better yet have a doctor take a look at them. At least she could still move. She was almost afraid to sit down again because working the stiffness out after the last rest took more energy than she had left to expend.

Colter couldn't see two inches in front of his face. He had never felt so afraid in his life. Even when his daddy was threatening to cut him up in little pieces and feed him to the dog, he hadn't been this scared. He hated the dark. He much preferred seeing the evil coming at him than wondering what evil lurked there in the darkness. At least he had Lacy. She had been quiet for the last hour or so, but he could hear her humming quietly now. It always confused him a little. He knew she thought better and fought better when she was singing to herself, but he also knew that she only sang when she felt agitated.

He had to smile at her choice of song. Lacy was singing a song called "A Week of Sunshine in One Touch." He didn't feel quite like they were spending a week in sunshine at all, but it had a nice beat and it cheered him up to listen to it.

"Ms. DeMark?"

"Yes, Colter?"

"Could you sing a little louder? I like that song."

"Sure, Colter."

"Ms. DeMark?"

"Yes, Colter?"

"Do you think we're almost to the end?"

"I don't know, but I hope so."

"Ms. DeMark?"

"Uh, Colter, since we're not in school, you can just call me Lacy. Okay? When we're back in school, you'll have to call me Ms. DeMark again, but for now, just Lacy will do. Okay?"

"Okay, Ms—Lacy?"

"Yes, Colter?"

"You can just call me Colt."

Lacy smiled in the dark. "Okay, Colt."

"Lacy, can I ask you something?"

"Sure, Colter—Colt."

"Do you remember that guy with the gun that came into the school?"

"Yes."

"I remember him too. I remember that you pinched his shoulder and he just fell asleep. Do you remember?"

"Yes, Colt."

"Well, can I ask you something about that?"

"Sure!"

"Why didn't you ever use that on me? Even when I bit you, you didn't use it on me."

"Well, there's a side effect to that move. When the person wakes up, they have a splitting headache and they are nauseated to the point of throwing up for hours. I didn't think it was a good idea to do that to a first-grader."

"Oh," he paused as he thought about that. "Thanks!"

"You're welcome. So would you like to sing with me?"

"Sure, but you'll have to sing something I know."

"Okay, you choose."

"Do you know the Space Skeedoo song?"

"Oh sure! It's one of my favorites." It wasn't really; it was a popular cartoon theme song, but Lacy figured that if she could keep him singing, he wouldn't panic on her. Of course, she wasn't sure who was going to keep *her* from panicking. The boy chose one cartoon theme song after another as they continued their march downhill. Finally, Lacy noticed that the path had leveled out. That had to be a good sign, she thought. But they still could not see even an inch in front of their faces. If they made it out of here in one piece and still breathing, she was never going to like darkness again. She used to like to sleep in total darkness. That was going to change. She would get a few cute little nightlights, one for each room. Okay, maybe two for each room.

Just when she thought that she was not going to be able to handle the cartoon theme songs or the dark one minute longer, Lacy felt a shift in the air.

In a few more steps, she could feel a little breeze! They made a tight turn to the right and could see light a few feet ahead of them! Colter squealed in delight and let go to run toward the light.

Lacy caught him and held him back. "Wait a minute, Colt. We have to watch our step. There could be a hole in the floor or a drop-off as you leave the shaft. We don't want to make it this far and then get hurt or lost again a few feet from the entrance."

They continued their slow pace until they turned again, this time to the left, and saw bright sunshine on a beautiful green field. They both ran for the entrance then. They had to shield their eyes in the brightness after the long hike in total blackness, but that didn't stop their celebration. Laughter bubbled out of both of them as Colter twirled and danced in the green grass of the meadow before them.

CHAPTER 4

Rock and Roll Is Not Enough

There was half of a sports bar left and only a couple swigs of water. Lacy gave what was left to Colter. She pulled her purse out and dug through it to find her cell phone. As soon as she found it, she checked the battery. She still had plenty of power and dialed Jeremiah's number. He could zero in on her phone location and be there to pick them up in no time. Surely there was a road around here somewhere. Nothing happened.

"Chits! There's no signal! What does it mean there's no signal! This phone is guaranteed to always get a signal! That's why ADD's get them!"

Colter's big blue eyes were watching her. He didn't know what to make of her mood. She wasn't singing, but she wasn't happy either.

"Colt, don't worry. We're out! We couldn't be too far from civilization. We just have to walk some more. I was sort of hoping that as soon as we made it out of that hole, I'd be able to call for help, but the phone isn't working. So we'll just have to hoof it a while longer. At least the sun is out and the place is beautiful!"

"Lacy? Which way should we go?"

"Well, let's see about walking back around to where my car is. Maybe we can find it without finding your dad." She suspected that her car had probably been ditched somewhere no one would find it for a good long while, but she kept that to herself, not wanting Colter to worry. "I doubt he left it in his driveway. In any case, there have to be people around here somewhere. If we find a house before we make it all the way around, we'll ask to use their phone. Before we head out though, I have to get out of my armor. I need to check my ribs."

She stepped behind a large rock and pulled her sweater off. She slipped out of the armor, moving stiffly and gingerly. The left side of her rib cage looked like it had been tie-dyed in blues and purples. It was a wonder she was still breathing! Oh well, there was nothing she could do about it now. She slipped her sweater back on with some effort and pulled the armor out from under her skirt. It hurt too damn much taking it off to worry about putting it back on.

She just hoped they wouldn't run into Colt's father any time soon. She'd have to be watching out for that stupid black pickup. They wouldn't be able to flag down a ride until it was almost on top of them to be sure it wasn't him. Their best hope was just to keep walking. She sure hoped they would be home tonight. She needed a good soak in her tub. Of course, a lovely glass of wine would be good too, or maybe some nice painkillers!

Lacy pulled her sweater back down one-handed and walked back around the rock. She was going to check Colter over and make sure he was doing all right, but when she looked at him, she noticed that his attention was directed on something out in the middle of the meadow. She followed his gaze and was amazed to see two men on horseback riding toward them. The men were dressed oddly. Well, in all truthfulness, they were only *half* dressed. They had dark boots and some kind of leather pants on with leather straps that crisscrossed their chests. But that was all except for what looked like a red patch on the front of their left shoulder at the point where their collarbone joined it. As they got closer, she noticed that the patch was really a tattoo outlined in black with some sort of design inside it. Their hair was about shoulder length and blew loosely behind them.

Well, there was no accounting for style these days. People were known to wear all kinds of odd outfits. At least they weren't too chubby to carry off the style. They actually looked pretty good. As they got closer, she reassessed her earlier observation. They looked pretty damn good! Lacy and Colter walked out toward the two men. At least they wouldn't have to walk anymore though she hoped their horse trailer and pickup were somewhere close. Lacy knew she'd had it, and she supposed that Colter was looking forward to a ride also.

The men were too close for Lacy and Colter to retreat by the time she could make out their eyes. These were not the eyes of friendly men. These were the eyes of vultures . . . predators. Colter saw the look in the men's eyes also, but even if he hadn't, he'd have known they were dangerous when he heard the first strains of music slip from Lacy's lips. She was singing some serious hard rock. Colter's dad used to play similar music when he and Tony had their drinking parties. Colter took a couple of steps back behind Lacy. When she started singing like this in school, he knew he was in deep trouble. She had never hurt him, but he never doubted that she could. He guessed he was about to see just what that music really meant.

"Well, well, wha' have we here? A whelp and a lady! An' they both look a bit the worse for wear." The first man spoke with an odd sort of accent. It wasn't exactly English and not quite Scottish. It seemed very out of place to Lacy and Colter.

The second man looked Lacy up and down from her head to her toe. She didn't appreciate the attention, but she didn't say anything, in hopes that they would still be able to finagle a ride out of here though her hopes were beginning to dwindle.

"Ah, an' the lady has a lovely singin' voice. That could be worth a bi' t' our laird, though we migh' have t' alter her choice o' song. I think we'd better take her and her escort int' our care." The two laughed at the "escort" who seemed to be hiding behind the lovely but filthy young woman. "We canno' leave 'em ou' here unprotected!"

The man's offer came off sinister rather than sincere. His eyes were still admiring Lacy's curves. She took a defensive stance at that point, convinced that this was not going to go well. Her response brought more laughter from the two men.

Lacy mustered her courage, hoping to send them on their way. She did not feel like defending herself with ribs that needed some healing time. "Maybe you should just turn those horses around. We are perfectly capable of protecting ourselves. Indeed we have been doing that very thing for the last few days without your help. I'm sure we'll be fine."

"Oh, a feisty lass! And she only pauses in her song t' speak, then goes righ' back t' it. Still, if ye were as good at takin' care o' yerself as ye say, ya probably would no' be lookin' quite so . . . disheveled." The man dropped down from his horse, revealing the reason for the straps that crisscrossed his torso. There was a sword strapped to his back! He approached Lacy quickly but stopped a few feet away and peeked around her to look at Colter. "Lad, what say ye? Is this yer mother?"

Colter took courage from Lacy who stood ready to pounce. The song had gotten louder, and the words were very well enunciated. He knew Lacy was ready to fight if necessary. "She is not my mother, she is my teacher. She's an ADD, so you might want to get back on your horse and leave now. She's dangerous when she sings. Take it from me! I ought to know! She has sung to me a lot in school!" His eyes rolled as he finished.

"She's dangerous when she sings?!" The two men were enjoying the exchange a great deal. Their laughter nearly unhorsed the second man.

"Well," Colter caught their attention as he spoke again, "just remember that I warned you! She's singing rock-and-roll songs now. The harder the rock, the harder you roll!"

Lacy wanted to look at Colter the same way the two men looked at him now. She wondered where he was getting all this bravado. But she didn't dare take her eyes off the man on the ground. She watched the one on the horse from the corner of her eye. She didn't think she could take them both at the same time. She could easily take them if she were not already injured and if she had been wearing something other than this stupid skirt. It was not tight, but it wouldn't allow as free a movement as her gym clothes would have. She should have changed as soon as they left the cave. Hindsight was 20/20!!

"Do ye know wha' the whelp is talkin' abou', Keif?"

"No, no' at all. Listen, I was thinkin'. Do we have t' take the lady t' our laird righ' away, or could we play for a while first? I mean, it's no' like she looks t' be in the best condition now. She needs a bath, for sure! We might want t' see t' tha' first."

They both laughed conspiratorially again as the man on the ground took a step toward Lacy. Colter ran away from him toward the rock, and while he was distracted by Colter's flight, Lacy took advantage of the situation and turned suddenly. At the same time, she threw her leg in the air and kicked him hard in the jaw. The man dropped like a rock. Lacy was amused that the line from the song she was singing happened to be "Baby, are you sorry yet?" She almost laughed, but first she had to deal with the second man. Keif was off his horse and running toward her.

Keif's eyes were livid with anger. His fists were clenched tight as he entered her circle of defense. He was ready for her to try the kick again and defended against it easily, but missed the real move when her other foot came up right between his legs. To his credit, he remained standing after that blow but was unable to defend against her right-handed uppercut. He was stunned, but managed to stagger forward, wiping blood from his mouth. The anger on his face was so intense it seemed a tangible entity taking over his body and lunging toward her. Lacy dodged him and stopped singing long enough to issue one more warning.

"Turn and leave now, you can take your companion with you. I won't hurt you if you leave right now!!"

"I'll leave after I've had ye and repaid ye plenty for my mouth!" He came at her again, the evil in his face radiating toward her. Before he could get within arm's reach of her, she swung around and kicked him directly in the nose. She heard a disturbing crunch of bones. Her body turned with the kick, and she followed it up with as much of a punch to his midsection as she could muster. After all, she thought, it was better to give him everything she had while she still had it to give. He dropped right on top of the first man. Lacy nearly dropped with him as pain reverberated throughout her chest area. Tears came to her eyes, and she had trouble just breathing for the moment. Dizziness swept over her, and she stumbled to the ground. She forced herself back onto her feet once more and took shallow breaths until the dizziness subsided. She wiped the tears from her eyes quickly when she registered Colter's approach.

Colter was running back to her, squealing with delight! "Wow, Ms—Lacy! That was awesome! They didn't even get a hand on you!"

Lacy took a shallow breath, trying to pull herself together again. "They weren't expecting a fight, Colter. They underestimated their opponent. Unfortunately, they will not stay unconscious and we need to get out of here. I don't have another punch in me right now." She reached down, checking pulses to make sure the men were all right, only to bring back the dizziness when she bent over. Both men were soundly unconscious. The man on top had a nasty broken nose, but other than that, they would both recover before too long.

Breathe, she just had to breathe before she passed out. She had to think of Colter. She needed to get him away from here as soon as possible. What person would be stupid enough to attack a fully trained ADD? Now what should she do? The immediate "what" was that she was going to throw up! Lacy couldn't help herself. Even with next to nothing in her stomach, everything that *was* there came up abruptly, and each convulsion brought on more pain! Colter was staring at her with panic in his eyes.

"Lacy, what's wrong?" He started to run toward her.

"Stop right there, Colter!!"

He stopped abruptly where he was but didn't take his eyes off her.

"I'm okay, Colter." She stood on shaky legs and began to walk toward him. "I'm just not feeling well because of my ribs. Give me a minute and then we need to go."

"We could take their horses!"

"Do you know how to ride a horse?"

"No, but I bet you do!"

"No, I don't know the first thing about horses, Colter. Schools are not attacked by horses often enough to make it prudent to train us in controlling them. And sometimes, if a horse is not directed by a rider, it will just wander back to its home. We do not want to be on top of them when they go home, especially if their home is filled with men such as these."

"I'm not sure what all you said, but I bet it means we're walking again!" The disappointment in his voice was easily interpreted. Lacy couldn't stop a small chuckle escaping despite the shock of the last few minutes and winced, as she paid the price in pain again.

"Sorry, kiddo! But I couldn't pull myself up on top of one even if I wanted to right now, let alone put you up there. Let's go."

"Uh, Lacy?"

"Yes, Colter?"

"Do you think you could do the same thing you just did again, only against say five . . . no, six guys?"

Lacy laughed. "I think it would take a harder rock song than I know!"

"What if I sing a little Jarhead Revival for you?" He suggested the popular hard rock band, named for the retired marines who formed it, hoping that he'd inspire her to start singing and soon.

Lacy had slipped behind the rock to change into her sweats. She sure wasn't going to get caught in that skirt again. This side of the mountain was weird! People talked funny, dressed funny, fought with ADDs, what next?

"You know Jarhead Rivival songs?"

"Yeah, and you are going to need it, I think."

"Why?" she finished, sliding into her sweats and stepping out from behind the rock. She immediately understood what Colter was talking about.

Colter was at the center of a half circle of six men. They were all standing by their horses except for the one that was leaning over the two unconscious men. Unlike her first adversaries, these men looked more like her old friend John Finley. They were a good head taller than she was down to the last man. Even though John had taught her how to take down a guy his size, she was certain that it would only work once, twice if she was very lucky, and with no upper body strength right now, her options would be limited. After that, the others would learn how to avert the assault. She would have no chance to defend either Colter or herself. On top of all that, she really didn't feel like fighting anymore even if she could. She began to hum as she looked for a way out of this mess.

"Umm, Lacy?" Colter was not calmed by her humming this time. It was too tame. There was no rock and roll in the tune. It was mellow for heaven's sake! "You want me to sing some Jarhead Rivival for you?"

Lacy stopped singing long enough to whisper an answer to him. "No, Colter, it wouldn't be enough. I can't take on six men by myself. I don't even have the advantage of a few of them still sitting on their horses. We need to think our way out of this one. We can't fight our way out."

Lacy had spoken quietly, hoping that the men had not heard her. The one leaning over the two bodies in the field finally strolled back and addressed the man in the center.

"They're both alive, Marek. She knocked them ou' cold!"

Marek was the tallest of the group. He was quite handsome with dark shoulder-length hair and light brown eyes. His facial features were well defined but a bit scruffy looking under a couple of day's growth of beard. Lacy noticed his strong build. How could she miss it? Just like the men she had beaten, he was wearing only boots, leather pants, and two leather straps that crisscrossed his chest. All the men were dressed similarly, only their pants varied in color from tan to black.

The only differences she noticed between the two men she had felled and this group were silver disks that each of these men wore at the point where the leather straps crisscrossed on their chests, the color of the tattoo that each bore—just at the crest of the chest right below where the collarbone attached at the shoulder—and the look in their eyes. The disk on the leather straps bore a design—a crest, she thought—with a small blue stone at the center. Each tattoo rested on a blue background the same color as the stone on the disk, but the tattoos varied in design. Their eyes bore the biggest difference however. They weren't looking at her as if she were a piece of meat, but rather with admiration. Truly, the one called Marek was actually smiling at her!

Lacy felt adrenaline coursing through her body again, for the—well, how many times had that happened today? She had lost count. She was beginning to wonder what her body would feel like if she never needed adrenaline. She thought she might like to try that. As Marek took a step toward her, she slipped into her defensive stance again. Although what she planned on doing when she was clearly surrounded was beyond her. Without realizing it, her song changed. The words came fast and perfectly from her throat.

Once again, Colter turned and ran a small distance behind her. He had heard the change in her song and was heading out of the way. He was pleased with her choice of songs. She was preparing to fight. She would win! She always won. But Colter didn't get far. One of the men grabbed him around the waist as he ran past him. That was all the provocation Lacy needed. He shouldn't have touched the boy.

She was a blur of motion. The man holding Colter was clearly not expecting the attack. She moved with precision, hitting him twice before he thought to turn away from her. His effort was to keep the boy out of reach of her assault, but turning his back on her was just what she needed. She had been trained to disable threats to the children without bloodshed, and she was an expert. She flew to his back, hitting the man's sword but still managing to cling with one arm around his neck. With the other arm, she pinched a nerve at the base of his neck. The man passed out, dropping to his knees first and releasing Colter. Colter dropped to his feet, turned to smile at Lacy, and ran for the rock again.

Lacy's feet had touched the ground again as the man's knees hit. She released him then, allowing his body to fall forward to the ground. Turning to the other men, Lacy expected an assault from behind and resumed her earlier stance, this time standing between Colter and the rest of them. To her surprise, although several men had started to draw their swords, the big man named Marek had raised his hand to stop them. She had dropped one of their men, but the big man would not allow them to attack her. What was wrong with the people on this side of the mountain? They just couldn't be real. She looked up into the eyes of Marek. He was smiling even bigger now! What was with that?

"If you will just get on your horses and leave, I won't hurt anyone else," Lacy told Marek in a shaky voice. "You can take your man with you, he isn't hurt badly . . . He'll have a headache when he wakes up and will probably be sick to his stomach, but other than that, he'll be okay."

Marek laughed. "If we leave, she will no' hurt us!" he yelled louder so they all could hear.

Laughter again! Chits! Lacy was getting very tired of all this. She just didn't have the extra energy in reserve to deal with all this arrogance yet again! Okay, this arrogance was well placed. Really, she wasn't going to get the jump on all of them and they knew it. Well, chits! She was going to have to take out the big guy—uh, . . . biggest guy. Then maybe, just maybe, the rest of them would develop a little respect.

Still, it would take a lot more physical strength to take him down, and her ribs were screaming already. Jumping on the guy who had grabbed Colter had required holding on with upper body strength. That had taken a toll on Lacy's ribs. Despite the adrenaline coursing through her body, the arm that had done the holding on was not responding well to mental suggestions that it rise above her waist. She had pretty much lost it as a weapon for the time being—unless her attackers were less than three feet tall—and these attackers were, most definitely, *all* at least twice that size. She didn't have the strength left to maneuver the big man the way John had taught her. And she was sure that the only reason she wasn't doubled over in pain was the adrenaline still surging through her. She would have to try diplomacy.

"Look, you can take your other two guys with you. Uh, and you can take their horses too! Just let us go on about our business, please. You don't want to mess with me. I'm an ADD. It's a federal offense to mess with an ADD or an ADD's charge." She pointed to Colter as she finished.

"We have no intention o' taking those two wi' us, they are no' ours. We were lookin' for them t' retrieve what they took from one of my holdin's but we will take their horses. You would no' have anythin' t' ride if we did no'. Besides, they belong t' ye now." As Marek spoke, the man who had inspected the two men was going through their pockets. When he finished, he took the saddlebags off the horses and looked through each of them briefly and then threw them up on his own horse.

"They belong to me?"

"Aye, ye felled their riders. We saw it."

"I don't want them. You can have them. The boy and I will be on our way. We have to get home. People will be expecting us. Sorry about your man. If he had left the boy alone, I would have left him alone."

"Galen should have been able t' take a woman. He'll be shamed, but it will no' happen again. Ye will ride wi' us. We will see ye home safely."

"I won't ride anywhere. We will walk, thank you anyway."

"Ye will no' be safe in this area wi'ou' us. We have no' found the others. Ye will ride wi' us."

"I can take care of us. Thank you for your concern." She amended quickly, "What others?"

Marek smiled. Truly she was an exceptional woman, but he doubted she had much fight left in her. She looked very tired and was favoring one arm though she tried valiantly to hide that fact. He did not answer her question but instead asked another, "What is yer name, Little Warrior?"

Well, chits! Lacy thought. She was not only losing energy, she was also losing patience. The man may be nice to look at, but he was annoying. She was mortified when he closed the distance between them in only two strides. She should have attacked then, but she was out of energy and beginning to feel the pain of her exertions. The song that sprang from her lips was weak at best. Lacy was sure that Colter would be disappointed. She had no fight left. She just couldn't react quickly enough. She knew she'd never be able to take him down in her present shape, and even if she did, what would she do with the rest of them? Chits, she hurt! She was so tired of fighting. She sighed loudly.

"ADD DeMark," she told him then resumed her song. All she ever wanted to do was teach. Now look at her! Here she was in yet another situation. She'd never heard of any county in the area where men rode around half dressed on horses, daring to attack and detain ADDs and their charges. Her mind was reeling as she tried to understand where they were and what was happening. Lacy caught herself staring into his eyes. They were hypnotizing. She might have gotten lost in them until she saw him glance up at one of his men and motion toward Colter. That was it! She'd take him down or die trying. No one was touching her Colter! The song changed in an instant.

Marek heard the change and wondered about it. A warrior woman who sang! Her voice was strong and pure. It was pleasing. He liked listening to her. He preferred the song she had started with to this one, however. The other had been relaxing, calming the spirit into a moment of rest. This one seemed to do the opposite. He was straining to hear every word.

"Just another barroom rumble," she sang a line from an old country song. She tried a surprise kick to his groin, he deflected it. "A cue stick causes quite a tumble." She sang as she turned in a blur and her back hit his abdomen. It was as hard as a rock, but she threw her elbow into it anyway. She felt the reverberations all the way to her rib cage, causing her to double over. With no air to support it, her song stopped. What in the heck did he do in the gym that she didn't do? It was like hitting a steel plate. With one more grand effort, she took hold of his arm, using the side of her body that seemed to be in the least amount of pain in an attempt to throw him over her back to the ground; but she wasn't fast enough. Everything hurt too damn much! With uncanny speed, he grabbed her around her ribs, holding her arms tight to her side. The pain in her ribs forced what little air she had left in her lungs out in a loud cry. Tears sprang to her eyes, and her legs felt like she'd just stepped off a small boat that had been out to sea for months.

Colter had managed to keep the rock between him and the man Marek had sent after him. He was very fast. He had spent a lot of time at school eluding people, but he had to admit that it was easier in a room with desks and partitions to crawl in and around. The big man was almost on him when he heard Lacy's song stop and a scream replace it. That sent him into full-force fear and rebellion. No one ever bested Lacy! He jumped up on top of the rock, using a little foothold he had noticed earlier. Going over the rock had saved him from running right into the arms of a second man who had come over to help the first. As soon as he saw Lacy in the arms of the biggest man, he ran to her rescue.

A six-year-old squirt of a boy was usually no match for a grown man, but Colter had been trained by the best, he thought to himself. After all, he had eluded and injured adults for the last three months in school. Didn't the principal and Lacy both have bite marks that matched his teeth exactly? Actually, he felt kind of bad about that, but he wouldn't feel bad about biting this man! He threw himself at the man, wrapping his arms around one leg.

"Let her go! Let her go, or I'll bite you so hard you'll have teeth marks forever!"

"Colter, stop!"

"No, Lacy! I won't stop. He hurt you and I won't let him hurt you again!"

"It's okay, Colter. He isn't hurting me now." The big man had loosened his grip on her as soon as she had cried out. He hadn't let go, but he was no longer hurting her; he was supporting her.

"Lacy—" Now Colter was in tears.

"There are too many of them, Colter. We can't possibly win. My ribs were cracked when we fell down the shaft. I can't fight until they heal. Let go of him!"

Marek spoke then. "How badly are ye injured?"

Lacy was surprised when the man's hold on her loosened further and he let her go, making sure she could stand on her own first. Colter let go of the man's leg then and ran to Lacy. He stood just in front of her, back to Lacy, facing the man. She stood on her own, but just barely. "Badly enough that I can't take you down," Lacy admitted.

Every ear in the clearing had heard her boast, sending them all into another annoying round of laughter. Lacy wasn't amused. She could have taken him down if she was healthy; she just wouldn't have been able to fend off every last one of them by herself. Still, she didn't think the statement warranted all this laughter.

Marek stepped toward the little warrior woman standing before him. As he looked at her now, he again appraised the woman who would fight a hopeless battle to defend a small child. The little warrior was quite pretty. She looked too small to be a formidable opponent, yet she had bested two of Laird Bremhall's men. And she had done it injured! He was pleased that she had left them alive. There was mercy in her, as there should be in a woman. He wished he could be there when the two men explained to their laird that a woman and a child had taken their horses!

Then she had taken on Galen, he mused. There had been a sword strapped to Galen's back, yet she had ignored it and done something to his neck that had put him to sleep. Galen was only now beginning to come around. He was groaning and blinking his eyes, trying to get them to focus again. He threw up next . . . repeatedly. It was likely that he would never live *that* down. Marek laughed to himself. Then his attention returned to the little warrior. She also had that sweet name, not the name of a warrior, but of a lady. What had the child called her? Oh yes, Lacy, that was it. She was an anomaly for sure.

The boy was snatched up into the capable hands of Marek's second in command, Connor. Connor managed to hold the boy tight despite the fiercest fighting a six-year-old could muster. Lacy watched him anxiously until the fighting suddenly stopped and was replaced by his delighted voice.

"You're taking me on the horse?"

"Aye," Connor responded as the boy's thrashing stopped abruptly.

"Lacy, I get to ride a horse! Can I steer?"

"No!"

"Please?"

"No!" Connor left no room for argument . . . or so he thought.

"What's your name?"

"Connor."

"Hi, Connor. Do you want to know my name?"

"I already know your name."

"Really? What is it?"

Connor sighed loudly as he set the boy on his horse.

Lacy wobbled on her legs as if she might fall down where she stood. Marek leaned down to scoop her up in his arms. She immediately reverted back to her training and sank into her defensive position, but one exasperated look from Marek's golden brown eyes stopped her flat and she relaxed her stance, wobbling almost to her knees, save for Marek. He scooped her up then and raised her to put her on his horse but was surprised to see terror in her eyes. Up to this point, he hadn't seen terror there at all. She had been brave and defiant, defending the child from six warriors. But now, when he gently raised her to set her on his horse, she looked quite like she might scream.

"Wha' is wrong? I'll no' hurt ye. I thought t' put ye on my horse only because o' yer injury. If ye prefer t' ride by yerself—"

"No!" Lacy responded a little too loudly, and her body tensed in his arms. She felt the recriminations from her ribs at the involuntary response of her muscles. She held her breath for a moment to let the pain subside and then continued. "I just don't do horses! I don't like them. Well, actually, I've never ridden one, but—"

"Ye are afraid o' my horse?" Marek looked at her incredulously. "Ye would fight six men t' protect a child, but ye are afraid of a horse?"

"I'm not afraid! Chits! I just . . . I don't ride them, okay?! Couldn't we just go in your pickup or something? You do have a pickup, don't you? All the country people have pickups. It's like a cultural theme around here," she added sarcastically.

"I have jus' picked ye up. Now tha' I have picked ye up, we'll be ridin' my horse."

"I didn't mean you should pick me up! I'm talking about riding in your truck rather than on a horse. Is your house far?" Sitting sidesaddle on the horse, she looked down at her hands, filthy from the cave, grasping the saddle till her knuckles turned white. "Wow, I really need a bath." She hummed a couple of bars and then said, "I really need to use a phone too. Mine is broken, I think."

The humming turned into singing softly as Lacy continued to try to sort out a very confusing day. *This day is just getting better and better*, she thought sarcastically. She was beginning to feel a little nauseated, no doubt from the bear hug he had used to stop her assault or maybe it was sitting on top of a horse for the first time ever. And now she was expected to ride the horse of all things! Well, she really wasn't up to walking either. So maybe the ride wouldn't be so long. There had to be a neighborhood around here somewhere close.

"Where is yer home?" Marek asked as he swung up behind Lacy.

"I live in Riverton."

"Where is this Riverton?"

"It's just on the other side of that mountain there. Aren't you from around here? Riverton is the biggest town in Walden County."

"I have no' heard o' it and the land on the other side o' tha' hill belongs t' me."

"What?"

"It belongs t' me. I'm Laird McKenzie. Quite certainly, ye are lost. We'll take ye t' the healer and have her look after yer injuries. Then we'll decide what t' do wi' ye from there." Marek reached around her and took hold of her front leg to slide it to the other side of the horse. Lacy squealed with the intimacy of the move but, once settled, thought that she felt much more secure this way and relaxed a bit.

Galen was crawling sluggishly up on his horse. With every painful effort he expended, the others laughed and teased him. *If it weren't bad enough that they felt the need to goad me like this, did they have to laugh so loudly?!* he thought.

"We're so verra sorry for ye, Galen. It must have been horrible bein' taken down wi' two fingers by such a fierce adversary!" teased Kenneth.

Brett rode up beside him and patted him on the shoulder. "If only we could have saved ye in time! Had we only known what strength the pretty little thin' keeps hidden in those two fingers, we'd have cut them off before she had the chance t' shame ye so!" More laughter followed. Galen took a swipe at Brett, missing him but causing him to dodge the blow, almost sending him to the ground. Galen enjoyed a brief grin, but it hurt too much to sustain.

—

Still focused on what Marek had just said about Riverton, Lacy wondered just how far they had come in the tunnel. She was sure they had only walked for a couple of days—three at the most. They had been forced to move slowly because of the dark. They couldn't have come so far that the people here would not have knowledge of Riverton. And what was with the odd accent? She shrugged, unsure of what to make of all this. She knew the surrounding area of Riverton—there wasn't any place like this—she was a teacher after all! Maybe just a first-grade teacher, but she liked geography. She knew . . . she sighed. Nothing, it appeared! The humming started then. It was a new song she had heard on the radio a few times called "Back to Just Breathing," and right at the moment, that's what she was—back to just breathing.

Colter turned around to look at her, which was no easy feat as he was sitting on a horse facing the opposite direction with Connor right behind him. The man was so big that Colter had to wiggle around and peek under his armpit. Connor was not happy with the wiggling and was struggling to keep him looking forward.

The singing stopped momentarily as Lacy noticed the commotion. "Connor, choose your battles better. Let him see what's going on and you'll have a much nicer ride today. Trust me on this one. Wait for a battle that is worth fighting." The humming resumed, and Connor reluctantly allowed Colter a peek behind him. Lacy was right. As soon as Colter determined that the humming was a thinking thing and not a danger thing, he settled down easily in Connor's lap and resumed the argument over who would "steer."

Marek was most interested in the song, or maybe it was the singer he was most interested in. Her perfect body was easily discernable through the odd pants she wore. She had what once was probably a pretty light blue sweater on, but it had seen better times. He wondered what the two had been through. She looked as though she had been fighting the world. Knowing what he knew of her, that was probably it. He thought she might have pretty hair under all that dirt somewhere, but it remained to be seen. The boy looked just about as ragged and dirty as she did. The only clean thing between the two of them was the odd pants she wore. Of course, he knew she had just changed into them as they were approaching the two earlier. Marek and his men had been watching the fight with the Bremhall men.

They had hurried when they saw the two men approach Lacy and Colter. They thought they were going to have a chase on their hands to save the woman and child and were most impressed that she had defended herself even in the tight-fitting skirt she had been wearing. He was very curious about her and wished to ask her what the two were doing out here without protection. But she looked tired, and he didn't wish to interrupt the beautiful song. Her voice was lower than most women he had heard sing, and the song had an oddness about it. It was pleasing but very different from the ones sung in his great hall during feasts. He would listen and let her rest. Then he would demand his answers.

As the song continued, Lacy had a thought; this must be one of those colony-type things where the people refused to use cars or anything with electricity. That had to be it. Funny how she had never heard of it, especially considering its close proximity to Riverton. Yes, that had to be it. Of course, usually you didn't have to defend yourself against those sorts of people. They were usually very peaceful. But there must be bad eggs in their baskets just like in the rest of the world. She was just beginning to relax, and the song was merely a hum now when she heard him speak.

"We'll stop by the lake so ye can clean up before we go on."

"What?" Lacy questioned. He couldn't be serious. No one took baths in lakes; good grief, you could catch your death of cold! "We can wait till we get home," she hurried to add.

"We don' know where yer home is," he pointed out. "And besides, Jeanette would no' appreciate it if we did no' take good care of ye while ye are under our protection."

"Having us bathe in a lake is taking good care of us? Never mind! I don't need your protection and I don't need Jeanette. I just need to go home. Then I can see my own doctor and take a bath in my own bathtub with *hot* water. I appreciate your concern and your help, but I don't need it. If you will just drop us off on the other side of that mountain, I'm sure I can get us home safely."

"Ye could no' defend yerself against anyone in yer state right now, though t' be honest, ye might be able t' knock them ou' with yer scent!" He was only chuckling so far, but Lacy found it just as annoying as the laughter from earlier.

"If you do not appreciate my fragrance, you could just let us go our own way. I wouldn't take offense at all!" She had turned her head to try to look at him so he would know she was quite serious. She had to look up into his eyes even sitting in the saddle with him. "Please." Why was she being polite? Hadn't he just insulted her? It wasn't her fault that she and Colter were filthy. It was that chits of an animal that called himself a father to Colter that had caused their present predicament. She was truly going to make that man pay for this!

"Ye need no' wait, we are here." Marek jumped off his horse and took hold of Lacy to help her down. As he pulled her off the horse, the sweater slipped up a bit, taking his hand with it. Two things happened as a result. The first was the searing pain that shot through Lacy, causing her to swear loudly. The second was the louder swearing from Marek when he first noticed her well-defined abdominal muscles and then again when he saw the bruising from her cracked ribs. He quickly set her feet on the ground but didn't let go of her. She was swaying. He gently picked her up in his arms, cradling her as he walked toward the lake.

"Ian!" he yelled over his shoulder, "Bring her bag."

Lacy found the situation quite unsettling. Being too sore to fight physically, she opted for verbal demands. "You can set me down now. I'm over it."

"Ye are no' over it. Ye should have told me how seriously ye were injured. I could have made the ride a little easier for ye."

"Really? You got a pickup in your pocket, do you? The ride was fine. I don't need you. I'm fine. Put me down, please."

He ignored her request to be put down and continued toward the lake. "I suspect that we are no' on the same path wi' the words *pick up*."

"Don't you mean that we're not on the same page?" He looked blankly at her. "Never mind. It's one word—*pickup*! You know, four tires and a steering wheel?!"

Marek looked blankly at her.

She shook her head as if to clear it of the ridiculous conversation. "What are you planning on doing? Standing around watching me bathe? Well, you can forget it 'Sir' Marek. I don't need a knight in shining armor. I'm well trained and can take care of myself."

"Ye canno' even stand on yer own ri' now. I will help ye."

"That is really sweet, but I am not some wimpy little girl! I don't need you!"

"Tha's what ye keep sayin', but I am no' convinced."

He had carried her through a stand of trees, and at the edge of the lake, he stopped and set her down on a rock. He took her bag from Ian and sent him back to the horses. Connor was right behind him with Colter. Colter was running after Lacy as Connor tried to keep up.

"Lacy, are you all right?!" Colter was yelling through the trees. "Lacy, where are you?"

"I'm right here, Colter. And yes, I'm all right!"

"Connor said we get to take a bath in the lake!"

"Connor has another think coming!"

"Lacy, I want to take a bath in the lake. I've never done that before. But you can't be here. I'm not taking a bath in the lake in front of you!"

"Nor I in front of you!"

Marek broke in then. "Is he no' yer son?"

"No, he is my charge. I am his guardian for the time being. He is my student."

"Connor, take Colter back t' the horses until the lady is finished wi' her bath." Marek ordered him.

"Come on, Colter. We'll come back soon."

As the two walked back to the horses, Lacy's eyes never left Marek's. She glowered at him, daring him to take one step toward her. She began to hum. He cocked his eyebrows up a notch as he listened.

"I have noticed something about ye," the big man said as he began to smile.

The humming stopped. "What would that be?"

"Ye hum when ye are nervous or frightened."

"No, I hum when I'm forced to fight or when I need to think something through."

"So which is it now? Are ye thinking it through, or are ye preparin' to fight?"

"If you take even one step toward me to help me bathe, I will be forced to fight you."

"If I did no' know how injured ye are, I would love t' see ye try. However, in the interest o' keepin' ye in one piece, I will turn my back while ye bathe but I would appreciate it if ye'd talk while ye bathe. If ye stop talkin', I'll be forced t' turn and make sure ye're all righ'. Ye may not think ye need me, but ye do." He started to turn but stopped when she spoke.

Lacy felt anger flush her cheeks. "So you will not leave us alone, you insist that I take a bath, and you will not leave while I do. Do I have the whole picture?"

"Pretty much! But do no' forget t' talk while ye bathe. Do ye have a clean tunic in tha' bag?"

"I have several clean tu—T-shirts in there. I work out twice a day usually."

"Work ou'? Work ou' o' what?"

"Work out! You know, exercise to keep in shape."

"Ye have t' work . . . ou' . . . to keep yer shape?"

"Yes, usually I work very hard, but I am a little sore right now. So I haven't been able to keep up my normal regimen. Give me a day or two. I'll get back to it. I noticed you work out a bit too!"

"Aye, I work ou' in the barn and the fields o' my holdin'."

Lacy laughed then. She liked his sense of humor almost as much as his eyes. She couldn't see them right now because he was looking down at something on the ground, but she could sure remember them.

"Why do ye . . . uh, . . . work . . . ou'?" Marek was hoping that he might be able to figure out just what she was talking about if he kept her talking. He wasn't sure why she had laughed, but he liked the sound of her laughter though he was sorry that it was followed by a groan as pain obviously shot through her in its wake.

"I have to work out for my job. We are required to go to the gym twice a day for an hour each time at least. Unfortunately, that little guy with me has caused more trouble than any three children I have ever had in my classroom. I am in the process of having him removed from his home. After meeting his father, I'm pretty sure I know where all the trouble began. As a matter of fact, he hasn't been a lick of trouble since we got away from his house and fell in the shaft!" Lacy began to think that little revelation through and began to hum again.

"I hate to interrupt such a beautiful song, bu' ye need t' bathe and we need t' be on our way."

Lacy's brows furrowed. She rolled her eyes and then answered him, "Fine, turn around, please."

Marek turned and Lacy gingerly pulled off the sweater. She couldn't believe how dirty and chewed up it looked. It had snags and tears all over the back. She was a little embarrassed that she had ever turned her back on anyone with the sweater on. Oh well, she quickly stripped and walked into the water. "Holy cow! It's freezing!" she yelled.

"I suggest ye keep yer bath short!" He chuckled.

She growled and washed as quickly as she could. She sang again as she bathed; it helped with the cold a bit. Surprisingly the cold also felt good on her ribs! The singing kept Marek turned away from her as well as helping her sort out her predicament.

It was a good thing that she had shampoo in her bag as well as conditioner though she only had use of her right hand. She pulled out her towel and quickly dried off. She had to admit that she sure felt better. When she took the time to look at her ribs, she sucked in air so fast that it hurt. She groaned and Marek started to turn. She squeaked out, "Stop! Don't turn, I'm fine."

"Are ye sure? Are ye in pain?"

"I'm fine. I just hadn't checked out my ribs this well before. The intense colors sort of surprised me."

"Aye, they surprised me too."

She blushed at his response but finished dressing, pulling her spandex sweats back on and her favorite bright coral T-shirt. The T-shirt was snug fitting and stretchy, very comfortable. She put her loafers in the bag and took out her tennis shoes. Once she finished dressing, she told Marek he could turn around. It was his turn to suck in a breath.

"Is tha' all the clothes ye have wi' ye?!"

"I only have my gym bag! We're just riding horses, what did you expect? A formal?!"

"What's a formal?"

"A long dress that goes down to your ankles, worn for formal occasions." Sheese! Where had this man been for the last thirty years?

"I expect ye to cover up a wee bi' better. I am traveling wi' men who have no' been home in a couple o' months."

"I thought you just lived around the mountain!"

"Yes, we do live just on the other side o' the hill, but we have been chasing the men ye caught for us since they raided one o' my holdin's. The raiding party split up into two groups. So we split up also. There were three in the group tha' attacked ye, so one is still missin'. But he won't get far. I sent two o' my men after him."

"You were chasing them? Why didn't you just call the police? Surely they could have apprehended them for you."

"Police?"

She rolled her eyes again. "It's like being abducted by the Mafia! Never mind!"

Marek took her gym bag from her and reopened it. He dug through it and pulled out her oversized sweatshirt. "Here, put this on!" He was scowling at the thing, wondering just what it was, but anything was better than watching her walk out in front of his men wearing what looked like a brightly colored second skin. He had to admit that he liked what he saw; he just didn't want anyone else to see what he was seeing. Wow, would he like to put his arms around her again! He almost wished she would hurt herself . . . just a little . . . so he could carry her back to the horse. What was he thinking?! He cleared his throat.

Lacy looked straight into his eyes with total defiance. "I will not put on a sweatshirt in eighty-degree weather!"

"Sweatshirt? Ye call this thing a sweatshirt? Does it make ye sweat?"

"It certainly would make me sweat today! Put it back, please."

"Ye will wear it."

"No, I won't!" Lacy was still staring at him. He was looking pretty stubborn about this, but he was just going to have to back down. It was too hot for sweatshirts!

He didn't budge or put the sweatshirt away. Lacy got the feeling that they were not going to go anywhere until she agreed. She finally rolled her eyes and reached for the bag. She grabbed the sweatshirt and stuffed it back inside. Marek took a step toward her with the intent of helping her put the sweatshirt on when she started digging through the bag again.

"Fine! I'll compromise with you," Lacy half yelled at him. "You do understand compromise, don't you?"

Marek didn't respond, but he did stop his advance and wait for her to rummage though the bag until she pulled out another T-shirt. This one was gray and oversized. Lacy hated it and only used it for emergencies. She guessed this was sort of an emergency. She was tired and ready to get home. She had to remind herself that she was not here to build lasting relationships after all. The gray T-shirt could have fit her old friend John. It hit her about halfway down her thighs and left enough room around the middle to fit another person in it with her. She pulled out a belt that she had inadvertently left in the bag after her last workout session and buckled it loosely over her hips.

The effect was less than stunning she thought. Marek, however, thought that this woman could not help looking alluring. If the truth be told, he could

---

49

find her a burlap sack to wear, and the woman would make it look good. He watched her pull out an odd-looking machine. She pushed a button on it, and it made a sort of growling noise. She pointed it at her head and made an effort to brush her hair at the same time. She couldn't lift her left arm high enough to either hold the odd machine or to brush her hair. She handed the noisemaker to him. Honestly, he didn't know what to make of that!

Lacy noticed his astonished face. She reached up with her good arm, turned off the blow-dryer, and looked up at him. "Would you mind holding that thing up and pointing that over here? I can't do it myself." He was staring at the blow-dryer, looking at it as if it were the first one he had ever seen. Lacy assumed he was wondering where the batteries were. "It's solar. I never understood the reasoning behind a solar-powered blow-dryer until this moment. I'm not much of a camper, so this is the first time I've actually used it outside. It was a gift. I'd have never bought it for myself because I have to put it in the windowsill at school to charge. The same person gave me the straightener also. It's solar too. I guess they will be helpful today though!"

The blank look on his face was comical. He clearly had no idea what she was talking about. Lacy would have laughed at any other time in her life, but after today, she didn't know how to respond to his obvious confusion. In frustration, she finally reached up, took hold of his hand, and looked directly into his bewildered eyes. "Look, just hold it up and point it at me. I need to get my hair dry so I can straighten it. Okay?"

Marek watched her turn the thing on again. He turned it toward his face to look into the barrel and was surprised at the wind coming out of it. He jumped and almost dropped it. Lacy was looking at him as if he was an imbecile. He didn't like that look! She reached over and turned his hands so that the thing blew back toward her again and began to brush her hair in front of the wind stream. Then he had it! It was to help her get her hair dry! It blew warm wind out, and Lacy was drying her hair with it! He would have to find out how it worked.

He yelled over the sound of the thing, "How does it work?"

"What?"

"How does it work?"

"I showed you! You just push the button and it blows air!"

"Aye, bu' how?"

"I don't know. I'm a teacher, not a manufacturer!"

When she finished, she began pressing her hair through another thing. As she worked, the lovely wave she had in her pretty blond hair was disappearing. The thing took the curls right out! He tried to stop her. She just slapped his hand away.

"What are ye doin' t' yer curls?"

"I don't feel like curls right now. I feel like straight hair. I haven't been clean in two or three days and I want to finish my hair, please."

"I like yer curls."

"I'm happy for you, but I don't feel like working with them. It's easier with straight hair although it is rather difficult to do with one arm."

When she finished, she repacked her equipment and ran the brush through her hair one last time. She put the brush back into her bag, then took it out again as she remembered that Colter would need it. When she looked up, she noticed Marek staring at her hair. He reached out to touch it. She held still for him as he first stroked her head and then began running his fingers through it. She would have stopped him except that his expression was filled with curiosity, and that made Lacy curious. What was going on with this guy? She'd ask him later . . . maybe.

Finally running low on patience, she caught his hand and pulled it from her hair. "Okay, Marek, leave the hair alone. We need to let Colter in here. If we don't let him have his bath, he'll fight us all the way to wherever we're going. I don't have a lot of energy left in me, and I'm tired of fighting."

Lacy turned away from Marek and headed back toward the clearing. Marek took the bag from her and followed her out. She had recovered a bit with the taking of a bath, but she still looked fragile to him. He stayed close to her in case she needed his support, but he couldn't seem to take his eyes off the beautiful yellow hair cascading down her back. He wondered how long the curls would stay away. If she carried the thing around with her, surely she had to use it often, so the curls would have to come back on a regular basis, wouldn't they? He wondered just how it all worked.

The bath had certainly done wonders for her. Her beauty when they found her had been something, but now she was radiant. A beautiful little warrior woman! Who could have known he would start out chasing marauders and end up with a beautiful warrior woman riding on his horse with him? It had definitely been a very rewarding day!

Colter had been entertaining the men with tales of their adventure through the dark mine shaft. The men had listened intently as he had told them how the landings had caved under them and how Lacy had kept Colter safe as they fell. He explained how scary it was when Lacy had blacked out and Colter thought she was dead. Then he told them how long they had walked until they had finally made their way out. He explained that Lacy had helped him by singing as they went. He told them about how Lacy had been his teacher and when she sang at school he knew he was in trouble. He told them to watch out when she starts singing hard rock stuff because that meant she was about to kick some butt. The men weren't sure what he meant about hard rock songs, so Colter began singing all the hard rock songs that he knew. The ones he knew were all from his father's repertoire, and even though the language was a bit strange, the warriors couldn't believe that the beautiful lady would sing these songs . . . even in battle! Colter insisted on teaching them some of the lyrics so they would be able to help her out if she had trouble coming up with a tough enough song for battle. He patiently explained how he had had to help her out before.

When Lacy stepped out of the trees and heard the songs the men were singing with Colter, she was mortified!

"What are you men doing?"

The men turned to look at her with wide eyes. They stared at the furious, beautiful lady before them, struck simultaneously by her beauty and her apparent indignation all at the same time. When they didn't respond immediately to her, she really tore into them.

"How can you teach a little boy such horrible songs?"

Ian was the first to recover. "What? We did no' . . . he—"

"Don't tell me he came up with those on his own? He's just a baby!"

Colter took exception to that remark. "I'm not a baby!"

Lacy ignored him and continued to chew the men out. "What has gotten into you? A little boy shouldn't be taught such songs nor allowed to repeat them. Shame on you all!"

Kenneth, a stocky man with blond hair and rugged looks, finally managed to respond to the irate lady. "Dear lady, he told us he learnt this song from you! The truth o' the matter is tha' none o' us have ever heard it before!"

"He what? Colter Stecks! What have you been telling these men?!"

It did not escape Colter's notice that Lacy did not wait for him to answer and had started to hum as she approached him. He knew the song and the look. Lacy had used it more than once in school. His eyes nearly popped out of his little head as he watched her storm across the clearing toward him. He hopped up and ran behind Kenneth.

"I'm sorry, Ms. DeMark! I didn't tell them you sang them. I told them to watch out for hard rock songs, but they didn't know what they were. So I sang them the ones my daddy used to play!" He heard her footsteps stop along with the humming as Lacy heard his response. He chanced a peek around Kenneth's legs to see if Lacy was still angry with him.

"Oh, that explains a lot. Gentlemen, I beg your forgiveness," Lacy said to the men and then turned back to Colter. "Still, Colter, you know what language is acceptable in school, am I right?"

"Yes," he responded somewhat slowly.

"That is the only language that is acceptable for little boys. Do I make myself clear?"

"I'm not a little boy, Lacy! I'm a big boy," he said defensively.

"Colter, do you really want to argue this point?"

"No." His voice was almost a whisper.

"Now apologize to these gentlemen, please." She was waiting for a fight. Colter never said he was sorry at school without a fight. She thought she might faint when he turned to the men without an argument and apologized.

"Thank you, Colter." She beamed at him, and the smile brought him out from behind Kenneth's legs and put a smile on his dirty face.

Lacy walked over to him and took his hand and pulled him toward Connor. "You need to go take your bath. Here's the shampoo, a brush, and the towel. Go on with Connor now."

"Take the little guy for his bath and try to hurry," Marek quietly told Connor while Lacy wandered out of earshot. "She's abou' had it. I would like to have a little more distance between us and Bremhall before we camp."

Connor nodded, waited for Colter to get to him, and quickly took him back to the lake. Lacy had found a rock to sit on. She looked exhausted to Marek. She only sat for a minute before she was up again. She wandered around for a bit and ended up back by the trees. Marek finally decided that she was looking for a place to sit where she could lean back and rest her ribs. She had wandered back to the tree line. She finally sat down on the ground and gingerly leaned up against a tree. She closed her eyes, and Marek watched until he saw her arm relax and her hand slide to the ground. Her arm slid down palm up, revealing an odd-shaped round wound on the inside of her wrist. He hadn't noticed it before. It looked like little teeth marks. Marek stepped closer to examine it. Sure enough, it was a bite mark! He wondered how that had happened. He would have to add that to the list of questions he had for her. It was more important that he let her sleep first. God knows she needed it! She had fallen asleep in a matter of about thirty seconds.

CHAPTER 5

The Healer

Being late in the day anyway, Marek decided that he couldn't make her move on until she had a little more sleep. He had his men set up camp. They built a fire and moved Lacy to a blanket close by. She never even stirred from her sleep. Colter curled up beside her not long after his bath. He managed to stay awake long enough to share in the men's meal, but not much longer after that. Marek covered them both with the second blanket from the Bremhall's horses.

Lacy's dreams were troubling. She was falling into the shaft again. The darkness was enveloping her and pulling her deeper and deeper into nothingness. She sat up suddenly and was jerked back to reality by the pain shooting across her chest. The pain caused her to suck in air suddenly, which brought on more pain. She tried not to cry or make any noise, but a whimper escaped her lips despite her best efforts. Damn, she hurt. Every muscle in her chest, back, and abdomen ached. Her left arm was so stiff she couldn't even lift it. Tears slipped silently down her cheeks. What she would give for a strong muscle relaxant!

Marek was there in an instant. He had been on watch and had seen her sit up suddenly. He sat down behind her and pulled her back into his chest. She resisted only a second, finding that it hurt too much to fight him. Surprisingly, she could breathe a little more easily leaning back a bit. She managed to take a couple of pretty good breaths.

"Bad dreams?" Marek whispered into her ear.

She nodded. "Marek?"

"Aye?"

"Could you help me stand up? I think I would feel better if I walk around a bit and loosen up my muscles."

"Are ye sure?"

"Yes, please."

Marek gently sat her back up, moved to her side, and scooped her up in his arms. Once he was standing, he set her feet slowly and gently back on the ground, still supporting her by holding her around her waist. She took a tentative step and let go of him. He walked beside her, watching her to make sure she didn't fall. As they walked past one of the men whose name Lacy didn't know yet, Marek kicked him lightly and said, "Brett! Wake up and take over the watch."

Brett dutifully sat up, shook the sleep off, and stretched. He was alert in that small moment of time. He stood and began to scan the area as he headed off to some vantage point that Lacy didn't bother to take note of. She was too busy paying attention to the throb in her ribs and the tall handsome warrior at her side. She stumbled on something in the dark, but Marek reached out to steady her before she fell. He had taken hold of her arm, and he pulled her in close to him as they walked. She didn't resist or pull away again. She leaned in to him. She was so tired. She wished she was home in her bed. She needed sleep, but the hard ground had made her so stiff she didn't want to think of lying back down again. She stopped walking and wrapped her good arm around Marek's waist. He was so warm and she was so tired . . .

He felt her begin to relax after wrapping her arm around him. She had stopped moving, and Marek reached down under her knees and pulled her into his arms again. He walked back to the camp, sat down, and leaned up against a tree. He settled Lacy against his chest and pulled a blanket over them both. She didn't move again until the next morning when her stomach began to protest the lack of food deposits in the last twenty-four hours. She woke up in Marek's arms.

She wondered if the hunger was really that important when compared to sleeping in his arms. She tried not to move or change her breathing. She was enjoying his warmth and the soft caresses he was providing up and down her back. That must have been what had awakened her, she thought. Her comfort was quickly interrupted when her stomach growled loudly.

She felt his breath close to her ear as he whispered, "Little warrior, you canno' take care o' yer hunger until ye wake up and neither can I."

Despite the smile that was clearly audible in his voice, Lacy felt a pang of guilt at having kept him from his breakfast so that she could enjoy his closeness. She stirred both reluctantly and cautiously, waiting for the pain to erupt when she did. Her ribs didn't disappoint her, but it wasn't as bad as it had been the night before. She wasn't sure if that was because she had begun to heal or if it was because Marek was so warm that he kept her muscles from freezing up on her. Whatever the reason, she was grateful, and since he had sat up leaning against the tree all night holding her, she decided to be grateful to him. It was on that premise that she turned carefully, looked up into those beautiful brown eyes, and kissed his shoulder, the only thing she could reach. She was a little embarrassed at the silliness of the gesture and hurried to explain herself.

"Thank you! I'm sorry you had to lean up against that tree all night. But every muscle in my midsection is screaming its thank you. You are the most gallant man I have ever met." Whew, where had that last statement come from? *Gallant?* She must be nurturing delusions because of the company she was keeping! She was beginning to sound like one of them. She was treating him like . . . a knight of the round table or something. She sounded like a dolt even to herself. She winced even as she turned back around and tried to sit up. What must he be thinking?

Marek had stopped thinking the minute her lips touched his shoulder. He hadn't gotten his mind working again until she had gotten to the part about him being gallant. If she knew what he'd been thinking about as he held her, as she kissed his bare shoulder, she'd have chosen a different word, he was certain! He'd then thought about kissing *her*, but he would have had to move her to get to her beautiful lips. He was afraid he'd hurt her if he did. He was going to kiss her, he promised himself; he just had to wait for a better time.

She was sure a pretty little warrior. He wondered where she had learned to fight using her legs to take down a man. She hadn't had to use her upper body much on the two Bremhall men, and that had saved her. If she had been dependent on upper body strength, she'd have been in trouble quickly. He and his men would have had to lead a merry chase to rescue her then.

He helped her sit up, supporting her back as she moved. Once she was sitting on her own, he stood up and then helped her to her feet. Marek could see that she was moving more easily now, but she was still cautious and slow.

The man who served her up a little breakfast introduced himself to Lacy as Kenneth. She thought she had met them all now. As she glanced around the campsite, she tried to remember each man's name. As she made her way around the circle, she noticed that Colter was missing as well as Connor.

She was humming again.

Marek moved close beside her. "What's wrong? There is no danger here. What are ye thinkin' abou'?" He had picked up on the humming faster than his men.

"Where is Colter?"

"He's with Connor."

"And where is Connor?"

"They will be right back. They are just in the trees behind us."

Lacy's humming softened but did not stop. He found her a place to sit comfortably to eat and sat beside her. Marek noticed that she relaxed a little as she ate, pausing the song with each bite though never ceasing completely, and kept glancing behind her to watch for Colter.

"He is safe. Connor will no' let anythin' happen t' him. If you wish t' sing, we would like t' hear the words."

"Hmm?" Lacy had not realized that she had been humming. It took her a moment to figure out what he was talking about. When she did, she just shook her head and forced herself to stop humming.

Marek was disappointed that she did not sing for them. She had a lovely voice, but alas, he had only heard it when she was frightened or worried. He wondered what it would sound like if she ever really *tried* to sing. It would be most enchanting, he thought. Hell, it already was. He liked that he knew when something was up with her. When she was distressed or agitated in any way, she would start singing. It was a dead giveaway. Unfortunately, he was going to have to train it out of her. If her enemies ever figured it out, she would be vulnerable. What a pity! It was a very endearing trait.

Connor and Colter came roaring out of the trees, Connor chasing and Colter giggling as he dodged and rolled away from him. Connor looked so serious that Lacy assumed that Colter had finally become himself again and was back at his games from school. She stood up and bellowed at Colter. The song she sang now stopped every one in their tracks, and Colter stopped running as if he'd hit a wall.

"Ms. DeMark! What did I do?" Colter's eyes were wide with confusion.

Lacy's song stopped as she answered him, "I don't know, Colter. Perhaps you would like to explain why Mr. Connor is chasing you all over the place! I thought we were through with this kind of behavior!" She was frowning at him and her face was flushed with anger. She was just not up to dealing with a misbehaving little boy. Most of the time, she didn't like having to deal with it at school and she wasn't even at school now! Why did she have to deal with it when she felt so damned bad?

Connor interrupted then. "Dear lady, we were only playin'. I was the . . . ," he faltered.

"You were the what?" Lacy prodded.

"Well, he was jus' showing me how fast he was when—" Connor looked decidedly uncomfortable.

"How fast he was when what?" she asked again.

"We were jus' playin'! Truly!"

Lacy's curiosity was piqued. "Tell me what you were playing, Connor, please."

"It would bore you, dear—"

"Stop calling me 'dear lady.' My name is Lacy." Lacy looked at Colter then. "Colter, what were you playing?"

"I was showing him how fast I was when I used to run away from you and Principal Ferguson."

"So, Connor"—Lacy turned a very intense brown-eyed gaze in Connor's direction—"you were pretending to be me?" For a very intense moment, no one moved or even took a breath. Connor stood stock-still. Then Lacy's eyes softened; her lips curled up at the corners and laughter erupted. Then came the moan of pain. She caught her breath and held it for a moment, waiting for the pain to subside. When she could talk again, she looked up into Connor's bewildered eyes. "You'll have to get faster—oh, and watch out, he bites!"

The men were laughing with her until the last part. Marek was the first to respond. "He really bites?!" He was glaring at Colter as the question of where her bite marks had come from dawned on him. "Come here, lad."

If Colter had been nervous when Lacy had started singing, he was shaking in his booties now! Marek had never looked at him like that. He wasn't sure if this might be the time to start running again. Maybe another demonstration of his incredible speed was in order. He started to take a step away and then thought better of it as he stared back into those hard golden brown eyes. He dropped his head and walked toward the big man.

Incredibly, Lacy came to his defense. "Marek, what are you doing? He's just a little boy! He doesn't know any better!" His hard eyes looked unforgiving, and it occurred to Lacy that she really didn't know what he was capable of, though for some reason, she doubted that Colter was in any real danger. Still, she kept a close watch on Marek for any sign of danger to Colter.

Marek reached up and took the child's chin in his hand. He pulled his head up until Colter was looking into his eyes. "Is tha' righ'? Ye do no' know any better?"

Colter tried to pull his chin from the man's hand, but Marek would not let go. Colter didn't answer right away.

"Marek, he is not your responsibility. Let him go! You are scaring him," Lacy warned.

"Colter, answer me." Marek did not acknowledge Lacy's pleading.

Lacy stood then, singing again. She paused the song to give Marek her ultimatum. "Marek, you will release my charge now! I will not ask again!"

Marek did not budge; he continued to stare into Colter's eyes. Colter held his gaze but did not answer. Not expecting Marek's next move, Lacy was unable to react as Marek's hand flew out and grabbed her wrist. His gaze had not left Colter's. She didn't stay stunned long; she reacted instinctively. Her legs came to her defense, but Marek had been expecting that since that was how she had felled the Bremhall men. He let go of her wrist and Colter's chin, caught her foot, and pulled her into his lap. He caught her weight before she managed to hurt her ribs any further. Once she was sitting in his lap, he grabbed her wrist again and thrust it in Colter's face. "Do you see this, Colter?"

The little boy's eyes filled with tears then. He looked down at his feet. "I'm sorry, Lacy. I shouldn't have hurt you like that, but Mama said—"

Lacy had started to fight Marek's hold, but she stopped when Colter spoke. "Colter, what did your mama say?"

"Mama said that I had to be real bad in school."

"Why would your mama say that?" Lacy could hardly believe her ears. She had thought that his father had been the culprit behind the horrible behavior. Was it really his mother?

"Mama said that the only way to get away from Daddy was to be really, really bad in school. She said that if I was bad enough, you would keep me away from him. She said that she couldn't keep me safe anymore, but that you would . . . if I was real bad. She told me to behave like Daddy does. So I worked real hard to do what Mama told me to do. I'm sorry I hurt you, Ms. DeMark."

"It's okay. I understand, baby."

"I'm not a baby, Ms. DeMark."

"Sorry, Colter, I call all my students baby sometimes. And I'm not Ms. DeMark until we're back in school, remember?!"

"Okay, Lacy."

"Colter, there will be no more biting . . . ever. Do ye understand? Warriors do no' bite!" Marek was still staring into the boy's eyes.

"Yes, sir," Colter replied.

"Now go and get your breakfast and then help the men pack up."

"Yes, sir," he said again and then he leaned around Lacy and hugged Marek's neck. Marek didn't know exactly what to do about that, but he finally wrapped his free arm around the boy and patted his back. "Colter?"

"Yes, sir?"

"Warriors do no' hug each other either." Marek whispered the reprimand in Colter's ear so the boy would not be embarrassed in front of the other men, but Lacy heard it and smiled.

Colter let go, and Connor fed him and put him to work helping to pack up the blankets and Lacy's bag. The little guy actually liked the whole camping thing. He had enjoyed sleeping out under the stars and sitting by the campfire. He didn't even mind packing it all up because that meant he was going to get to ride a horse again.

"Connor?"

"Aye, Colter?"

"Am I riding with you again?"

"Aye."

"Can I steer, today?"

"No."

"Why not?"

"Ye do no' have enough experience wi' horses."

"Connor?"

"Aye, Colter?!"

"How am I supposed to get experience if you don't let me drive sometimes?"

"*Drive?*" Connor was confused by the word.

"Yeah, *drive*! You know, steer the horse." Colter was clearly exasperated with Connor's lack of vocabulary!

Connor just smiled at him. He couldn't fault the child's logic. "I'll think abou' it, Colter. Maybe I'll let ye 'drive' when we're on McKenzie land. Fair enough?"

"Sure!" Colter's face radiated sunshine after that.

Connor thought he had earned a little peace—silly thought.

"Connor?'

"Aye, Colter?"

"When will we be on McKenzie land?"

"I'll let ye know."

"When will that be?" No one was surprised at Connor's exasperated groan.

Lacy was a little disgusted with her fighting abilities of late. She couldn't seem to get it together! If Marek had really been an enemy, she'd have been dead after that last fiasco. Here she sat in his lap as evidence of her incompetence. And here she sat in his lap, still as evidence of her attraction to him! She was so mortified by her ineffective attack that she finally scrambled to get out of his lap. She pushed off him a little too hard on her left side, and the pain was shooting through her again. She groaned but continued to struggle.

Marek would have liked to keep her there while his men finished packing up but decided that he should help her up before she hurt herself further. He supposed that she was not happy about the ease with which he had stopped her attack earlier. He knew that warriors never liked to be bested, and she probably was no exception even though it was probably easier for her since she was a woman. Women were softer and weaker after all! It was expected that they would not be able to best a man. He lifted her to her feet and then stood up behind her. As an afterthought, he pulled her back to his chest and wrapped his arms around her. He decided to try to comfort her. She was not very receptive. She tried to push away, but stopped when he began to whisper in her ear.

"Ye were forced t' repeat a move tha' I have already seen ye do. I know ye have no upper body strength. I know yer weaknesses. It made it easier than it would normally be. Do no' feel bad."

"I am a highly trained ADD! I should be better able to protect my charge! If you had been of a mind to hurt either one of us, you could have. You may be right, but I don't have to like it!" She didn't raise her voice. In truth, she didn't wish for any of the men to hear their conversation. As she spoke, Marek turned her around in his arms to face him. She would have fought him, but any fighting brought on a swift remembrance of the injured ribs. "Please, let me go!" She barely whispered the demand.

"No. We have t' leave and I need t' put ye up on my horse again . . . unless ye'd like t' ride one o' yer horses on yer own." He wasn't sure if perhaps she was so angry that she wouldn't wish to ride with him so he'd given her the choice. He needn't have worried. The look of horror that swept across her face at the contemplation of managing a horse on her own almost made him smile. He managed to keep a straight face as he waited for her response.

"I would prefer to ride with you, please," Lacy whispered, feeling like such a wimp. She could look a man like Colter's dad in the face and stand and fight, but put a horse between her legs and fear racked through her like it racked through a five-year-old with a monster under the bed. It was illogical, she knew, but she had no idea how to even stay on top of the thing without Marek's arm around her, especially when the thing got into a run. The thought of that nearly brought tears to her eyes because the damn thing would jog first, and that bounced her ribs around.

Marek sat her on his horse. He overheard her next comment as he swung up behind her.

"I hate horses!"

"Do ye now? Why?"

"Well, let's see, it might be because they have no windshields, heated seats, or CD players. Or it could be because they provide too bumpy of a ride. Perhaps they are just too damned high off the ground! I'm not sure, I just miss my car!"

"I'm no' sure I quite understood anythin' ye just said, but perhaps it would help if ye explained what a *car* is."

"A car."

"Yes, what is a car?"

"You've got to be kidding!"

"I do no' think so."

Lacy thought about what he was saying and finally got the joke. "Oh, I forgot, people in this part of the country prefer pickups to cars! Haha! Just for the record, pickups are just fine with me!"

"So ye like it when I pick ye up then?"

"Never mind, I'm not in the mood for this."

"Lacy."

"What?"

"Are ye afraid o' heights?"

"No, why?"

"Well, ye said tha' horses were too high off the ground."

"I'm sure I won't mind quite as much when it doesn't hurt to get on and off of one."

"Ah, I imagine so. Perhaps I need t' teach ye how t' handle a horse. If ye understand them, ye will no' dislike them quite so much. They are a nice break t' walking. Faster too!"

"Okay," she conceded. "First off, where are the brakes?"

"The brakes?"

"Yeah, how do you stop this thing?"

"This is no' a thing, it's a horse."

"Yeah? What's her name?"

"She's a he and ye ought t' show a wee bi' o' respect!"

"Okay, what's his name?"

"Thor."

"Thor? Where did you get a name like that?"

"The healer named him. She assured me it was a name o' great respect in her homeland."

Lacy was giggling when she asked, "Where is her homeland?"

"I do no' really know. She is a verra private person. But someone paid her wi' this horse. He was a wee bi' more horse than she was comfortable wi', so she traded him t' me for a less spirited horse. She had already named him."

"He's beautiful . . . for a horse." She could at lease honestly say *that* about the big blond horse. Somehow, Lacy kept picturing him with a winged helmet and had to stifle a giggle. "I think I'll just call him Marek's ride!"

"Whatever pleases ye, lass."

The trip seemed to go on for a lot longer than Lacy had anticipated. Marek decided to use the time to ask questions and demand answers. He wasn't sure just where to start. He guessed he better start with the important things.

"What were the two o' ye doing ou' in the middle o' tha' field wi'ou' protection?"

"We were there by accident. We . . . I . . . it's a long story."

"We have quite a ways t' go, so start at the beginnin'."

"Yeah, well, hmmm . . . I am not privileged to tell you everything. But I can tell you that I was trying to keep Colter safe from his father and uncle who were trying to kill us. I took Colter into a mine shaft to hide and we fell through the floor . . . several times! It was an old shaft! That's how I hurt my ribs. Then when we discovered that we weren't going to be able to climb out, we began looking for a second way out. We found it after probably two days in there. I'm guessing, of course, you tend to lose track of time in the dark.

"After what seemed like forever, we finally saw light. We exited right by where you found us. There is a cave there . . . at least that's what it looked like from this side. Anyway, we had just made our way out and tried to use my cell phone to call for help. It couldn't pick up a signal and then those two guys showed up. They were more interested in lechery than in being helpful, so I did what I'm paid to do. I protected Colter and myself to the best of my ability . . . which was somewhat limited by injury . . . which is why you are now escorting us."

Marek had been listening closely to every word. There were a couple of things he wanted more information about. "Why was Colter's father trying t' kill ye both?"

"I can't tell you anything about it, really, it's a privacy thing, you understand. I could get fired if the school district found out I was discussing it. You already know that Colter and I were involved so I can use our names, and his father and uncle are . . . well, don't worry about them. When I get back, I'm going to *so* make those men pay! By the time I'm through with them, they will be in no position to ever hurt Colter again."

Marek understood most of what she had said but was a little appalled that a school would burn her for talking about a child; at least he thought that was what she meant. He'd never heard it called *fired* before though.

"Had they hurt him before this?" He couldn't believe any self-respecting man would hurt a little boy! That was cowardice, for heaven's sake!

"I can't say any more, Marek. I've sworn an oath. Please don't ask me."

"Aye, I understand oaths. I'll not push ye, Little Warrior." He was quiet for a moment before he continued. "What can ye tell me abou' the sale fone?"

"Cell phone. Hmm . . . well, it's just a cell phone. It is top of the line. Since I'm an ADD, I'm supposed to have the best of the best. It should be able to pick up a signal from anywhere, but it isn't picking anything up. It's as if the damn satellites had all fallen from the sky!" She pulled the cell phone out of her pocket and handed it to Marek. "Maybe you can get it to work!"

He was still trying to figure out the "satellites" remark as he took the little gadget from her. Marek turned it over and over in his hand. Then he pushed one of the buttons on it, causing it to beep. It startled him and he dropped it. He pulled his horse to a stop and hopped down from its back.

"What are you doing?" Lacy asked, having missed the whole beep-and-drop moment. She was more terrified at having been left on top of Thor by herself.

"Sorry, I dropped the . . . uh . . . cell . . . phone."

"You dropped it? Crap! Now the damn thing is probably really broken!" She started to ask him to give it back but wasn't willing to let go of the saddle on which she now had a death grip.

Marek swung easily back up into the saddle with her. He was still examining the little phone. "It beeped!"

"Yeah, well, they do that!"

"How does it work?"

"It isn't working! Weren't you listening? It isn't picking up a signal! Otherwise, I'd have called Jeremiah and he'd have come to get us! Would you mind sliding that back into my pocket? I'd do it, but I'm busy holding on."

"Who is Jeremiah?"

"A coworker. He taught the other first-grade class at my school."

"This Jeremiah is a man and no' a woman?"

"Yes!" Lacy's puzzled look was lost to Marek since he couldn't see her face.

"So he teach's the wee ones how t' fight?"

"No. He doesn't teach them how to fight! We are trained specifically to keep them *from* fighting! He teaches them reading, writing, arithmetic, science, social studies, the usual. Where have you been for the last century?"

"Well, I have just never heard o' a man teaching anythin' bu' fightin', huntin', or the family trade."

Lacy didn't even respond to that statement. She sat in bewilderment in front of this odd, very naïve man.

Marek pulled her back into his chest and pried her hand from the saddle and put the phone into her palm. He was frustrated but decided that the little warrior had been through too much to talk coherently. These odd machines would require some study. Maybe Murray could figure them out. He was good with gadgets and managed to keep the mill working. He'd get him on it soon.

When the group rounded a small crest, the horses, sensing they were close to a rest, sped up to a trot. Lacy tried to hold her ribs as still as possible when she saw the horses in front of Marek's speed up. She closed her eyes and tensed for the jolt she figured was coming. Marek had anticipated the horses' normal tendencies to speed up when they got close to the healer's house and to home, and he was already pulling on Thor's reins. He noticed Lacy tense up and pulled her back into his chest again. His arm was across her waist, and he was gently stroking her side as he spoke.

"Do no' worry, Little Warrior, I will no' let him trot."

"Where are we?"

"This is the healer's cottage. You can see my holding from here." He pointed to a much larger building in the near distance. Lacy noticed grass, people, buildings, and more horses . . . but no cars. She also noticed that most of the men were dressed similarly to Marek, but the women wore either long tunics that fell from the shoulders to the ankles or leather pants like the men, with a long tunic over them that hit about midthigh. Both types of tunics were brightly colored. They also wore loose-fitting belts around their waist that dipped attractively over the hips.

The healer's cottage was a simple place built from stone and pine logs. There was a small shelter in the back for the healer's horse, and Lacy noticed that she also had a chicken coop beside the horse shelter. Not far from that was a good-sized vegetable garden. The healer must have been good with plants as the house sported several flower pots full of brightly colored flowers.

Marek jumped down from the horse and took Lacy by the waist and slid her down to her feet. He was careful to set her down lightly and to make sure that his hands did not slide up this time. He was smiling at her as he set her on her feet.

"Better this time?"

"Yes, thank you." She smiled back at him. Her gaze lingered a moment on his eyes and then his face. Those warm brown eyes were so gentle. His face was tanned from being in the sun, and his shoulder-length brown hair had a gentle wave to it also. Still, there was a power in this man. It was evidenced in the way he spoke to his men, to Colter, and to Lacy. And if he had never managed to open his mouth, she'd have seen it in the muscles in his arms, chest, and legs. She had felt it every time he had lifted her or comforted her. She felt safe with him. It was a lovely feeling.

Marek thought sure that she would shake off his hold as soon as he set her on the ground and was pleasantly surprised when she gazed up at him. He had the urge to touch the beautiful blond hair as she studied his face, but he couldn't take his eyes from hers. He saw a peace in those deep brown eyes that he had not seen there before. She was relaxing as he watched. He wanted to pull her to his chest and just hold her there. His little warrior intrigued him. She would sing during a fight . . . why did she do that? He didn't know, but in time he would understand it. Then he would break her of it. She was not singing now, yet he knew she maintained a warrior's awareness. She would sing in an instant and defend in a heartbeat, even injured and in pain as she was. She would fight even if she knew she couldn't win. He would keep this little warrior. He had made his decision. While the healer worked on her ribs, he would tell his men.

Marek leaned down as he focused on those lovely lips. He meant to have that kiss he'd been thinking about since this morning, but he was distracted by a scream echoing behind him. He let go of Lacy and turned while drawing his sword and was poised for an attack in the amount of time it took Lacy to hum the first two bars of a song. The scream came from the front door of the healer's house.

The healer was a stocky woman—not fat, but muscular, Lacy thought, with dark hair and bright blue eyes. Her eyes were what caught one's attention. They were merry and warm and quite, quite beautiful. They were the blue of a cloudless summer sky, and her rosy complexion along with her smile that easily revealed itself in her eyes, even when not on her lips, endeared her quickly to strangers. Lacy was no exception. She couldn't break her gaze from the smiling woman's face. The eyes looked familiar to Lacy, and in the next minute she understood why. Colter was staring at the woman with a look of pure joy, the joy that was echoed in the healer's eyes.

"Mama!" Colter was scrambling to get off the horse and out of Connor's arms.

"Colter! Oh my! Colter! Is it really you?!" The woman looked as if she were going to have a heart attack right there on the spot. Her face drained of all color, and she grabbed at the neckline of her tunic. Then she seemed to pull her wits together and she ran to Connor's horse, reaching up for the little boy.

"Mama!" Colter flew into her arms. The hugging began in earnest in accompaniment with the tears. Both of them were crying. Colter just repeated *mama* over and over again.

Lacy stood in awe. She hadn't even bothered to relax out of her fighting stance. She just gawked at the two in disbelief. She was so thunderstruck, she even stopped singing. Marek noticed that. He turned to look back at Lacy. The question in his eyes brought her back to herself. She loosened her stance and shrugged her shoulders at him.

"Colter, how in the heck did you get here?" his mother asked.

"Lacy and I fell down the shaft. Dad and Uncle Tony were chasing us. We had to get away, so Lacy made me go in the mine. I told her you said not to go in there, Mama. But Ms. DeMark picked me up and went in anyway. We fell through the floor. But don't worry, Mama, Lacy kept me from gettin' hurt. But I think she got hurt. That's why we came, so you could help Lacy."

Colter's mother turned her gaze on Lacy. What had Lacy been thinking about the woman's smiling eyes? They weren't smiling now! She definitely didn't look happy as her eyes bored into Lacy's. "You took my son into an old rickety mine shaft? You could have killed him!"

"Well, it was either hide in the shaft and defend him from there, or wait for your husband and brother-in-law to shoot us or beat us to death with a baseball bat. What would you have had me do?"

"Listen to him when he tells you something! You could have both been killed!" she said again. She set Colter down and walked toward Lacy. She stopped suddenly and took another look at her. "You're his teacher!"

"Yes, I am. I was serving a summons to your husband to attend a hearing to discuss the educational placement of your son for the next semester when he decided on another plan of action. He picked up a bat and swung it first at me and then at your son when Colter tried to defend me. I dropped your husband with a well-placed kick, and your brother-in-law took over with a shotgun. At that point, I noticed your son running toward the woods by the house and I followed to get behind him so that his 'loving' Uncle Tony wouldn't get a good shot at him. I saw the shaft and shoved your son in. He yelped about not going in, but there wasn't a lot of time to deliberate. I thought to stash him and turn to face Tony when I found that a bit of the floor was missing. We fell to the floor below. I landed on my back with Colter on top of me."

"It's a wonder the floor held you!"

"It didn't, we fell again, but Colter landed on top of me again, so he didn't get hurt."

"Mama, Lacy kept me tight in her arms and wouldn't let me wiggle. She kept me safe, Mama. Don't be mad at her."

Lacy continued the story, hoping to get it over with before the woman could interrupt. It would be good to get it all out. "We fell two more times. The last one knocked me out for a bit. When I came to, Colter was screaming at me and we sat in total darkness. I felt around and found my purse not far from me, it had a flashlight in it. When I turned it on, I discovered my gym bag. Your husband had cleaned out my car and thrown it all down in the hole with us. I decided that he probably wasn't going to call anyone to come get us out, so we found our own way out."

"You were coming to take Colter away then?"

"Yes, and while we're at it, Colter tells me you are responsible for the bite on my arm, the numerous kicks, punches, pinches, and all-around terror he inflicted on me and his classmates! So if you wish to yell at me, you are going to have to explain yourself first!" Lacy was furious. She took a threatening step toward Colter's mother, but she wasn't singing. Colter noticed this and so was not worried for his mother.

"Oh, sorry about that. I didn't know how else to protect him. I wanted to leave with him, but Dan is a pretty frightening person. When I finally got up the nerve to tell him I was leaving and taking Colter with me, we had a horrible fight." The woman stopped talking for a minute. "Oh, by the way, my name is Jeanette."

Lacy was surprised by the sudden change in conversation, but she understood a moment later as she watched Jeanette deliberate over something for a moment and then address her son, "Colter, would you like to go inside the house and check it out? You'll be staying here from now on. There are cookies on the kitchen counter. You may have only two." Her son ran into the house as her eyes followed him. As soon as he disappeared, she continued. "Dan dragged me out of the house and locked me in the shaft. I knew that he'd probably just let me starve to death out there. After all, if I ever got out of there, I would sneak off with Colter sooner or later. He knew that."

Lacy noticed that Jeanette was watching Marek and his men closely. They had taken the horses over to a grassy area to graze and were tending to their needs. Jeanette dove into the story then like a man on a mission.

"With that conclusion drawn, I knew that the only way out was to find the way myself. My father built that shaft and I had spent a lot of time in there with him. I knew it like the back of my hand. It had been built with two floors and a tunnel that opened out on the back of the hill. What I didn't know was that there had been a cave-in, resulting in a third floor. Though I only fell one floor, it surely hurt. I limped my way out and headed around the hill. Only there was no Riverton on this side of the hill. My home was gone and my life was gone. So I went back to the cave, determined to find a way out of the shaft from the locked door. But there is no getting back from this side that I have found. The little cave stops just about five feet inside the entrance."

"What?!"

"The best that I can figure is that we dropped through some kind of time warp, or a wormhole maybe would be a better description. We aren't really anywhere in the history of Riverton or the surrounding area. If we had dropped back in time, we would be standing here among American Indians. Instead, we are here in the midst of an odd adaptation of Scottish clansmen. The accent is close, but not quite, their jargon's off, and instead of kilts, they wear—"

"You're telling me that I'm in another space and time and there is no way back?"

"Isn't that what I just said?"

"Stop it! Why are you doing this? That can't be true! An alternate time and place?! That's just crazy! It's not true! I'm going home!" Lacy turned to leave.

"Think about it, Ms. DeMark. What have you seen since you walked out of that shaft?" Jeanette looked at Lacy with a gentleness that hadn't been there before.

"I've seen . . ." Panic filled Lacy's eyes as she turned to meet Jeanette's. "They didn't know what a pickup was . . . or a car . . ."

"No, they wouldn't. There aren't any here. They still use horses. There are no lights, no phones, no motorcars, not a single luxury." She sang the last part to the tune of *Gilligan's Island*, a very old sitcom theme song whose reruns still entertained the early morning television junkies in Riverton.

"I don't believe you. That can't be right. I'm going back to the shaft." She turned to leave again and ran right into Marek. She winced but managed not to groan when pain rippled through her chest. "Please move."

"No, Little Warrior, Jeanette needs t' look at yer ribs. Ye can get t' know each other later." Marek watched Lacy's face. He had seen that look before when Jeanette first came to them a few months ago. Wherever these women came from must be very different from here. He remembered how Jeanette had worked so hard to get back to the cave she said she had come from. He had finally taken her back, watched her enter, and waited. She had reemerged a short time later. The look she had on her face then was now echoed on Lacy's face. It was a look of disbelief that bordered on panic. He was waiting for the humming to begin, but Lacy looked instead as if she were going to faint. She staggered a moment, and all color drained from her face.

Realization came upon Lacy with a vengeance. She remembered Marek's bewildered look at her blow-dryer and hair straightener. She remembered how he looked at it as though it were the first one he had ever seen. Then there were the comments about cars and pickups and how they had been misconstrued. And where was Riverton? It should be right here! There should be streetlights and streets with cars on them, but there was only the holding and a few scattered cottages like Jeanette's in the valley before them. He hadn't known what police were either. And the phone! He had dropped her phone just because it beeped at him; he hadn't known what it was!

Lacy had never felt this alone and vulnerable. She had not even felt this helpless during her ADD proficiency exams. Her opponent had been John Finley. She remembered looking up into the face of that hulk of a man and thinking, "Bring it on!" Her classmates had claimed later that the song she had been singing had distracted him, allowing her to hold her own with him. No song came out of her mouth now. She felt sick. The area around her seemed to tilt. Her vision began to close in on her, allowing first only a tunnel of sight and finally going out like a television picking up only snow. Finally, it went black altogether.

Marek caught her before she hit the ground. He easily cradled her in his arms and followed Jeanette into the cottage. He laid Lacy out on a cushioned window seat of sorts and turned back to Jeanette. He started to say something but was interrupted by Colter, whose eyes were the size of small saucers.

"Mama, what's wrong with Lacy? Did she die?"

"No, honey, she didn't die, but she's had a . . . bad . . . day. She'll be all right, you'll see."

Placated, Colter went back to eating his third cookie as he watched.

Marek was still staring at Jeanette as he asked the question that had been on his lips before he had been interrupted, "What did ye say t' her?!"

"I just explained that she can't go back where we came from. I haven't found a way back in all the months that I've been here and she won't either. She didn't take it very well."

Colter's face lit up. "You mean we get to stay here and ride horses and stuff?" Jeanette nodded at him with a smile.

"Where did ye come from, Jeanette? Ye've never shared tha' wi' me," Marek continued.

"Marek, I don't know how to tell you that. We came through an opening in that cave that doesn't open back the other way. At least I couldn't find it. And your men went into the cave after I did. What did they find?"

"Nothing bu' a small cave."

"Right! I don't know why we're here, but we aren't going back. She isn't taking it as well as I did."

"As I recall, ye cried on an' off for a month," he reminded her. Marek couldn't help but be pleased that Lacy was stuck here. It would make it easier when she found out that she now belonged to him. His men had been pleased with the choice. They had wondered what kind of woman would finally be chosen by their laird. They had known he would be interested in this woman when they had seen her drop Bremhall's men.

"Yes, but I didn't faint, did I?!"

Marek couldn't help smiling. "No, ye did no' faint. Ye should check her ribs. They look pretty bad."

"I think I'll wait until she's awake. I wouldn't want her to wake up to a new shock, like a stranger poking around her midsection. If I hit something sore, she might straighten up suddenly and really cause some damage. I'd rather she be ready for any pain I might cause."

As if on cue, Lacy's eyes began to flutter. She groaned. "Where am I?"

"Here we go again!" Jeanette came closer to her. "You are in my cottage and I need to check your ribs. Are you okay with that?"

"Yes." Lacy seemed resigned to her situation. "Marek, would you mind turning your back again?"

"I've already seen the bruises."

"Yes, but hopefully, you haven't seen everything! And even if you have, that doesn't mean you have to see it again."

Marek smiled but turned away. Jeanette sent Colter outside, pulled the curtains close, and then turned back to Lacy.

"You could leave the room, you know," Lacy commented.

Marek grunted, "No' likely. Ye are under my protection now. I need t' know what care ye will need t' recover."

Lacy sat up gingerly and unbuckled her belt. She wiggled gently out of the oversized T-shirt but needed a little help out of the smaller T-shirt. Jeanette helped her out of it and took a good look at her ribs. She helped Lacy remove her bra as well. Then she began to push and probe, feeling for breaks. She was very gentle, but even so, Lacy had to stifle a groan or two. She was very worried that any noise or quick intake of breath would have Marek turning around. She kept her eyes on him throughout the examination.

Fortunately, her ribs were not broken but only cracked. Jeanette wrapped them snuggly for support and helped Lacy get dressed again.

"It will just take some time for them to heal. So no lifting heavy objects . . . or, for that matter, fighting off warriors or defending helpless children for at least a month. I'll give you something for the pain."

"Thank you, but I will not sit around doing nothing if a situation arises." Lacy was thinking that the list sort of knocked out a good portion of things she usually did. And if in fact she couldn't get back home, she was out of a teaching job also. What in heaven's name was she going to do with herself? She was lost in a strange . . . other place. History here was probably different. Who knew if they had books for teaching, let alone paper and pencils! Perhaps a trip back to the cave would be the best use of her time. She could hide and evade, now that she knew what enemies were out there.

Jeanette was watching her face, knowing exactly what Lacy was thinking about. Hadn't she been thinking the same things a few months ago? That prompted her next question. "You'll see to it, Marek?"

"I will."

"You will see to what?" Lacy looked into Marek's arrogant face.

"I will see t' yer following o' the healer's instructions."

"You are keeping me prisoner then?"

"No, ye are free t' come and go, but I will be comin' and goin' wi' ye."

"When you are feeling better, perhaps you could begin teaching the children here. They need a good teacher, Lacy. You'd have to learn a different history, but I'm sure you are up to it. Perhaps you could study while your ribs mend," Jeanette said encouragingly.

"Thank you, but I'm going back to the shaft. I want to go home."

"Ye will have t' wait a few days. I need t' see t' the needs o' my holdin'. I would be happy t' take ye back for a look after tha'." Marek would take her back, he thought, after he was sure that she would not leave. She would be his. He had made his announcement to his men. Now he would just have to break the news to his little warrior.

"That won't be necessary. I can find my own way. Now that I know what dangers there are around here, I can easily avoid detection. But thank you for your offer."

"Ye will no' leave wi'ou' me."

"Suit yourself, but I'm going now."

"No, ye are no'." Marek was calm but adamant as he spoke to her.

"You can't stop me."

He just smiled.

Jeanette was watching the whole exchange with a strange look in her eyes. "Marek, are you claiming this woman?"

"I am."

"Are you prepared to mark her as such?"

"What are you talking about? He can't claim me! And he sure as heck isn't marking me . . . whatever that is!"

Marek's nod was all Jeanette needed to see. "Lacy, you are staying, honey." Jeanette smiled nervously at her. "You are in no condition to fight this, and you have no one to fight for you. The good news is that Marek is a very good catch."

The look on Lacy's face was readable by everyone. If it hadn't been, the song was a dead giveaway. She was ready to fight right now. Her body tensed. She rose slowly and took a step toward the door. Marek's golden brown eyes stopped her in her tracks. She couldn't tear her eyes away from him. They held her mesmerized. She was impressed again by the strength she saw there. In her present condition, she could not even consider physically trying to get away. She would have to wait. She would hate it, but she would wait.

"Okay, you win. I can't fight well right now. I will stay for a week. Then I will go. You will not be able to stop me. I *will* go," she promised. "Until then, I would appreciate an explanation about this claiming and marking thing please."

Marek was more than happy to explain. "I have claimed ye as my own. Everyone in my holdin' will treat ye as my ward until ye are marked as mine. After that they will treat ye as my lady. As my lady, ye will be charged wi' the running o' the household and the raising o' my children."

"Really?! Just how many children do you have? Pray, tell! And just how much raising will get done in the span of one week?"

There was a growl of laughter from him then. "Ye will be the first t' know when I begin havin' them." He rose from his chair, still laughing, and headed out to dismiss his men and bring his horse around. "Come wi' me, Little Warrior, we will be late for supper. Do no' keep me waitin'."

"What in the heck is he talking about? How will I be the first to know when—" Lacy's mind began to unravel the conversation, but before she had completely nailed it all down in her head, Jeanette came to her aid.

"Marek has just told you that you will be his wife. It's a little different here than in our world. Basically, he claims you and then he marks you as his. After that, you are forever his wife. There is only one way out of this situation. Someone has to challenge him for possession of you and that someone would have to fight him and win. Of course, if that someone happened to win the fight, you would become his! Since no one will fight Marek for his choice in a woman, you are technically his already. He will wait the allotted time for someone to challenge, but then he will take you. Don't look so horrified, Lacy! He is a very kind man. He will protect you and take good care of you. There will be many unhappy single women after his announcement today."

"Today? He will announce this travesty today? I will not agree to this."

"Women do not have that choice here."

"*I* will fight him for me."

"*You* will lose. You would lose even if you were completely healed, but most assuredly, you will lose with your ribs in the shape they are in. Remember that back home, you are one of the most highly trained warriors in the world, but here the men are not like the men back home. These men are trained for battle from the time they are old enough to aim a good punch. Besides, there has never been a challenge by a woman. I'm not sure it can be done."

"It will be done! I will fight him one way or another!"

"Well, at least wait for a month. I would hate for you to actually break a rib. You could puncture something important and kill yourself. I can't heal many internal injuries. I was a nurse before I married my husband, but I don't have the equipment here or the medicines to help you much if that happens. Please, be careful!"

"Hmmph!"

"Lacy, give Marek time to demonstrate the kind of man he is. You may find that being his lady might not be so bad." She lifted both eyebrows as she smiled.

Her statement was met with a roll of Lacy's eyes as she stomped out the door.

"Marek? May I have a word with you?"

He took her by the waist and put her on his horse once more and swung up behind her. "Aye, ye may speak t' me. Ye may always speak t' me. I have claimed ye."

"Yeah yeah, about that. I don't want to be claimed. I'm flattered, but I am not . . . I don't want to . . . Thank you, but no thank you."

"It is no' yer decision, Little Warrior."

"Actually, it is my decision. I will not be claimed by you or anyone else. I will choose my own . . . man. Okay?!"

"Ye will choose me. I have claimed ye. If ye have someone t' fight for ye, I will accept the challenge, o' course. Do ye have someone t' fight for ye?" His eyes twinkled.

"Yes, I do."

He raised his eyebrows as if he were skeptical. "Who might this unwise man be?"

"He's . . . she's me! I will fight for myself if I must."

"Women do no' fight."

"I do."

He had to agree with her there. She had been doing nothing but fighting since he had met her. Marek seemed to be thinking the situation over.

Lacy was a little unnerved to see the corners of his mouth turn up a bit as she glanced up at his face. He sure had a nice face, she had to admit. She particularly liked how it looked when it seemed to be just near breaking into a smile as it was right now. She'd have relished it now, except that she was quite certain that she didn't want to know what he was thinking just then.

He didn't keep her waiting long. "I will agree t' this fight, but we will wait six weeks for yer ribs t' heal first."

"How chivalrous of you!" she said sarcastically. "But the longest I'll wait is one month!"

Marek ignored the comment. "When ye are flat on yer back beneath me after the fight, ye will be mine wi'ou' argument, Little Warrior. Agreed?"

With no intention of ever finding herself flat on her back beneath this handsome but arrogant warrior, Lacy agreed. "But if you find yourself flat on your back looking up at me, you will admit defeat and allow me to return home. Agreed?" Lacy shot his own words back at him. "Oh, and just so everyone understands, when I defeat you, in one month, no one else gets to claim me!"

"Agreed!"

CHAPTER 6

The Laird's Lady

Lacy was quite surprised to see all the people turn out for the approach to the holding. She felt a little conspicuous sitting in Marek's lap on the horse. She stiffened and tried to sit forward, but Marek pulled her back into his chest. Though she felt uncomfortable with the attention she was drawing with that little move, she was mortified with what happened next.

Marek stopped the horse amidst his people and called out to them in a loud voice, "I have claimed this woman today. Ye will treat her as such." He then kicked the horse into motion again and continued toward the main building. Lacy was squirming around to try to face him, her face turning a dark shade of pink.

"What are you doing?" she asked as she finally managed to get turned around enough to face him. Though it was a little awkward, she did not let go of the saddle, even with one hand.

He didn't answer her verbally. He smiled down into her angry face. Her eyebrows were pulled so tightly together that only creases in her skin separated them. Her beautiful brown eyes were mere slits, and her teeth clenched together so tightly that he could see the muscles working in her jawline. Marek found the whole effect fascinating. How he would have liked to just kiss her! He'd been thinking about it the entire day, but now was not the time. She would need some time to get used to him. Instead, he pried one of her hands off the saddle and laced his fingers through hers. She tried to pull away from him but found herself too unsettled in the saddle and ended up clamping hold of his hand to steady herself.

Lacy was sure she would have punched or slapped him or something had she not been so surprised *and* sitting on this infernal horse! Instead she sat there like a total twit, not even noticing the cheers from the crowd as she stared at the smile that spread over his face. She finally managed to raise her eyes to meet his. They were smiling also. She sighed unconsciously and continued to stare into those beautiful golden brown eyes. Well, she hoped she wasn't staring but glaring instead.

"That was not so bad, now was it, Little Warrior?"

"That was . . ." Lacy struggled to recover her wits. "That was embarrassing! What were you thinking? I have not agreed to this arrangement. I notice that you did not tell them that I would be fighting on my own behalf for my freedom!"

"No, there is no reason t' tell them tha'. Ye will no' win in any case!"

"Oh yes, I will! You may be built like . . . like . . . very well built, and you may be a warrior, but so am I! I've been trained in . . . lots of things!" She was losing her concentration and beginning to babble!

Laughter was all she heard. He was laughing, and his men were laughing. Lacy was not! She thought that maybe if she could just sing, she could get her thoughts back together, but no song came to her. She just sat there in silence, staring into those golden eyes.

Marek half expected to hear a little of that hard rock that Colter was telling them about. His little warrior was just sitting there, gazing into his eyes in silence . . . finally! It occurred to him that she was lost completely in the moment. It pleased him considerably to know that he could command her complete attention as well as she commanded his.

Dropping her hands, Marek slid off the horse and reached up to pull Lacy down to him. She glanced around the stable. His men were all there, smiling up at her. She turned a beautiful crimson color, and finally the humming started.

"Sometime, Little Warrior, ye will have t' sing t' us properly."

The humming stopped abruptly. "Properly?"

"Aye, when ye are no' nervous, fightin', or thinkin' verra hard!"

A great comeback eluded her, so she settled for total denial. "I am not nervous, fighting, or thinking at the moment!"

"No?"

Realizing that she had just admitted that she wasn't thinking, at least not clearly, Lacy turned an even brighter shade of red. "That's not what I meant! I am thinking and it would take more than the likes of you to make me nervous. As for fighting, I might have, but I was being polite!"

Marek had taken her hand and turned to lead her into the house, but he turned back to her with a smile. "Really?"

"Yes. I would have punched you over that ridiculous remark, but I didn't want to insult you in front of your people. Well, that and my ribs hurt too much for a successful execution of a good left hook."

"Little Warrior, I am greatly lookin' forward t' our little sparrin' match. When I have ye on yer back, pinned t' the ground, ye will apologize t' me for insultin' me so."

"I insulted you? I insulted you! You just announced to everyone here that I'm yours! I am not yours! I don't belong to anyone! I am Lacy Rene DeMark, ADD, and very proud of it! No one gets me unless I say so! And stop saying that part about having me on my back pinned beneath you! It's infuriating!" She was shouting loudly, arms held straight and rigid at her sides with her fists clenched.

She exited the stable, head held high, shoulders erect, and with absolutely no idea where she was going. But she thought she just might try that left hook if she didn't leave right then. Unfortunately for her, everyone heard the song she began singing as she made her way into the sunshine.

Marek sighed loudly as he watched her exit.

"I think maybe she is no' verra happy wi' the pending nuptials! Just wait till she finds ou' abou' the markin' ceremony!" Galen smugly pointed out. "Ye may be wishin' that ye'd chosen a woman a little closer t' home."

"Do no' worry! She'll come around. Besides, the hunt is nearly as much fun as the feast!" He paused for effect. "And, Galen, she was furious wi' me, but I'm still standin' . . . What happened t' you?"

Before Galen could come up with any sort of retort, Marek was out the door to go find his wandering little warrior.

Marek caught up with Lacy as she rounded the corner of the main building. She didn't see him coming, caught up as she was in the sights and sounds of the bustling little holding. It seemed as though everyone had someplace to go and something to do, and they were more than happy to get it all done while the beautiful weather made it so pleasant to accomplish those goals. Women sat outside mending laundry, working in little gardens, keeping an eye on children, and visiting with each other. The men were busy also with various chores, some of which Lacy had never seen accomplished before.

As she strolled in front of the large building, something caught her eye. She saw a man sitting by a brick structure with an opening in it. Inside was a blazing fire. At first she thought he might be cooking, but as she approached, she noticed that he held a long tube of sorts. It had to be at least a yard long, and there was a dark blue sort of ball at the end. He had just pulled it from the brick structure and was blowing into the opposite end. As she watched, the blue bulb expanded into a lighter blue. She continued to watch as the master glassman worked to form a beautiful pitcher, the main body a lighter blue than the handle. He deftly finished the creation as she watched. As he finished and set the piece down to cool, he turned to her and bowed.

"Good afternoon, milady. May I help ye?"

Lacy was surprised to see more of his creations in a corner of the little shed area. She saw pitchers, glasses, vases, and jugs in a variety of colors and shapes. She was even surprised to find piggy banks and small animals among the menagerie. She smiled up at the man. "I have never seen anyone actually blow glass before. You do beautiful work."

The man smiled shyly at the compliment. "Perhaps ye would do me the honor o' choosin' somethin' from my work as a gift from me t' the laird's lady."

Lacy's face flushed. "Thank you . . . but . . . no, I couldn't," Lacy stammered over her answer. The laird's lady, for heaven's sake, she didn't belong to anyone. She had merely stumbled into this mess. She started to explain about the challenge to come in one month but was interrupted by the gentleman.

"Please, ye will insult me if ye say no." His eyes were gentle and sincere with a friendly smile behind them that she could not refuse.

What was it with these guys and being insulted over the littlest things? she wondered. "Okay, in remembrance of this most auspicious day and your kind generosity, I will accept your gift."

"Ah good," the man beamed. "Choose anythin' that pleases ye."

Lacy had chosen the one she wanted even before he had finished speaking. She could see a little pond the man had fashioned out of a mirror where he had added glass lily pads, little frogs, and several swimming ducks. By the side of the pond stood a lone little duck, looking out over the pond but not touching the water. The little duck personified exactly the way Lacy felt in this strange place—like a duck out of water.

"I would like the little duck that stands by itself away from the other ducks that swim in the little pond."

The man reached over the pond and picked up the little duck. He wrapped it in a small square of cloth and handed it to her with a bow. "Is there anythin' else tha' strikes yer fancy, milady?"

"Sir, there are many things here that would strike the fancy of a woman with eyes in her head. Your work is lovely. But for now, this will do me. I thank you." Lacy bowed to the man and turned to go. Even as she bowed, she wondered if that was customary here or not, but it was the nicest form of respect and honor she could think of to thank the man.

She still had not noticed Marek trailing a bit behind her. As she left the booth, he caught the eye of the master glassman and pointed to the blue pitcher he had just finished. He then nodded to some matching glasses and held up ten fingers. The master smiled and nodded.

Lacy opened the little cloth covering as she walked and took out the lonely little duck. He was quite lovely. His graceful little neck was a tiny bit longer in proportion to a real duck, giving him a graceful artistic quality that Lacy found most appealing. The light shone through him as she held him up to admire him. She had decided that he was a boy duck as soon as she had chosen him. "You'll be my good luck charm, Ping!" she spoke to him as if his little glass ears could hear it all.

"Ping?" Marek joined her now, curious about her choice.

Lacy jumped at his voice. "You scared me! I could have dropped him!"

"My apologies, Little Warrior." He took her elbow and began leading her toward the big building.

"Have you been following me?"

"Aye!"

"How long?"

"Since ye left the stables."

"Why? I can take care of myself!"

"I am fairly sure ye do no' know yer way around here yet and I thought ye might be interested in a little food. Ye have no' eaten since this morning."

"Oh." Lacy looked down at her feet. "That was thoughtful of you," she said a little sheepishly. "Thank you."

"Ye need no' thank me for carin' for my lady."

Angry, defensive walls went up immediately. "Marek, I'm not your lady! I'm just Lacy. I don't need—"

"Anyone. Yes, ye've said that. But what were ye plannin' on eatin' if I did no' take care of ye?"

The gravity of her situation hit home with his last comment. She was in a foreign land with no money, no income, no friends or family. She was really alone! And no amount of defensive training was going to change that fact. Glancing down at the little duck in her hand, the emotions of the day came to a head.

I will not cry in front of a total stranger . . . I will not cry! she thought as a tear spilled down her cheek. Keeping her head bent down and avoiding his gaze, Lacy managed to pull herself back together. "Point and set . . . you win this round," she whispered.

He wrapped his arm around her and smiled. "Aye, I win a lot, Little Warrior. Ye should remember tha'."

Panic and sadness were immediately replaced with anger. She wiped her eyes with the cloth the duck had been wrapped in and looked up at him scowling. Though she preferred the angry feeling to the panic, she couldn't quite hang on to it as she stared at the handsome man. He was facing forward, leading her through the courtyard to the front door of the building. He was so tall. Her head barely came up to his chin. Should he wish to rest it there, he'd have to lean down just a bit. His face and upper body were tanned. She wondered if he had a big *X* on his chest and back where the leather straps crisscrossed and kept the sun's rays from touching his skin. The thought of a big white *X* in the middle of that perfect muscled chest brought a smile to her lips. A flush of red swept up through her neck and cheeks when she realized she was staring at his chest as he led her through the door to the building. She glanced up just in time to see him looking down at her with a smile on his lips. She looked away quickly to hide her embarrassment.

"I'm curious abou' somethin'." Marek had stopped walking for a moment. Lacy stopped, turning slightly toward him. "Yes?"

"Why the wee duck? There were many things in the glassmaker's shop tha' ye could have chosen. He'd have given ye anythin'. Why did ye choose a wee thumb-sized duck?"

"Hmm. Well, I suppose it's because he wasn't in the pond, he was standing outside by himself watching. He was out of his element. In the water, he would be fast and sure of himself. He could duck down under the water for protection or swim away quickly. He could mingle with the other ducks and eat at his leisure. But outside the water, he is alone and defenseless, no food, speed, or companionship. He is a duck out of water. I could relate."

"Ahh, and the name. Ye called it Ping. Why Ping?"

"I'm a schoolteacher, and each year I read the story of Ping to my students. He's a little duck who gets separated for a time from his family. He eventually finds them again, but he has learned some valuable lessons along the way. Ping just seemed like a natural fit."

"Ye're feeling a little lost, are ye?"

It was a minute before she could answer. It seemed that tears were just below the surface again. What an emotional roller-coaster she'd been on today! Her voice came out as a whisper once again. "Yes, I am."

"Do no' worry, Little Warrior, I'll take care of ye. Ye're mine now."

"Marek, I'm not yours!" she repeated, but the conviction had not the force of her earlier declarations.

"So ye keep sayin'. But ye are mine, lady. Whatever ye need, I'll provide it. If ye need protection, I'll give it. When ye need clothes or food, I'll provide it. If ye need to talk, I'll be here, and if ye're afraid, Little Warrior, I'll hold yer hand." His hand wrapped around hers. It was warm and strong. He squeezed gently, sending small bolts of electricity through her body.

The shock waves rippling through her surprised Lacy. Without thinking, she squeezed back, her eyes locked on his. The smile in his eyes was warm and tender. He reached up and wiped a tear from her cheek. She hadn't even been aware that one had escaped. Too late, she realized that more had developed.

Chits! Here she stood crying like a baby in public and holding hands with a total stranger! *Stop it!* she screamed in her head. *You are an ADD, Lacy! Get it together!*

"It's all right!" he whispered into her ear as he pulled her to him. "I've got ye." Her tears flowed uncontrolled down her beautiful face, and Marek melted inside. He would have promised anything to her to stop the tears. He pulled her more tightly to him and pressed her head gently against his chest.

—

Kissing the top of her head, he said, "If there is any way I can get ye home, I promise I will." *Blast! Now why did I promise that?* he thought. *I'm a fool! That is the only explanation!*

"Thank you, Marek. You really are a sweet man." Lacy began to get herself under control. "You wouldn't happen to have a Kleenex on hand, would you?"

"A what?"

"Oh, uh . . . a handkerchief?"

"Come wi' me, we'll find ye one."

He led her through an entryway down a dark hallway to the left of a large staircase. He stopped her in the hallway, asked her to stay there, and left. He was only gone for a moment before returning with a handkerchief. After wiping her eyes and blowing her nose, she looked up at Marek.

"So do I look a total wreck?"

"Ye look beautiful!"

"You are either weak in the eyes or the perfect gentleman."

"I have very strong eyes, and I can assure you that I have never been described, t' my knowledge, as a *perfect* gentleman. Therefore I must be tellin' the truth! Which I am."

She smiled. He took her hand and placed it on the crook of his arm to lead her into the dining hall. Looking up at the staircase, she supposed that the bedrooms were upstairs. The room they now entered was large with one long table up close to a huge fireplace. There was a fire burning in the hearth, but it was small, owing to the warm weather. There was a teapot suspended over the fire, and steam escaped its spout. Most, if not all, of the men that had been riding with Marek were seated around the table. She and Marek joined them, and Marek passed her an apple from a large basket of them that sat in the center of the table. There were several young boys standing near the entrances watching the men eat, and Marek signaled to one of them. The boy disappeared through a nearby door, returning a short time later with two platters of food. He placed one in front of Lacy and one in front of Marek. Another boy set two blue glasses and a large blue pitcher in front of them. Lacy recognized the pitcher at once.

"The pitcher!" she exclaimed.

"What?" Marek asked innocently.

"That is the pitcher the glassman was working on today! Marek, did you . . . You did, didn't you? I . . . you . . . didn't do that for me, did you?"

He sat watching her as did everyone at the table. It was impossible to read his face as he waited for her reaction.

"I thought ye liked the pitcher and maybe ye'd feel more at home if . . . ," he stopped speaking when she looked into his eyes. She bit her lip to keep from tearing up again.

'Marek, that was very thoughtful of you. You are a very sweet man," she said for the second time that day.

The serving boy who had placed the pitcher in front of them had not dared to move as he watched the emotions play out across Lacy's face. He still stood beside her.

Lacy finally pulled her eyes away from Marek's and looked up into the boy's freshly scrubbed face with golden brown eyes, much like Marek's.

"Thank you." She smiled at him.

"Ye're welcome, milady."

"Lacy. Just call me Lacy. What is your name?"

The boy looked nervously at Marek, trying to decide what the proper thing to do was when a guest improperly addressed a serving lad. Marek nodded to him, and he returned his gaze to Lacy. "Eric, milady."

"Eric, how old are you?"

Totally confused with this unnatural conversation, Eric stammered, "Uh, . . . ten, milady."

"What grade are you in, Eric? And please just call me Lacy."

Eric's eyebrows shot up at that question. "Grade, Mi—" He looked desperately at Marek.

"It would not be proper for him to call you Lacy," Marek informed her. To the boy he said, "Milady will be fine."

"Oh sorry, Eric." Lacy looked away from Eric and into Marek's eyes briefly before returning her attention to Eric. "In school . . . what grade are you in? You do have a school, don't you?" She was met with blank stares all the way around the table. "I thought you needed a teacher."

"Oh! Ye mean a bell room." Marek turned to his men. "She means a bell room."

"A bell room?" Now it was Lacy's turn to look puzzled.

"Aye, the children are called t' a room t' learn by the ringin' o' a bell. So we call it the bell room. It's the place they are called t' begin their training."

"What kind of training?"

"The boys are taught t' hunt mostly by their fathers, but they learn how t' fight when they're called t' the bell room. The girls are taught t' cook by their mothers, bu' they sometimes learn another trade, like needlepoint or quilt makin' at the bell room by women who volunteer for such."

"Where do they learn reading, writing, arithmetic, health, science, and history?"

"I guess they just pick it up as they go. Bu' if ye'd be interested, we would no' mind having a teacher tha' could help with the pickin' it up." Remembering the little duck, Marek thought that Lacy would adjust better if she had a task.

His thoughts aside, he hadn't expected her to take to the suggestion quite as well or as quickly as she did.

"I'd like that!" Lacy smiled first at Eric and then at Marek. "When can I see the class . . . uh . . . bell room?"

"Well, we do no' really have one . . . It is sort of supplied by the person who is teaching."

Lacy began to hum a bit, stopped suddenly, and spoke, "Oh well, we need a permanent one then. I'll also need something for the students to write on and with. Some tables, chairs, and whatever books you can supply would be helpful. I will need students to arrive in the room beginning at eight o'clock in the morning and they will be released at three o'clock in the afternoon, so they will have to bring a sack lunch and something to drink. I would like to have children between the ages of five and ten at first. We'll see how that goes and then we can expand it to include the older children after I'm better organized. About how many children live around here?"

A glance up at the men around the table took Lacy by surprise. All of them, looking quite stunned, had stopped eating abruptly and were staring right at her. Indeed, Galen was staring at her with his mouth hanging open, a forkful of food not an inch from his lips.

"What?" she asked as she threw her hands out palms up.

A meaningful glance around the circle of men by Marek sent them all back to eating. Their eyes dropped at once, everyone of them intent on the next bite of food on their forks. Marek reached out and took her hand. He brought it back down to the table and her other one followed suit.

Lacy looked suspiciously around the table, finally stopping when she came to Marek. "Care to explain?"

"Well, it migh' take us a bit t' put that together for ye, Little Warrior. Perhaps in the meantime ye might like t' look over the books I have available in my library." Marek was going to have to play this one carefully, he thought. He didn't want to squelch her enthusiasm. He did, after all, want her to become a part of their little community. So he opted not to tell her that most children were needed at their own homes to help with chores. Those who weren't needed at home as much helped out here in the main building of the holding. Perhaps he could work it out to have the children in the bell room from eight to ten or maybe even eleven in the morning, but nothing after that! He'd break it to her after he showed her the library.

"That sounds great!" came her cheery response. Lacy lapsed into silence as she ate. Getting the school going wouldn't be so hard, she thought. It was a small area. How many children could there be? Once she got it up and going, perhaps she could find an educated woman to take it over when she left. Even if it didn't keep going after she left, at least she'd have something to occupy her time here besides her exercise routine and avoiding Marek. And speaking of that last thing . . . avoiding Marek, she needed to accomplish that at all costs. The man was insufferable. It seemed that anytime he was close enough, he was holding her hand, wrapping his arms around her, or picking her up! The man couldn't keep his hands to himself! That was when she finally noticed he was still holding her hand.

Her brow creased, and she tried to wiggle out of his hold. Marek had turned his attention to a conversation on his other side, misinterpreted Lacy's effort to escape, and laced his fingers between hers, pulling her entire hand into his lap as he did. She rolled her eyes, resigning herself to the momentary loss of her left hand. The men around the table seemed oblivious to the situation, and she had at least begun to relax, having avoided *that* little snippet of embarrassment when she caught Galen's eyes. He was looking right at her, a broad grin on his face, having no doubt as to her true intent and subsequent failure to execute.

CHAPTER 7

A Wee Thin Line

Two weeks had flown by with Lacy finding herself most often engrossed in Marek's personal library. It did not include very many children's books, but she had discovered a few nestled in a box stored high on a top shelf near the back. She had been looking over a few histories of the place, reading a couple in her room at night, with intent to read the rest in the next week. Presently, she had a stack of about twenty books sitting on a small table in her room that she thought the little school could use. However, there had been no progress toward the establishment of a place to begin the school. Marek had been called away from the holding. There had been some news of an attack on a village in the south of his holdings, and he and the men he had had with him when they found Lacy had headed out the day after her arrival.

His absence was a good thing as far as Lacy could see. This meant she could pretty much come and go as she pleased without fear of running into him and being detained with unwanted hand holding or embraces. They *were* unwanted, she told herself . . . even if they were very pleasant. In any case, the longer he stayed away, the better for her.

Most of her movements were now unfettered with pain. The bruises were yellowing and beginning to dissipate. She had decided that today, she would go for her first run. She thought it was best for the time being to forgo the usual sit-ups and push-ups, etc. She didn't think that straining her ribs unnecessarily was a very good idea. Better to allow them complete healing before she fought Marek. She would wait until the third week of healing before she began working on her upper body again. The need to have it in tip-top shape before the fight was important, but she couldn't rush the healing. It would just take time.

She finished tying her tennis shoes, stood up, and took a last look in the mirror. She had been wearing long tunics that Marek had supplied to her. They worked just fine for sifting through the library, but exercising in them was out of the question. It was a good thing she had a pair of sweats in her bag. Heaven knows what the people will think of her outfit as it is, with the snug-fitting

T-shirt. If she had had to wear her shorts, there might have been a small uprising! She tied her hair back in a ponytail and headed out the door.

Running quickly out of the walled section of the little holding, Lacy made her way to the ridge above it. The view from up there might help her to visualize where she was and the best way back to the cave in the event that she really did lose to Marek and had to escape on foot. She would hate to break her word to him, but she couldn't stay here. There was nothing for her here. It seemed that having a school was only important to her, and keeping students engaged when no one cared to have them there would be even more difficult than keeping them in school back home where parents needed the free babysitting.

She also missed her bathtub. The little house she owned in Riverton didn't have much, but the bathtub was an old one made of steel, insulated on the outside, and enclosed in a beautifully tiled encasement. It kept the water hot a lot longer than a normal bathtub did. She had purchased the house for the tub almost exclusively. The house had required a lot of fixing up, being as old as the tub had been. But she had done it, and now it was a lovely little home. Oh, to be in her own house with a nice glass of wine and a hot bubble bath!

Putting wistfulness aside, she concentrated on the trail and the views around her. The view on the ridge was breathtaking. It overlooked the little valley with the holding nestled close to the foothills. She could see for miles here and noted rolling hills and small mountains in the distance. As she ran farther across the ridge, she could make out Colter's house in the distance. It was walking distance from the holding, and Lacy had made her way out there once, just to check on him. It had been a lovely day and the library had gotten stuffy, so she had gone to visit. A couple of Marek's stable men had walked with her. One of the two had injured his hand pretty badly, and they were going to see Jeanette about it.

Colter had been happy to see her, but disappointed that she was working on starting another school. "I thought we were done with that!" he whined.

Lacy had chuckled and reassured him that he would probably be well over the age of attending school by the time she got it going if things kept to their present pace. His big smile told her that he would be counting on that! The visit had ended when Jeanette had finished with the injured man's hand and asked the two to please check on her horse. It had been behaving oddly. It was skittish and irritable. They had discovered nothing physically wrong with the horse and inspected the area, looking for signs of animals or other disturbances. They did find some human footprints in the area and supposed that someone had been out for a walk and had disturbed the animal. Jeanette thanked them for checking, and they paid her with a tanned rabbit fur. They offered to walk Lacy back to the holding, and she had accepted. They had a nice visit owing to the older one's dry sense of humor and Lacy's easily manipulated laughter.

They had made it back in time for the evening meal and said their good-byes as they went their separate ways.

She remembered the day as she ran across the ridge behind the healer's house and down a slope onto the road below. It was the same road from which she had first seen the little holding. It looked much the same today, the weather being warm and sunny, and the spring colors flourishing in the sunshine. There was one little difference. Lacy was moving in the opposite direction.

Having not run for a week and a half, Lacy's breathing was a bit labored. Sucking in the air needed to sustain the pace required her to stretch her ribs a bit, but the pain was not overwhelming. It felt more like an intense bruise. Still, she thought she better slow down to a walk for a bit and allow her lungs to revert back to a lower intake of air. Being injured was the pits! She loved the feel of endorphins racing through her body and was quite certain that unless she kept up her normal pace, she'd not feel them. On the other hand, she didn't wish to reinjure her ribs and cause a delay in healing.

She had been walking for only a short time when she heard it. It was a snap of a twig like someone had stepped on it. It could be the wind in the trees or an animal, but whatever it was, it put Lacy on guard. Her humming was barely audible listening as she was to her surroundings as she walked. Turning around at this point seemed prudent, and Lacy thought that running back would also probably be a good idea.

Changing course, she was immediately confronted by two men. She did not recognize the faces, but the evil in those eyes was almost tangible and reminded her of the Bremhall men. They were also missing the metal crest in the crosspoint of their chest straps, and the tattoos near their shoulders sported a red background rather than blue. They had to be more of Bremhall's men!

"Ah, just who we were lookin' for, I think!" this from the taller of the two. He was a stocky man with long, greasy black hair and black eyes made blacker by the bushy eyebrows over them. "Is this the lass ye saw with Keif and Brady?"

"Aye, tha's her! I could hear her singing then too! Get her and let's go! McKenzie could be back any time now."

Lacy didn't stop to wonder why they wanted her. In a split second, she turned to her right and took off running toward the ridge. She figured that trying to fight them both at the same time might not be the wisest choice. She was still injured and didn't have the advantage of one of them still sitting on a horse this time. Of course, she did have the element of surprise, and she could have taken them, she knew, if she had been totally healthy and perhaps even without being totally healthy. But good judgment had her trying to outrun them instead. She would only fight if forced. Jeanette had been very clear about not fighting for a month. Lacy would try to acquiesce to her wishes.

The men were quick. Lacy was having difficulty staying far enough ahead of them to keep from being grabbed. She ran straight up the hill to the ridge, choosing the most difficult path she could in hopes that her training and physical abilities were better than theirs. Rocks cascaded down the slope, causing Lacy to slide a bit on her way up. Fortunately, she could hear them having the same difficulties.

Her breathing was ragged, and though the song she would like to have hummed could not find passage out through her throat, it still sang through her mind. She centered then, concentrating on the task at hand and the words of the old song. The path before her became clear in her mind's eye. Everything she remembered about the area that she had noticed on the way here was etched with fine detail in her memory. Singing did that for her. It allowed her to focus amid surrounding chaos. It did its job now, even though the more important effort of sucking in enough air to sustain her speed of flight restricted the flow of the song from her lips.

Ahead, amidst a flourish of smaller saplings, stood a very large tree. She had noticed it on her way up the slope. It was a landmark of sorts. Just on the other side of it was the narrow path leading down through the bushes and rocks to the back gate of the holding. She would be hidden from sight to the sentries until she reached the last group of bushes a hundred yards or so from the holding. If caught within the bushes, she would be easy to kidnap . . . or worse. But the path was also the shortest route back to the holding of which she knew. Her eyes focused only on the tree, the path, and speed. She barely noticed that her ribs were screaming in loud protest. The adrenaline had kicked in, and her speed increased.

There was a loud expletive echoing behind her as one of the men noticed that her speed had not slowed but had indeed increased. There was a loud crash as the second man knocked the other out of the way and poured on the speed himself. He was a noisy pursuer, and Lacy could make out every footfall the man made. He was gaining on her!

The tree loomed just ahead of her. As she cleared one side, she reached out for a piece of it to hold on to as she swung around it. The jolt on her arm stretched her already screaming ribs. Lacy let out an abrupt and very loud shriek of pain but didn't slow her pace. The shriek caused her to lose her song for just a minute and with it her focus. She stumbled on the path, thinking that surely the man behind her would have her in a moment. She felt him reach for her, his fingers brushing the back of her shirt. But the T-shirt was snug fitting and he couldn't get purchase, his fingers sliding off.

Bushes whipped at her as she flew down the path, the song once again in her head. She could see the clearing up ahead. It would only take a minute to break through. How close was he now? The opening was almost within reach when the man made a dive at her. He caught her legs, throwing her to the ground. Lacy hit hard. There were stars in front of her eyes, but she kicked her legs free, nailing her attacker in the nose and rolling onto her back.

The man made another dive at her, but Lacy was ready. She got her legs up and caught him in the abdomen, throwing him over her body and onto the ground behind her. She had turned over and was standing again in less than a second. The other man had caught up to them by that time and was running toward her like a freight train. He looked huge coming down the hill at her. A quick glance at the first man offered a bit of relief. He was still down, moving haltingly to get up. Lacy turned to face the second man. She stood still; a loud heavy rock song sprang from her lips. He looked a little startled but continued his advance. Just as he dived toward her, she stepped quickly into the brush around her. The man landed squarely on his staggering cohort. As the two men wrestled with each other striving to regain their footing, Lacy sailed over them toward the opening once more.

She glanced back over her shoulder as she hit the open field, never seeing the man in front of her. Their bodies collided, knocking them both to the ground. They rolled fast and hard across the ground. Using every bit of strength she could muster, she began to fight with everything she had left, her fists flying in a blur as she tried to position her legs between her and the man.

Marek took two very solid hits, one to his jaw, loosening two teeth and the other to the stomach before he could pin Lacy to the ground and get her to see and understand that it was him. As soon as it registered, she collapsed, lungs heaving, pain shooting through her chest. She was vaguely aware that Marek's men were already up the path and in hot pursuit of her assailants. Though Lacy had faced many situations that had required her to fight, for some reason, this one took its emotional toll on her. She was shaking and as frightened as she had ever been. Her mind raced back to the night she and Colter had run for their lives. She didn't remember being this shaken then! What was wrong with her?

Marek released her arms when he saw recognition come into her eyes and helped her into a sitting position. As soon as he did, she wrapped her arms around him, pulling him close and burying her face in his chest. Just as abruptly, she pushed away and let loose a tirade of foul words. She tried to stand and perhaps to run after them. Marek had other ideas.

Wrapping her tightly in his arms, he sat with her, talking to her in a quiet, soothing voice. She wasn't sure what he was saying over her own exhortations, but it didn't seem to matter. It was reassuring just to have him there. What she didn't notice was that his eyes did not leave the entrance to the hidden path even once. There was intensity in his stare. He would have liked to be the one chasing down the filthy heathens. But he would not leave her either alone or with one of his men. He had seen the terror in her eyes, though she covered it with all this false bravado. It had surprised him. He had thought that nothing but a horse could inspire that look in her eyes; he smiled at that memory. Well, no, she had not been *that* terrified even of his horse.

His little warrior had quieted, he noticed. He wrapped his palm around her neck and nudged her to look up at him.

"Better now, Little Warrior?"

"Yes, sorry. I don't know what got into me. I don't usually fall apart just because a couple of goons feel the need to chase me all over kingdom come." She made an effort at wiping the sweat off her face with the tail of her snug-fitting T-shirt. The view Marek got of her midsection as a result made him take a deep breath. He stopped her and pulled her shirt back down into place.

"It isn't the first time I've been chased." She managed a sort of snort just short of a chuckle. "The last time they had a gun pointed at my back."

"A gun?"

"Yeah, it's a hollow tube that, with the aid of an explosive black powder, spits out a little piece of metal that travels so fast you can't even see it. If it hits you in the right place, it can kill you in a heartbeat. If you're lucky, it could just cause you a lot of pain and suffering."

"Ye had one of these pointed at ye and ye were no' as scart then as ye were today?"

"I can't explain it. Normally I would have turned and fought. But I ran instead. Some ADD I am, huh?!"

"Perhaps it was a combination o' things tha' caused yer reaction, Little Warrior. Ye said ye feel ou' o' place here. Maybe ye're feelin' just ou' o' control enough tha' ye canno' handle even one more element o' chaos. Besides, sometimes it's better t' run than t' fight." He stood up then, pulling her with him. "I'm sorry I was no' here for ye sooner."

"You were here in the nick of time. Thank you!" She cocked her head sideways and looked back up into his golden brown gaze. "How did you manage that, by the way? How did you know to come here? Did you know I was in trouble, or was I just lucky?"

"Well, I'm thinking that the devils that attacked ye were the lucky ones. Ye have a mean punch, Little Warrior. My jaw and my stomach may need some extra care after this." He was rubbing his jaw as he spoke.

"Yeah, well, your middle is as hard as a rock! My healing may be delayed by a week or two! Still, I'm sorry. I thought you were one of them."

"I hope so. I would no' want t' think ye hit me like that on purpose!" He managed to bring a smile to her lips. Ah, when she smiled, it warmed him down to his toes. "As it turns ou'," he thought to explain, "the attack on the village was a diversion. It was meant t' get my men and me ou' o' the way for a bit. As soon as we realized it, we turned around and came home as fast as we could. It took us four full days o' hard ridin' t' get back. I was no' sure what we'd find when we got here. I thought they'd have attacked by now. So it was wi' great relief tha' we rode up the lane toward the holdin' and everything appeared in good order.

"We had just come into view o' the holdin' when I saw movement down this path. Ye canno' see it from the holdin' walls, but from the road, I saw ye streak around the tree and head down the path. I then saw two men in hot pursuit. I could no' tell who was doin' the runnin' away and who was doin' the chasin' from this distance, especially only catchin' a glimpse as ye ran past a small opening in the foliage. But we made for the opening in the path as fast as we could. When I heard ye scream, I thought I knew who it was, but when ye started singin' . . . then I was sure. I just canno' figure ou' why they waited so long t' attack ye. They had t' have known we'd be back as soon as we figured ou' their little ploy."

"Well, assuming they were after me, and I think they were, perhaps they waited because I never gave them an opportunity until today. I have been recovering and going through your library. So I haven't really left the confines of the holding. Well, except for the day I went to visit Jeanette and Colter. But two of your groomsmen came. One of them had gotten his hand caught in a gate and banged it up pretty badly. It just so happened that Jeanette had been having trouble with her horse being very skittish lately. So after Jeanette patched up the injured hand, the two went out to check on her horse. They noticed footprints around her cottage and thought that it had just been people from the holding walking behind her stable coming back from hunting. Then the two of them walked me back to the holding, so I guess they just haven't had opportunity."

"Today, I had decided that it was time to start my exercise regimen again," Lacy continued. "I was pretty sure I could run, if not anything else yet. I made it across the ridge to the road heading out when I heard something. I turned around to head back and ran right into those two barbarians." She paused and looked up at Marek. "They aren't your men then."

"No, they're Bremhall's, I expect. We'll know when my men get back wi' them."

"Why would they come here and risk being caught just to get at me?"

"Hmm, well, I'm no' sure about tha' just yet. But when the men get back, I'm sure we'll find ou'. For now, perhaps ye'd like t' head back t' the holdin'. If ye like, I'll have a bath drawn for ye."

"Smell like I did when you first met me, do I?'

"Oh no, Little Warrior! I'm thinkin' ye might just like a bi' o' warm water for relaxin'." He smiled down at her. Taking her hand, he began to walk her toward the holding, leading the horses behind them.

Lacy found it quite disconcerting to be walking in front of the horses. She kept glancing over her shoulders to make sure they weren't too close. Marek, noticing her discomfort, moved her to his left side and the horses to the right.

He pulled her close to his side, wrapping his arm around her waist. Pulling her close reminded him of what she was wearing.

"Lacy," he paused as he thought how to broach the subject, "might ye find . . . must ye . . ." In frustration, he finally spit it out, "Ye will no' wear tha' tunic again!"

"What? You have to be kidding, right? Look at how you're dressed—No, look how you aren't dressed! I at least have everything covered! I didn't wear my shorts for your benefit, but I will not wear a long tunic while running! It's just not going to happen, so get used to it or let me go home!" She shrugged out of his hold and would have run the rest of the way back to her room had it not been for the dull ache in her ribs. *Damn ribs*, she thought. As it was, she settled for walking quickly, if stiffly, ahead of Marek.

He caught up to her and pulled her back into his side. "I did no' mean t' upset ye. It's just tha' seein' ye dressed this way causes me t' think o' things tha' . . . Well, if I'm thinkin' them, then perhaps every man in my holdin' is thinkin' them too. It's just no' prudent t' dress this way, Little Warrior. It provokes . . ." He was gesturing helplessly as he tried to explain.

"Really!" Lacy sarcastically replied.

"Really!" Marek looked at her in earnest as he responded, almost sending Lacy into a fit of giggles. She resisted the urge.

"Marek, I'll stop wearing this outfit to run in when you and your men start wearing shirts. Until then, it's like the pot calling the kettle black and I will not change my ways. You are free to take me back to the cave if this is not agreeable!"

"Ye compare apples t' oranges, Little Warrior. My attire, or my men's for tha' matter, allows us t' be ready t' fight in a moment's notice. And it does no' affect women the way yer attire affects men!"

"Yeah right! And God didn't make the little green apples either!" she quoted an old country song she remembered from her childhood. Her mom had loved the oldies, and as a result, so did Lacy.

Marek was stopped short at that statement. When Lacy did not stop with him, he dropped the reins to the horses and reached out to take her hand and pull her back to him. He looked into her dark brown eyes. A lock of golden hair had escaped her ponytail and blew across her face. He was smiling at her at first, but the smile turned to a scowl as a thought clearly crossed his mind.

"What?" Lacy asked him innocently. Sometimes, she noted, when he took her hand and looked at her with that smile, she wanted him. Sometimes, she thought she might just be persuaded to stay with him rather than return to her own home . . . sometimes. But then sometimes, he looked at her with the scowl she now saw on his face and all it provoked was confusion, curiosity, and insecurity. She looked away, trying to pull her hand out of his. He held it tight and reached with his other hand to her face, drawing it back to look at him.

"Ye are tempted by my men's lack of attire?" He looked almost worried.

"No, never mind!" She made another effort to turn away from him again. He pulled her back. "Tell me!"

"No. Forget it. Let's just get back to the holding. Once I've cleaned up, I'll change. You win! I'll do as you say until I get back to the cave. Deal?"

"No deal! Ye will tell me if ye are tempted by my men's lack of attire!"

Lacy's frustration level was peaking about now. "I said *no*, I'm not tempted by your men's lack of attire, all right?!" she yelled at him in frustration! "I'm tempted by *your*—" She stopped herself before the words were completely out of her mouth, but too late to keep her meaning from Marek.

A wide smile burst across his face. "Ye want me, Little Warrior!" He rocked up on his toes and back to his heels, arrogantly enjoying her discomfort.

"Well, it's kind of hard not—Marek, can we just drop this? It won't make any difference anyway."

"Aye, it makes a world o' difference t' me. Ye want me!" His smile was almost contagious.

"Wanting you is a lot different from needing or loving you! It's just a chemical reaction to your . . . presence! For heaven's sake, can we please just change the subject?!"

"Aye, there may be a difference, Little Warrior." Marek did not change the subject. "But knowing ye want me is a definite step in the right direction. And I warn ye, lady, there is bu' a wee line between wantin' and lovin'." He leaned closer to her, his handsome face only an inch or two from hers, his eyes lingering on hers, persuading her to cross that wee line. His arms wrapped around her waist, gently molding her to his body.

Her hands went defensively to his chest, but she couldn't quite muster the push against him that would break his hold on her. Instead they lingered there, resting against his considerable chest muscles.

Holy Toledo! He feels good . . . so good . . . , she thought. The leather strap that ran over Marek's left shoulder stopped Lacy's hand. She hadn't even noticed that her hand was moving toward his neck until it slid under it, caught for the moment. She could feel his muscles contracting as his hold on her waist tightened.

He leaned in and whispered in her ear, "Just a wee thin line."

His cheek pressed close to hers; he held her there. She leaned her forehead on his chest and just enjoyed the moment. She concentrated on the feel of his warm breath diffusing through her hair. She noticed the softness of his hair blowing across her cheek and the warm arms that embraced her. Suddenly, she was in one of those "sometimes" moments. But the vulnerability of the moment was staggering. They were standing right outside the back gate of the holding, and Lacy began to feel the eyes of the gate guards burning into her back. Reluctantly, she pulled her head up and turned a bit to look at the holding gate.

"Aye, they're watchin', Little Warrior. They're tryin' t' decide whether or no' t' come out and take the horses, or t' leave us undisturbed for the moment."

"Do ye think there'd be anyway at all t' have it both ways then?" she mimicked his odd almost Scottish accent.

Marek's chuckle was low and almost a growl. "Pretty good, Little Warrior. Another month or two and we'll have ye speakin' wi' ou' tha' odd accent!" He looked back toward the holding gate. Answering her question, Marek looked back at her and said, "I wish it could be both ways because I'm afraid tha' the moment I let go o' yer lovely waist, the spell will be broken and I will find myself once again havin' t' woo ye into another moment such as this. Still, I promise, I'll think upon it tonight when I'm driftin' off t' sleep."

Now it was Lacy's turn to smile at him. She looked briefly into those golden eyes and then pressed her lips lightly to his. "So will I." She pulled away then and headed toward the holding gate. She thought she heard a sigh from behind her, but it could have been one of the horses' heavy breathing.

CHAPTER 8

The Picnic

The hot bath that Marek had ordered drawn for Lacy had restored her to a general feeling of well-being. Her ribs felt better, and her muscles had relaxed. She dressed in the long emerald green tunic that the maid had left out on the bed for her. She would have preferred a pair of the leather pants and three-quarters-length tunic that some of the women wore, but after the argument she and Marek had earlier, she opted to go with the flow . . . for a bit, anyway.

The tunic was an overlay to a creamy silk undertunic, the outer green one being slit up the sides to the waist. She had been given dark brown sandals to wear with it and a lovely green-stoned pendant necklace to top it off. She took the time to straighten her hair, pulling a bit of it back into a braid. Stepping in front of the full-length mirror in her room, she thought she didn't look half bad. Being close to lunchtime, she decided to go down to the kitchens to see if she might be of some help to Marta, the cook.

Marta was a chunky woman with a delightful sense of humor. She had dark shoulder-length hair that never completely stayed up in the barrette where she clipped it every morning, so a lock or two was always hanging down in front of her face. Hazel eyes set off her friendly face, and olive skin highlighted the silver rings that adorned each finger. She ran an efficient kitchen mostly because her staff adored her. She had the habit of working hard at her own chores to finish early enough to be able to help her staff finish theirs. This inspired her staff to try to outdo her in an effort to be able to help *her* once in a while instead of the other way around. Most of the last week, she had allowed Lacy to help with little things, like cutting up vegetables or sorting through the cupboards for specific ingredients, but today, she took one look at the pretty woman standing in her doorway and shooed her out again.

"Ye will get tha' lovely thin' all dirty, ye come in here like tha'! Go find somethin' else t' do, love!"

"There isn't anything else to do! I've done all I can to get a school ready and now I have to wait for Marek to find me space! I've cleaned my room, done my workout, read all I can stand to read for the time being and I'm bored!"

"Well, why don't ye go into the hall and practice using that lovely voice for somethin' other than preparin' for battle!"

"I might if there was a piano or guitar around!"

"Oh well, if ye're meanin' an instrument, . . . I think I might be able t' help ye ou' there."

Marta led her out the kitchen door up to the main hall. She pulled a curtain back to reveal a type of piano. It looked a little different than the ones to which she was accustomed, the keys being all the same white color. It was a smaller keyboard also, the keys narrower. She sat down on the little bench before it, her back to the main part of the hall. She was glad of that as it faced a window and Lacy could see out into the compound as she played. She soon discovered as she played that the half-step notes were in the right places, just a little more difficult to distinguish, the defining point on the odd keyboard being one green key in the middle, which she soon discovered to be the equivalent of a middle C.

It took some practice, but she found that playing the little piano was easier if she kept her eyes closed. This effectively allowed her to "see" the keys as they would be on her own keyboard back home. It was still a little unsettling to push a flat key that would have been a black key and raised a bit on her piano. Still, the tone and clarity of the piano was surprising. She began to enjoy herself as she stumbled through a few old favorites. Music had always been easy for Lacy. She had learned to play the piano at a young age, and her parents had even tried to get her to commit to a musician's life. But Lacy had wanted to be a teacher.

She laughed at that. She would be safe at home right now, probably sitting in the lap of luxury, if she had done as her parents had wanted. As it turned out, she had been in one of the most violent jobs in society, had fallen into the shaft, and was now trapped in another . . . what? . . . dimension? All as a result of that one decision. Her parents were dead now. They had been in a plane crash the summer after Lacy's first year of teaching. The thought of them now changed the music she was playing. It reflected the sadness of the memory. When she realized the change, she stopped and thought for a moment, coming up with a song that she used to like to sing. It was a fun upbeat song with a silly story. At the finish, she heard a very familiar and quite robust giggle. She turned to the familiar face of Colter as he skipped across the room and scrambled up to sit beside her on the bench.

"Colter! It's nice to see you!" She laughed then. "I can't believe I just said that!"

He just grinned at her as he said, "Lacy, can you play another one?"

"For you?! Anything! What do you like?"

"Surprise me!"

Lacy not only surprised Colter, she also surprised a number of other people who had come in for the noon meal. Her beautiful voice rang clear in the hall. She had her back to them, and as they entered, they kept their silence so as not to disturb the lovely voice. She played through anything she could remember as Colter sat beside her, swinging his feet back and forth to the beat. A couple of times she played songs he knew and he sang along with her at the top of his lungs . . . mostly . . . mostly on key. It was at the end of one of his more exuberant renditions that the crowd that had gathered in the back of the room finally announced their presence with applause and laughter.

Lacy, startled by the audience, nearly fell off the bench but recovered quickly. Standing, she pulled Colter up to stand on the little bench, took his hand, and the two of them bowed deeply. They were overdoing the bow and gesturing toward each other to whistles and hoots. When the ruckus died down, one of the cooks came out and asked Lacy to please sing a love song for them. Lacy smiled shyly and sat back down at the little piano to oblige her. Colter, uninterested in mushy love songs, was off to find something to eat, having noticed a cake being set on the front table.

The song she chose was a favorite of hers. It fit her voice perfectly. It was a sweet song filled with the longing of secret and forbidden love. As she sang, she began to think of Marek. She wasn't sure why, but the thought of him made the music come alive. The notes carried through the main hall and out into the hallway to the front door. Marek heard it as he entered through that door.

He stood frozen for a moment, lost in the lovely voice. He finally moved, softly, through the hallway to the main hall. Entering from this door rather than the one closer to the kitchen, he had an unobstructed view of Lacy's profile.

Blond hair cascaded across her shoulders, the sun glinting off it in yellows and golds with just the hint of copper. The green tunic accented her very feminine figure, parting at the waist to reveal the creamy silk of the undertunic. Her facial expression matched the longing of the song as she stared seemingly into the face of a long remembered lover. The entire effect left him totally motionless at the door. He dared not move or even breathe lest he spoil the vision. He wondered whose face she envisioned as she sang.

The song ended, but the spell over the crowd took a little longer. It was a full minute before the applause began. It was probably a minute and a half before Marek could gather himself well enough to take a step toward her. It occurred to him that she had been wasting her talents teaching school. Or, if she was as talented a teacher as she was a singer, Colter must be a genius by now. In any case, he was having trouble breaking the spell she had cast upon him. He could neither move toward her or away from her. His eyes were riveted on the beautiful little warrior.

Marek watched her as she turned and smiled shyly at the crowd, rosy blush coloring her cheeks, her smile radiant. He watched her as she turned from the crowd toward the door from which he had just entered. Those dark brown eyes saw him then. There was a startled look on her face, and then the look changed to . . . what? Was she embarrassed? No, that wasn't it. It was as if she was suddenly uncomfortable though. Why would she be uncomfortable? What an enigma she was, and oh my, what he would give to hear her thoughts right now!

The applause had humbled Lacy. She usually sang only for her own enjoyment but had never been uncomfortable with an audience. However, this audience had gotten rather large, and she was anxious to make her escape. She rose from the bench, turned to smile at her impromptu fans, and headed for the door. A hasty escape at this time would be very nice. She was quite surprised to see Marek standing in her path.

Oh no! she thought. How long had he been standing there? She wondered what he was thinking about now. He had the strangest expression on his face. It was as if he had wanted to say something to her but was at a loss for words!

Lacy took a hesitant step toward him, pulled herself together with a little shake of her head, and walked toward him. Well, she told herself, she was really walking toward the door, not necessarily toward Marek. So why did her pulse quicken and the palms of her hands get sweaty?

Get it together! she thought. *He's just a man for heaven's sake!*

Marek was thinking similar thoughts himself. When she reached him, she smiled, murmured a greeting, and headed toward the door. It took him a minute before it dawned on him that she was leaving the building. He turned and ran after her. The door was open, and she was stepping out into the sunshine when he caught up to her.

"Lacy, have ye eaten lunch yet?"

"No, I was . . . I just needed to get away from the crowd . . . I don't usually have an audience. I thought perhaps I should make my escape before . . ." She giggled nervously. She had been about to say "before you came in," but she caught herself in time.

"Before what?"

"Oh, never mind, it—nothing . . . I just needed air."

"Would ye consider havin' lunch wi' me? We could make it a picnic. I know a place completely devoid o' crowds."

"I wouldn't want to trouble you. You're probably hungry—"

"No trouble at all. Please, wait right ou'side in the sunshine and I'll only be a moment." He started to turn toward the kitchen when he felt her hand on his arm. He turned back to her. "Aye?"

"Marek, this place . . . we don't have to ride horses to get there, do we?" She bit her lip subconsciously as she waited for his reply.

He smiled down at her. "Sweetheart, ye really have t' get over this fear o' horses."

Lacy paused a moment, taken by surprise by his use of the endearment *sweetheart*. Then she defensively straightened her shoulders and glared at him. "That's not it, it's just that I'm wearing this lovely dress and I'm . . . well, it's not mine . . . I wouldn't want to get it dirty . . . "

"It is yours and ye will no' get it dirty."

"It's mine?" The surprise took the glare right out of her eyes as she looked down at the lovely green tunic.

"I told ye I would take care o' ye. If I do no' want ye runnin' around in those second skins, I had better be offerin' ye something else t' choose from, aye?!"

"Yes but, Marek," she countered as she realized she was getting sidetracked from her original point, "about the horses . . . it can't be very ladylike to ride in one of these . . . " A quick glance up into his face again found him smiling broadly. Lacy sighed and gave up. "Okay, fine! I admit it! I am afraid of the horses. Can we walk?"

He reached out and touched her cheek lightly. "It'll be all right, Little Warrior. I promise." He left her then and hurried back into the holding.

Lacy sat on the little stone bench next to the door and waited anxiously. Horses! Oh, what she would give to get him back to Riverton and into her car. Then he'd see who was doing the cowering and who was saying, "It'll be all right!"

Marek caught Galen in the hallway near the kitchen. "Galen, get two or three men t' ride ou' t' the pond. Have them secure the area for me. I will be takin' Lady Lacy ou' for a picnic. I do no' think tha' Bremhall will have men here twice in one day, bu' it's best t' be sure. Also, have Ian set up watches around the perimeter of my holdin's. Bremhall was no' successful today, bu' I do no' expect him t' give up so soon. Spread the word tha' we need t' have a gatherin' t' decide what needs t' be done t' discourage further visitations."

"Aye! Marek, do ye think it's wise t' risk a picnic?"

"Bremhall will no' cause me t' live my life differently than I have been. I'll take precautions, bu' I will no' hole up inside and forget t' live. And I do no' want my lady t' have fear on my lands and today would be the best time t' risk it."

"I know ye do no' want the lady t' fear, bu' in her case, a wee bit o' fear might be a good thing."

"She has all the fear she needs livin' in a strange land far from home and havin' t' learn t' ride a horse. Honestly, I've never seen a lass so scart o' horses!"

"Aye! So are ye walkin' t' the pond?"

"No, we'll be takin' Thor. Speakin' o' tha', bring Thor around t' the front."

"Tha' would be my pleasure, Marek!" Galen smiled widely.

"Galen, leave Lady Lacy alone! Do no' tease her abou' her fear o' horses! It could come back t' haunt ye. Oh and, Galen, tell the men t' keep close eyes on their women and children. Do no' let them ou' by themselves . . . just t' be safe."

Galen nodded as he turned to go gather the men and prepare Thor.

Marek wasn't gone long before Lacy looked up to see Galen bringing Thor around the corner. She closed her eyes, wishing she had opted to stay in the crowded main hall for lunch. When she opened them again, she looked up into the smiling face of Galen. Every thought going through her head must have been readable on her face because he was clearly having a good time with the whole situation.

"Going ou' for a wee ride, aye?! Not havin' second thoughts are ye now? We did have a set o' brakes installed just for yer use, milady." He began to chuckle to himself at his own little joke.

"You know, Galen, I'm feeling much better now than I was the first time I met you. I'm sure that I could be persuaded to put you to sleep again if you care to continue this discussion!"

This remark brought on a full gale of laughter from the big man. "Aye, ye got me once, but I had my hands full at the time and I was no' expectin' an attack by a lady now, was I?"

Lacy stood and walked down to the wooden railing where Galen was tying up the horse. He finished wrapping the reins around the railing and began rubbing Thor's nose affectionately. She stood on a step just beside him, looking up into his mischievous smile.

"So you'd be willing to have a rematch then?"

"Aye, anytime ye like, milady! Though ye might want t' clear tha' wi' Marek first. He might no' appreciate ye challengin' his men t' a fight! Ye could get hurt, after all, no' tha' I'd hurt ye, bu'—" He was midsentence when he felt her hand on his shoulder just for the briefest moment. He would have been too tall for her to get a good hold, but she was standing on the step that gave her quite an excellent advantage. She squeezed firmly, and Galen was out for the second time! She caught him on his way down and struggled to lower him to the ground. She didn't want to hurt him, of course, just get him to show a little respect in the future. He was very heavy though, and she almost dropped him. Thank heavens, her ribs were feeling better.

Once he was safely on the ground, she turned and walked back up the steps to the little bench and had just sat down when Marek came out with a picnic basket tucked under his arm. Marek looked down at his sprawled-out warrior with confusion spreading across his face. He turned to look at Lacy, who sat most seriously, also observing the prone warrior.

"What happened t' him?"

"Oh, him?" Lacy asked innocently.

"Aye, him! What happened, Little Warrior?"

"He's learning to show a little respect." She stood and took Marek's offered arm and walked down the steps toward her nemesis. They stepped over Galen's unconscious body together. Then a thought occurred to her. "Marek?"

"Aye?"

"Maybe we ought not go so far for a picnic. Two thugs tried to steal me away, after all. I haven't seen the return of your men, so I'm assuming they have either lost them and given up or are still out in hot pursuit. Either way, it might not be very safe to venture so far."

"We are goin' t' have t' address this habit ye have o' insultin' me and my men, Lacy. They would never quit before they have finished their duty!" When he looked at the worry in her face, he perceived the real trouble behind her fear. He took a deep breath, turned her toward him, and addressed the problem. "Lacy, ye are going t' ride the horse. But I will be with ye. Do no' worry, Little Warrior. I will no' let ye fall. Besides, the men have returned."

"They have? Did they catch them?"

"Aye, my men are questioning them now. We'll soon know wha's goin' on."

"What if they don't talk?"

"They'll talk! Ian and Kenneth are most talented at information gatherin'." He smiled sweetly at her. As she opened her mouth to speak again, Marek stopped her with a finger to her lips. "Now, shall we go?"

With a heavy sigh, Lacy closed her mouth, looked at the horse in resignation, and allowed Marek to lead her to it and set her on top. She took hold of the saddle and waited for him to swing himself easily up behind her. He handed her the basket, reached around her, and took the reins. Lacy took the basket nervously with one hand, keeping the other locked on to the saddle. At Marek's urging, the horse began moving, taking Lacy's breath away.

She didn't even realize she was holding her breath until Marek wrapped his arm more securely around her, pulled her back into his chest, and whispered "Breathe!" into her ear. "I will no' let ye fall, Lacy. Trust me."

"Okay, I trust you, but what if—"

"Lacy, ye are insultin' me again!" He rolled his eyes and reached out to loosen her grip on the saddle. He held her hand then, bringing it up to his lips for a quick kiss. Since his arm was now completely around her shoulders, his hand holding hers merely an inch from her face, the kiss on her fingers took Lacy's complete attention. She noticed he had shaved since this morning, his cheeks looking smooth and clean. His dark hair shone with red highlights in the sunshine as it hung loosely in careless waves around his perfect face. His eyes held such tenderness as he leaned in to kiss her hand that Lacy could not have taken her eyes off him even if a battle had raged around them. His eyes closed as his lips found her hand, but Lacy's did not. Ripples of electricity lapped through Lacy's stomach like waves on a pond.

He looked up then into her dark brown eyes. "Better, Lacy?"

"Yes." She barely got the answer out. If he had not been so close to her, he'd have never heard her. His eyes left hers then and began to guide the horse in what Lacy thought might be a southern direction, though as she thought about it, she really wasn't sure which way was which. Everything she thought she knew about the land surrounding her was in question. The educator inside her thought about asking, but she didn't want to spoil the moment with directional drivel. So she kept her silence for a minute longer. Then it occurred to her that Marek had been calling her Lacy rather than his preferred favorite, "Little Warrior." Curiosity overcame her wish to revel in the moment, and she finally spoke.

"Marek?"

"Aye?"

"You called me Lacy."

"Aye, is that no' yer name?"

"Well, yes, but you always call me Little Warrior. Why the sudden change?"

"Do ye no' like it?"

"I like my name just fine, but somehow it almost seems like an insult coming from you."

"Oh well," he paused a moment as he looked quickly around the meadow. They were heading toward a stand of trees now, and Marek seemed to be a little preoccupied with the surroundings. But he continued as the horse made its way into the stand of aspen trees. "Ye were no' actin' like a warrior now, were ye? Ye felt an awful lot like a woman, with normal fears in need of some protectin'. I rather enjoyed feelin' needed for the moment, even if it *was* only due t' a wee horse. Ye are usually telling me how ye do no' need me, but when I get ye on a horse—"

"A wee horse!" she mimicked his accent, making him chuckle. "Listen, Marek, I am no more frightened of this four-legged fur-lined bag of bones than you would be of my four-wheeled leather-upholstered car on a freeway! It's all what you're brought up with, after all!"

"Car on a freeway?" he asked, eyebrows raised.

"I'll draw you a picture sometime, or better yet, maybe I'll be able to take you back with me and show you! Suffice it to say that my car can travel at speeds in excess of one hundred miles per hour, though in all truthfulness, I usually keep it around seventy-five since that is the speed limit on a freeway."

She couldn't tell by his face whether or not he believed her about the speed of her car. He just grunted some unintelligible word and pulled her back into his chest again as the horse sort of skipped up a little embankment. Then they were there. It was a small pond, surrounded by trees with a grassy beach area around the edge on which the horse now stood. It was quite lovely, and still. There was not a breath of breeze on the pond, and the glassy reflection of the surrounding trees was glorious.

Marek slid down off the horse, reached up to take the basket, and set it on an old tree stump. He returned to the horse to help Lacy down, but she had already taken hold of the saddle and slid off herself. He smiled broadly at her.

"Ye've just taken the first step, Little Warrior. Ye slipped down off the horse by yerself!" There was pride in his voice as well as a smile on his lips.

"Yeah, well, don't get all proud of me. I'll still need you to call me Lacy when we get back on that thing to go home."

He shook his head with a chuckle. "I've really go' t' take the time t' teach ye how t' ride." He stepped forward and took her hand to lead her to the stump.

"Why would you want to do that? I'm only going to be here for another couple of weeks, and you said yourself that you like my dependence on you when we ride."

"Well, ye are no' leavin' in two weeks, Little Warrior. I've claimed ye. As my lady, I'll be wantin' t' keep ye close. That bein' said, I must teach ye t' ride."

"Sweetheart, and I use the term lightly, may I remind you that you agreed to allow me to fight for my right not to marry."

"Ye need no' remind me." He smiled at her. "But, sweetheart, and I use the term quite seriously, ye will no' win, so ye might as well get the ridin' lessons ou' o' the way."

"You don't understand, Marek. I don't have any talent with animals at all! My own dog bit me when I was a child! I don't understand animals. They don't like me and I don't much care for them! I don't like riding horses even if you do have your arms wrapped around me, much less if I'm on one by myself! You know I would fight to the last man for something I believed worth fighting for, but riding a horse is not an act of defense . . . It's a mode of transportation. I have no place to go, save home, so if I can't walk someplace, . . . I won't go! So there is clearly no need—"

"Lacy, ye will learn t' ride a horse! Now stop frettin' over it and let's eat."

"Marek! You don't seem to—" Before she could finish, Marek pulled her to him and kissed her. He wasn't sure why; well, yes he was. He had wanted to do that since the day he met her. But he had managed to hold back. So what had gotten into him today? Maybe it was her ridiculous fear of horses. Maybe it was how beautiful she looked in the green dress. Maybe it was the song in the great hall. Maybe it was stepping over Galen and knowing exactly how the man had ended up laid out on the steps. Maybe it was how she felt in front of him in Thor's saddle. Maybe it was her stubborn streak that fought so ardently to avoid learning to ride or being claimed by any man without her consent. Maybe it was the way she fought with a song on her lips. Or the way she protected Colter. Or maybe, just maybe, it was all of that put together.

Whatever it was, he couldn't seem to stop himself. From the first touch, he knew he was lost. The warmth of her lips surprised him though why he would think they would be otherwise, he didn't know. He guessed it was that they felt so much warmer than his own. And soft. Heaven help him, they were so soft. He had to get closer; even though he was sure it could get no better than this, the need for more was overwhelming. Still, he pulled back, trying to rein in the emotions and lightning bolts ricocheting throughout his body.

Whatever Lacy had been meaning to say left her mind completely. The man could kiss the thoughts right out of her head. She thought that with the electricity shooting through her body, she could easily light an entire city for a day. He tried to break the kiss, but she pulled him back, demanding more. He pressed his lips again to hers, pleased with her response, and then his lips parted in unison with hers. They shared breath, lips, and tongue. Once again, Marek pulled away, this time going back for two or three short sweet lip-to-lip touches before stepping back, holding her at arm's length but still staring into her eyes.

The intensity of the moment did not dissipate as Lacy thought it would when he pulled away. Though he had stepped back a couple of feet and now only touched her where their hands were joined together, their eyes were still locked on each other, their breath heavy and uneven. This was a dangerous place to be. She couldn't drop his hand anymore than she could stop breathing, but to stand there and hold it allowed the electricity full rein in her body. She managed to close her eyes. *Control, control, get control of yourself*, she thought.

When she opened her eyes, he was smiling at her again and only inches from her face.

"It is a beautiful song," he whispered close to her ear.

Chits! She was singing again! She hadn't realized it until he spoke. The song stopped. *Come on, Lacy*, she thought to herself again, *get a handle on it!* She pulled her hand out of his, turned toward the basket, and made an effort to open it as she sat on the edge of the wide stump. Her hands were shaking, and she fumbled with the latch. It hadn't helped to pull her hand away. It still reverberated with the warmth of his touch, and just thinking about that sent another sweet shiver down her spine.

"Breathe, just breathe." She had spoken out loud, which she realized only when she heard his laughter. She felt the blood rise in her cheeks and didn't dare to look up at him. She thought she had better work on controlling her mouth when she was shaken up.

He didn't wait for her; he sat down beside her, reached out, and took her chin in his hand. He nudged her face up, but she avoided looking into his eyes at first. He held her there and waited. Slowly, her eyes crept up from his strong jaw, to the dazzling smile, past his perfect nose to those golden brown eyes. But it wasn't amusement she saw there now; it was desire, bold and clear!

"Marek . . . ," Lacy started but couldn't quite finish.

In an instant the look was gone, replaced with an everyday happiness at just being outside on a beautiful day with good company. He finished opening the basket and helped Lacy lay out the lunch. Marta had included fried chicken, some raw vegetables fresh from the garden, and four fluffy rolls, cooled a bit now by their short trip but still fresh, soft, and warm. Marek had stuffed in a bottle of wine and a couple of glasses and poured her one as they sat together on the grass, enjoying the view with the meal. With their backs against a fallen tree, they fell into small talk as they sipped and ate.

They were silent for a bit, just enjoying the varied wildflowers that grew in the area and the sounds of little critters out and about in the fine weather. The birds chirped overhead, and Lacy closed her eyes, enjoying the heat of the sun on her face and shoulders. She breathed in the scent of trees, grass, and flowers.

"It's lovely here," she said softly, eyes still closed.

"Aye, it is." Marek was closer to her than she had thought, but she didn't move away. She smiled, rather enjoying his close proximity.

He took her hand in his again. He was rubbing his thumb along hers when he spoke to her again.

"Lacy, what's it like where you come from? Ye talk all the time of things that I canno' even imagine and dangers I've never known. Wha' draws ye back there? Is it . . . do ye have a man there?" he asked nervously.

She turned to look at him as she answered, "No, I don't have a man there. I'm a teacher. Where I'm from, teachers are among the most highly trained people in the world. We have to be." She started out speaking with a bit of pride but added the last statement a little sadly. "It takes a lot of time. A teacher's social life suffers."

"Ye like teachin' then?"

"Yes, I do. I also like staying in such good shape."

"Aye, I like your shape too!" he commented with a bit of false lechery in his eyes; well, at least Lacy thought it was false.

"So why are teachers made t' stay in such great shape?" he asked.

"Well, a few decades ago, some well-meaning people thought it would be a really good idea to protect children from abuse. They meant well, but they went way overboard. It started out innocently enough. You could no longer spank a misbehaving child at school. When poor behavior began to get worse, the behavioral gurus told us that we had to put them in a time-out area, like sitting in the corner until they calmed down. Then they wouldn't let teachers correct a child in any way that might hurt their self-esteem, so corners were out and we made special rooms for them. Then they switched to a regimen of positive reinforcement. That meant that you ignored the poor behavior and only responded to good behavior with positive remarks or rewards. Instead of helping, what ended up happening was that children who were inherently well behaved were ignored while we concentrated on waiting for poorly behaved children to display even a single good behavior that we could reward. When that failed, we frantically tried to bribe badly behaved students into behaving better with stickers and prizes. That didn't work either!

"From there, they began to take rights away from parents too. They no longer allowed parents to spank errant children. A parent correcting a child with a firm swat to the backside could end up in jail if someone found out about it. It's considered abuse. The result of all this protection is unruly, out-of-control children. Kids are smart. As soon as they figured out that no one could touch them, they began ruling their homes and the schools. The behavioral problems in our classrooms have gone from bad to worse.

"There was a time when a severe behavioral issue would have a child expelled from school. This allowed teachers some ability to maintain classroom discipline. Everyone was able to come to a safe place to learn. Everyone followed the rules or they suffered the consequences. Unfortunately, now, the consequences are so lenient that students pretty much do as they please. So schools have become battle zones. Children as young as Colter . . . or younger are behavioral nightmares. They kick, bite, punch, swear, and spit to get their own way. The consequence for such behavior is a trip to a quiet room where they lay around on soft pillows in a dimmed room with soft music played for them until they calm down.

"Our high schools are riddled with drugs and drug dealers. Depressed students are in the habit of bringing guns to school and shooting at faculty and other students. Theft is as common as catching a cold and learning . . . Actual learning is a distant second to staying alive long enough to get a diploma and get out of there."

"What are guns again? Ye told me tha' Colter's uncle chased the two of ye wi' a gun pointed at ye. Since we have a bit o' time, perhaps ye could describe it t' me."

Holding her hand up in the shape of a gun, Lacy described the workings and the purpose of a gun to Marek in as much detail as she knew. His eyebrows rose higher and higher as she explained. Anger rose in his face as she retold the story about Colter's and her escape on the night they fell through the floor of the shaft. Their conversation lagged as the wheels turned in Marek's head. She could see him thinking things through as she watched his face. She could almost see the many different ways he could affect the slow and painful demise of Dan and Tony Stecks.

Finally, he spoke, "And ye are wantin' t' go back t' tha' world? Why would ye want tha', Little Warrior? Here ye can teach wi' ou' the poorly behaved children. If one o' them misbehaved, the lad would answer t' me as well as t' his father. Ye would no' be havin' any problems in the classroom."

"Well, I get the feeling that teaching is more important to me than a formal education is to your people. I've done my part in setting up a school. I've gathered the materials I will need. I've paper and writing tools, a chalkboard and chalk. I've pilfered your library to find books I might use to teach reading and writing. I've even read a few of your books on the history of the area. But I have not, to date, been given a space in which to hold school. I also gather that getting some of the students into a classroom will be challenging because they have so many chores that must be done. I understand that, so I'm not offended, but how can I be a teacher when I have no classroom and no students? As you have noticed, I don't know how to do many other things. My food was mostly premade for me in my world, so I don't know much about cooking . . . though I could learn . . . except I hate cooking. I can't ride a horse to save my life . . . nor would I want to! I have a brown thumb and animals hate me. What's left? I am a pretty good warrior, but I notice that most of your women do not go with you on raids or stand watch to defend the holding. I can sing, and I know music and could teach that, but aren't we right back where we started?"

"I'll find ye a place t' teach and students t' work wi' as soon as I can, but I'm sure ye'd find a place t' fit in, Little Warrior, whether I helped ye or no'. In the meantime, do no' think tha' the music ye provided today was no' worth the time t' sing it. It boosts morale, raises spirits, and inspires people in their work and their imaginations. A fine song, delivered masterfully can inspire a work o' art, a new invention, a deeper faith, and a man t' act courageously. It can cause the uptight t' relax, the lazy t' work, and the lover t' act. Ye're very badly needed here whether ye know it or no'."

"I have not noticed, was there a great lack of lovers acting before I sang?" She giggled.

"Well, I was single until ye started singin'."

"You are still single, sir!"

"No, I've claimed my wife. I'm no longer single."

"The woman you've claimed has not claimed *you*, you know!"

"Oh aye, she has, she's just so used t' fightin', she feels she must continue!"

"You think?"

"I know!"

"And just how would you know?"

"She told me wi' her very own lips no' thirty minutes ago."

"She did not!"

"Aye, she did!"

"Marek, I have never said—" She saw him staring at her lips then and stopped midsentence. The desire was back in his eyes when he looked up into hers, electricity flying between those golden brown eyes and her dark brown ones once again as it dawned on her that indeed her lips sang two different songs, one loudly protesting what the quiet, physical message relayed so completely.

CHAPTER 9

The Unlikely Guard Dog

The rest of the afternoon was frightening but exhilarating as far as Lacy was concerned. Marek had decided that it was time to start the riding lessons. The first step was to get Lacy used to the horse, and he insisted that she feed Thor an apple that he produced from the basket. This required standing close enough to the horse for Lacy to hand him the apple. She found the close proximity to the horse's nose quite disconcerting, but as Thor took only the apple and not her fingers, she considered it a success. Marek was not so sure. He watched as she stood as far away as possible and leaned over, stretching out her arm until she nearly fell on the ground in front of Thor.

The second step was getting Lacy close enough to rub Thor's neck. In an effort to avoid the whole leaning thing again, Marek stood behind Lacy, taking small steps forward while pushing her in front of him. When he got her close enough to touch Thor, he reached around her to rub Thor's neck. As he leaned over Lacy's shoulder, he noticed that her eyes were squeezed shut and she was holding her breath again.

"Lacy," he whispered, "breathe! Then open yer eyes, he's no' goin' t' hurt ye."

"Yeah, so you've said . . . repeatedly . . . but couldn't we start with a smaller horse? Or maybe a large dog? You know, just give me a little time to get used to the idea first?"

"Lacy, open yer eyes! For heaven's sake, ye are a warrior! Ye've dropped men twice yer size."

"Well, yes, but I've never been trained to drop a horse! I don't know what to expect! Like, does he bite? What if he steps on me? What if I fall off while I'm riding?"

"He does no' bite unless ye get in the way o' his mouth when he's eatin' and he does no' see ye, and even then, he would stop biting' as soon as he felt yer flesh. He's a vegetarian! If he steps on ye, it will hurt verra much, and if ye fall off, try to fall on soft ground!"

"You are not helping!"

Marek sighed in frustration. "Lacy, what if ye happen to be fighting and yer opponent socks ye in the nose?"

"Well, I would get a bloody nose and my eyes would both swell up and turn black, of course!"

"Aye, well, just like a fight, defensive or offensive, everything is a risk. Ridin' a horse is a risk, but so is defendin' a wee lad. But if ye get good at ridin', yer horse just might save yer life one day."

She sighed loudly, her back pressed tightly against Marek's chest. "It's that important that I do this?"

"Aye, it's tha' important."

"Okay, you win . . . but how about you stand in front and I'll pet him from behind you?"

"Lacy!"

"Never mind!" Her big brown eyes opened up, and she reached out her hand. It was shaking, but she finally stroked the horse down the neck and patted his shoulder. Thor took it all in stride and turned his head toward her. She had closed her eyes again just as she patted his shoulder and never saw it coming. He nuzzled her, leaving a little apple juice slobber on her left cheek. Now her eyes were open wide! She was as surprised as Marek that she didn't scream, but then she supposed that being petrified with fear had frozen her vocal chords along with every other muscle in her body. She didn't move anything, not a muscle, not an eyelash, as she watched Thor turn away from her and head a few feet away to nibble on a thick juicy patch of grass he'd been eyeing for a bit.

"Ye did real well, Little—" Marek was interrupted by Lacy's sudden attempt at running. She turned a complete one-eighty and ran right into his chest.

She started babbling immediately, "It's okay! I'm all right! It wasn't so bad! He's a good horse. I'm fine, really! The horse is fine, he's . . . just . . . eating! But I'm good!" She rambled on for a bit, trying to stop the shaking and pull herself together. Finally the babbling changed to irritation, and Marek was pretty sure she was regaining her sanity. "What a wuss! I'm such a wuss! Why can't I do this with a little decorum?" She was no longer shaking and was just beginning to make a little sense again when she felt a nudge in the middle of her back.

She looked up at Marek. He was looking a little worried as he stared back into her eyes.

"Are ye all right?"

"He's right behind me, isn't he?"

"Well, Lacy, he's . . . yes, he's right behind ye, but do no' worry. He likes ye! He's wonderin' if ye have another of the sweet apples on yer person."

"Oh." She didn't move but closed her eyes and began to sing. She felt another more insistent nudge to her back. Finally, she paused the song long enough to ask, "Uh, *do* I have another sweet apple on my person?"

"Yes, can I leave ye for just a minute to get it for ye?"

"Yes. Marek?"

"Aye?"

"Hurry, please."

He smiled, let go of her, and moved to the stump. He pulled another apple from the basket and handed it to a very stiff Lacy. She was singing again and managed a weak smile as she turned around slowly. Thor was only about four inches from her nose. He nudged her again under her chin, and she held the apple out to him. He took it gently from her hands and munched it as she reached out to touch his nose.

"It's so soft!" She stopped singing and started to stroke Thor on the nose with a little more confidence. It was not long before she had both hands on *his* face and a large smile on *her* face.

"Be careful, Little Warrior, he'll"—Thor was faster than Marek and completed his sentence by nibbling a little kiss on Lacy's cheek before Marek could finish the warning—"kiss ye." Marek waited for the panic to register in Lacy but was surprised instead when she giggled. He thought he might faint himself when Lacy leaned over and kissed Thor back . . . right on the nose!

She turned suddenly around and caught Marek around the neck. Her smile was radiant! "He likes me! He really likes me!" Then she hugged Marek with all her might. "Thank you! I was so scared, but he's great! And he kissed me! Isn't he wonderful?"

"Aye, he's wonderful!" Marek was hugging her back with just as much enthusiasm. Damn, she felt good. "Lacy, love, could ye do me a favor?"

"Anything, Marek. He likes me!"

"Yes, so ye've said. But, Lacy, would ye mind showin' this much enthusiasm for me when *I* say I like ye?"

Her laughter was louder now. She stared into Marek's beautiful eyes, torn between the urge to stay right where she was and the equally strong desire to continue the lesson. Reason finally won out as she decided that she better continue with the lesson. After all, the urge to stand in Marek's arms was not fleeting, but the urge to learn more about Thor might be. If too much time elapsed before she touched him again, she might become afraid and have to go through this all over again. She pulled her hands down to Marek's chest and turned in his arms to face Thor once more.

"What's next?"

Marek's eyebrows shot up. "Are ye ready for more then?"

"Yes, what's next?"

They spent the next couple of hours taking the saddle off and putting it back on then removing the bridle and replacing it. Marek showed her how to check the hooves and assured her that he'd show her how to clean them when they made it back to the holding.

"Can we go now? Then you could show me what to feed him and how to brush him down."

"Aye, we can go. Maybe tomorrow, ye might like t' have yer first lesson on top o' the horse."

"Ah, my first driving lesson! Can I wear my workout pants?"

"No, ye cannot wear those second skins. The men—no, ye canno' wear them! I'll get ye a pair of the ladies' leathers and a tunic."

"Well, all right but, Marek, I'm wearing my workout pants to run in. Those leathers won't work for that. Okay?"

"Lacy, those things are indecent!"

"Marek, I need to be able to work out . . . Would you rather I wear my shorts?"

"What in the world are *shorts?*"

"They are very comfortable short pants. They hit me about here." She demonstrated the length of the shorts with her hand on her thigh.

Marek's eyes were about the size of the apples they had just fed to Thor. "No! Ye may absolutely NO' wear shorts t' run in! For heaven's sake, Little Warrior, do women have no modesty where ye come from?"

"Women?! The men dress the same way, only sometimes, like yourself, they don't wear shirts! What do you think that does to the women? At least we keep our shirts on, for crying out loud!"

"Ye've argued this point before! A man wi'ou' a shirt really bothers ye?"

"Oh, not at all, I quite enjoy it! I like to watch the way the muscles ripple when a man is working. Shucks, just watching you walk across the courtyard is amazing! Didn't you notice that my eyes nearly popped out of my head when the six of you rode up to Colter and I the first time? I have never in my life seen six beautiful chests all at the same time. Usually there are some skinny ones or fat ones in there, but you six were a feast for my eyes."

"Really!" Irritation was creeping into his voice though he kept his facial expression neutral.

"Oh really! Why, it was a complete pleasure to hop up on Galen's back to put him to sleep. All that power so beautifully packaged. It was a delight to touch even though I did have to let go rather abruptly. And then there was you. You wrapped that incredible chest around me . . . Well, actually, that rather hurt, but the view from there . . . well, there were four other perfect chests all around! Come to think of it, the six of you could put together the hottest six months of calendar pinups I've ever seen!" Lacy had turned her back on him to put the remainder of the picnic back into the pretty basket as she teased him further. She struggled to keep the giggles out of her monologue. "You know, Marek, you are absolutely right, why bother going back home when the views here are so much more . . . titillating!"

"Titillating!" Marek roared. "Ye've been . . . ye think my men are—what's a pinup?!"

Turning to face Marek, Lacy collapsed into a puddle of laughter at the look in his eyes. He caught her up in those wonderfully strong arms, his hand catching her chin and pulling it up to look into his face. She'd been laughing so hard that her eyes were watering.

"A pinup, Lacy?" he prodded.

"It's a picture of a particularly beautiful body that one posts on a wall to look at throughout the day. A calendar pinup would be a picture of a beautiful body attached to a monthly calendar. They are quite popular at home."

"And did ye have many of these on yer walls?"

The seriousness with which he asked these questions had put a halt to the giggles, and Lacy stood staring back just as seriously.

"No, I thought they were degrading."

"Then why do ye talk so?"

"To tease you!" She smiled then.

"So ye were no' starin' at my men?"

"Haven't we discussed this before?"

"Lacy!"

"How could I?" She took a deep if shaky breath. "They were standing around you! I was, however, staring quite blatantly at you"—she made a poor effort at his accent as she finished—"or did ye no' notice, Huge Warrior?"

He smiled at her imitation. "I did notice ye were lookin' at me. I just did no' think ye were admirin', rather that ye were lookin' for weaknesses. Now I know why ye failed so miserably! Ye were distracted by all tha' . . . let's see, how did ye put it? Oh yes, by all tha' power in such a beautiful package!" Marek was chuckling now.

"Yeah, well, I was more impressed with how little effect my elbow to your abdomen had. I remember wondering just what you did in a gym that I hadn't been doing. It was like hitting a metal shield!"

"Do no' worry yerself, it was a pretty good hit, but ye did no' have all yer strength. I was verra surprised at the solidness o' such a hit from a woman."

"Well, when you are impressed with the hit and the thought of me being a woman doesn't even enter your mind, let me know!"

"Hmm, sorry, Little Warrior, if it's ye tha' hits me, I'll always be thinkin' abou' ye being a woman." He leaned down and kissed her briefly. "We need t' get back t' the holding. Ready t' mount up?"

"Yes. I believe I am! Are you going to show me how to get up there by myself?"

"Aye, but no' right now. I'll wait until ye're wearing yer new pants." Disappointment was written all over Lacy's face. "I'll get ye some tonight! We can start in the mornin'. Will tha' be all righ', Little Warrior?"

Her smile was all the answer he needed. He took her by the waist and perched her neatly on top of Thor. He handed the basket up to her and swung himself up behind her, pulling her back into his chest. This time he didn't have to pry her hands off the saddle. He reached around to take the reins, but she caught his hands in hers and pulled them up to her lips. She kissed them each then turned toward him.

"Marek?"

"Aye?"

"Thank you! It was a wonderful picnic!"

A smile appeared on his face. "Aye, it was!"

Once Thor had been returned to his stall, Marek demonstrated how to brush him down and feed him. Lacy had helped a bit but mostly had stood by Thor's head, stroking his nose. She stood back as Marek fed him though so that he wouldn't mistakenly bite her. They said their good nights to Thor and headed back to the main building. Dinner was just being served as they entered.

The crowd looked up as the two came in, and everything got quiet. Lacy wondered what they were all staring at when she realized that she and Marek were holding hands. Surely that couldn't be it, could it? She looked down at her attire, but it looked none the worse for wear. She glanced over at Marek to check out his looks. He looked radiant! He was smiling back at his people, his hair tousled but handsome, and his face sun flushed and relaxed. He had an expression of quiet triumph. He pulled her toward the front table and pulled a chair out for her to sit in.

He leaned over Lacy for a moment and whispered in her ear, "I'll be right back, I'll bring a plate for ye. Ye might want t' mend things wi' Galen a bit though, aye?!" He inclined his head toward the young man sitting at the end of the table.

Lacy whispered back, "Galen needs to mend things with me! He's the one that was doing all the needling! He was making fun of my fea—inability to bond with animals! He had the nerve to laugh as he told me that your men had installed brakes on Thor!"

"Oh, aye, I can see yer point! Remind me never t' tease ye abou' yer fea—inability t' bond wi' animals, Little Warrior."

She rolled her eyes at him but stood to move to the end of the table as Marek headed toward the kitchen.

"Uh, Galen?"

"Aye?" Though the reply was stiff, the man stood and turned to her, still looking a little green. Every eye in the place was on them.

Lacy leaned in close to make it appear that she didn't want everyone overhearing the conversation. But she spoke just loudly enough for the closest of Galen's companions to hear every word.

"I just wanted to thank you."

"Thank me?" he asked incredulously. His brows grew together suspiciously as he glared back at her.

"Yes, I know you only let me knock you out again so that I'd feel better about losing the fight with Marek when we first met. I had a hard time dealing with that loss. Your gallantry is unsurpassed and I thank you. However, please don't do it again. If I don't knock you out on my own merits, it's still not a win." She kissed him on the cheek, smiled at him, and headed back to her seat.

Marek returned a moment later with two plates of something that looked like potpie to Lacy. He noticed the change in the atmosphere immediately. Looking around at the faces of his men, he noticed that they were looking at Galen with what could only be described as respect. Galen, he noticed, could not keep his eyes off Lacy.

"What enchantment have ye unleashed on my men, Little Warrior? And what did ye do t' Galen, kiss him? He canno' keep his eyes off o' ye!" Marek scooped up a bite of the potpie and stuffed it in his mouth.

"Yes."

Swallowing, Marek looked at Lacy. "Yes wha'?" Marek took another bite.

"Yes, I kissed him."

Marek choked, coughing repeatedly to get the offending chunk out of his throat. "Ye did wha'?"

"Marek, are you all right?" Lacy had turned to slap him on the back, but he caught her hand and repeated his question.

"Ye did wha'?"

"I apologized and kissed him on the cheek! He accepted my apology, and I came back to my seat! What did you think I did?"

"Ah, ye apologized! Tha's good! I ... well, he ... well, he ..." Marek turned to Galen then and bellowed, "Galen! Have ye nothin' better t' look at then?"

Galen swallowed hard, nodded and turned to Ian who was sitting on the other side of him, and dove into conversation.

"Oh and, Galen?"

"Aye?" He kept his eyes on Marek as he turned back.

"Could ye have Thor ready for riding first thing in the morning? I'll be givin' Lady Lacy her first ridin' lesson."

"Oh aye!" Galen looked at Lacy, and they shared respectful nods.

After dinner, Marek walked Lacy to her room, kissed her—all too quickly as far as either of them were concerned—good night and left. It had been a wonderful day; well, not including the chase that had started it all. Still, the afternoon had more than made up for that little escapade.

She took off her dress and pulled on her shorts and a T-shirt and ran through her evening workout, trying to include a few push-ups and sit-ups. She could not do as many as she was used to doing, but at least her ribs didn't hurt much anymore. She would have to work up to her usual routine. The bed had a canopy made out of solid wood that could have supported the weight of a couple of sides of beef, so Lacy used it for a pull-up bar and made an effort at resuming that part of her workout as well. But her ribs weren't quite ready for pull-ups, so after only one attempt, she thought better of doing those tonight. She went through her normal routine, and a little over an hour later, she gave herself a wash down with the water in the basin beside the window. Feeling sufficiently refreshed, she turned to the bed.

A pretty nightgown had been laid out sometime during the day. Lacy pulled it over her head and was just about to crawl in bed when she heard a knock at the door. She opened it to peek, and there stood one of the maids holding a pair of black leather pants and a lavender tunic.

"Laird McKenzie wanted ye t' have these, milady."

"Oh, thank you!"

"Will there be anything else ye might want?"

"No, thank you. Good night!"

The maid bowed and returned down the hallway. Lacy closed the door and held the pants up to her waist. She slid them on under the nightgown just to see if they fit. They did! They fit amazingly well!

"How does he do that?" she asked out loud. Or did he have one of the women guess the right size? She'd have to ask him that in the morning. She slid out of the pants, folded them neatly, and laid them on a chair with the tunic. Bed was looking quite good about now, and Lacy crawled in, enjoying the feeling of clean sheets and a warm blanket. She was asleep in no time, dreams of the afternoon flitting through her head.

Marek headed straight to the interrogation room. When he entered, he found Ian and Kenneth sitting by themselves.

"Where are the prisoners?"

"We've already tucked them in t' bed." Ian smiled wickedly.

"Aye? An' what did ye learn?"

"We learned tha' Bremhall is no' runnin' things at his own holdin'!"

"The laird tha' is in charge now wants a closer look at the lady tha' took ou' two o' his warriors by herself."

Marek looked disgusted. "I knew we should have killed those two. I just thought Bremhall would take care o' it for me!"

"Aye, bu' do no' worry, Marek. The new laird *did* take care o' it for ye. Bu' now he wants Lady Lacy. He sent them after 'the warrior woman who sings'!"

"He specifically asked for the warrior woman who sings?"

"Aye!" Ian confirmed.

"That's interesting. How did he end up as laird? Does no' sound like Bremhall t' let another take his place."

"The new laird has a verra scary weapon!"

"Oh? What kind o' weapon could tha' be?"

"They called it a gun."

Marek's face went pale. "Are ye sure?"

"Aye! What is a gun?" Ian noticed Marek's reaction and stood.

Marek shared all that Lacy had told him about guns. It was a sobering discussion.

"So what are we goin' t' do abou' this new laird?" Kenneth asked.

"We are goin' t' have t' face him sooner or later, bu' for now we will have t' double the guard and watch over Lady Lacy any time she leaves the holdin'."

The sun woke her early in the morning. She had neglected to close the curtains the night before, and the morning rays drifted over the windowsill and onto her pillow. The air smelled of wildflowers and farm animals . . . well, the residue of farm animals. That reminded Lacy; she had a riding lesson today!

Throwing the covers back, she jumped out of bed and slid into her leather pants in a matter of seconds. She slid out of the nightgown and into the pretty lavender tunic, topping it off with her belt slung gracefully over her hips. She put on her sandals and laced them up. She took a couple of minutes to make the bed and straighten the room and then was out the door and down the steps.

The door to the courtyard was slightly ajar, and she sailed outside and down the steps, pausing only long enough to grab an apple from a bowl near the doorway in the dining hall. She almost skipped across the compound to the stables. The stables were still pretty quiet. The horses had been fed, but no one was around at the moment. Thor seemed as happy to see her as she was to see him. Lacy climbed up on the gate of his stall and reached over to stroke his nose. He came right up to her and gave her a slobbery horse kiss, sending Lacy into a fit of giggles.

"Look what I have for you, Thor!" She held out the stolen apple. Thor munched as Lacy hummed to him. "Now where do you suppose your master is this morning?" Lacy leaned over the gate a bit to scratch behind Thor's ears. In doing so, she accidentally hit the lever that opened the gate. She didn't notice right away. Climbing down from the gate, she headed out the door of the stables to go in search of Marek. The gate creaked open, and Thor followed her out. She turned at the noise, only to discover the great horse standing right behind her.

"Thor! What are you doing? You have to wait here. I'll go get Marek. Stay!" She backed away, and Thor followed her.

"Thor, turn around and go back to your stall!" He continued to follow her.

"Please?!" She had backed out of the stable and stood in the sunshine, staring helplessly at the horse. He nudged her with his nose.

"Fine! Follow me then . . . I guess!" She turned and headed toward the main building. She peeked behind her again, and sure enough, Thor was still following her across the compound. Her nerves took over and she began to sing. When she reached the steps to the building, she made another effort at getting Thor to wait at the bottom.

"Thor! Stay . . . . stay! Stand right here and stay!" She reached under his head and pushed on his neck. He stopped! She was thrilled!

"Good boy!" She turned and raced up the steps, opened the holding door, and was pushed inside by the big horse that had followed her up the steps and into the foyer!

"Thor, back up! You silly horse! What would your master say?"

"He would ask, 'What in heaven's name are ye doing, Little Warrior?'" Marek stood on the steps above Lacy, watching her try to push the horse back out the door—with little effect at all, he noticed.

Lacy turned slowly, smiled nervously up at the handsome man on the steps, and replied, "He followed me home! May I keep him?"

Marek couldn't believe his eyes. Here was his little warrior who only yesterday had been mortally afraid of horses now standing right under the head of a horse, trying to push it out the front door of his house. And it wasn't just any horse! It was the biggest horse in his stables! He didn't know whether to laugh out loud or yell at her. What was the woman thinking? Why had she let the horse out of his stall in the first place? She could have been trampled—though in all truthfulness, he doubted that Thor would trample her. He seemed to like her . . . a lot!

"Marek, I think I can explain. I hope I can explain! You see, Thor . . . Well, I mean, *I* went out early to visit Thor and climbed up on the gate to reach him. I must have accidentally opened his stall, and when I came back to the house to get you, he . . . he . . . he . . . followed . . ."

At first it was just a chuckle, but within a minute or so, Marek was sitting on the steps with his head thrown back in gales of laughter. It was contagious! Lacy began to giggle with him and before long was laughing out loud too. She scooted up the steps to take his hand and pull him from the stairs.

"You . . . ," she began between giggles, "you . . . have to help me get him out of here! He might poop or something!"

That didn't help anything. Marek couldn't even stand at this point, and tears were streaming down his cheeks.

"Oh! Laird McKenzie! What is yer horse doin' in my hallway?" Pauline the housekeeper had poked her head out of the main hall. Her eyes were squinted suspiciously at him as if he had been trying to put something over on her.

"I'm sorry, Pauline! It was my fault. Thor followed me in!" Lacy apologized.

"Well, why don't ye just get him t' follow ye out!"

"Oh, good idea." Lacy giggled. "I should have thought of that!"

Lacy pulled Marek to his feet and dragged him down the last few steps past the bulk of the large horse and out the front door with her. Thor turned awkwardly in the small quarters and followed the two of them out. They walked hand in hand until Thor squeezed in between them, the big blond horse nuzzling Lacy with his large soft nose until she giggled and scolded him affectionately.

Marek helped Lacy get Thor back in his stall and insisted that they get some breakfast before they started the riding lessons. As he turned from the stall toward the main hall, Marek sighed heavily.

"What's wrong?" she asked as she caught up to walk beside him.

"Well, I'm not sure exactly, bu' I think I'm jealous o' my horse!"

Smiling brown eyes stared back at him. "Are you? Why?"

"Oh, I do no' know . . . maybe it's because the horse can kiss ye all the way across the compound and elicit only giggles and feigned scoldin'. If I did tha' t' ye, ye'd be yellin' from here t' eternity! I believe the words would be somethin' like, 'I don't need ye, Marek! I do no' need anyone!' Oh, no wait, what ye'd really say is, 'I do no' need ye, *Sir* Marek!'"

"I did say that, didn't I?"

"Aye!"

"Well, it's still true. I don't need you"—she watched his face drop almost imperceptibly—"but I like you . . . a lot!" She watched as his lips turned up at the corners just a bit. "Oh and, Marek, horse kisses not only do not invite a wagging tongue to gossip, but they are also not nearly as much fun to think about later!" Lacy felt the blood rush into her cheeks at her own admission.

"Are ye suggestin' that my people have waggin' tongues?"

"Well, they are people, are they not?"

"Aye, I suppose they are."

"And are you not the most eligible bachelor in the holding?"

"Well, I do no' know about tha'. Galen is still single as is Kenneth and—"

"But you are laird of this holding, yes?"

"Well, aye, but—"

"There you have it! The most eligible bachelor in the holding! And when the most eligible bachelor in the holding kisses a young lady, tongues will wag."

"I do no' believe that, Little Warrior! Perhaps we should test yer theory." Marek stopped and pulled her into his arms.

Lacy wiggled out of his embrace. "No need, look up at the window to the dining hall!" Marek looked up just in time to catch no less than seven people staring down at them. Of course, as soon as he looked up, they all scurried away.

"Oh aye!" Marek smiled at her. "Breakfast?"

"Oh aye!" Lacy almost had the accent perfect. She and Marek laughed as they entered the main hall.

Riding lessons went very well. Once Lacy had lost her fear, she was a daredevil in the saddle. She seemed to mold to Thor like custom gloves to the hand for whom they were made. It was not long before Lacy could get into the saddle almost as easily as Marek. He had the advantage of height, of course, but Lacy was fast! They worked on speed, control, turns, stops and finally jumps. Marek was amazed at the ease with which Lacy learned and executed the maneuvers. In only a week's time, she had progressed faster than any student he had ever had before. He supposed it was the intense physical training she was used to that enabled her to move so easily with Thor. Whatever it was, she was something to watch!

He had been looking for a horse for her other than Thor, but then something changed his mind. It happened one day when he was out working with his men. They were practicing with their swords and training the younger men when Marek looked up to see Lacy out for her daily run in the field near them. Thor was right behind her. He followed her like a little puppy. But the next thing he saw made him decide to give Thor to Lacy and find another mount for himself. As Lacy, true to her word, ran along the trees in the sweats that she loved and Marek hated, she suddenly stopped short. Marek heard the singing at the same time he saw both Lacy and Thor come to a screeching halt. Thor had been trotting just a few paces behind Lacy, but after initially responding to a very near yet unseen threat, the horse suddenly shot forward to Lacy's side. He stood between the threat and Lacy. Lacy wasted no time in jumping up on Thor's back, and the horse was turned and running before Marek could blink.

A loud bellow from Marek had him with no less than five of his warriors running toward the threat in the trees. It couldn't be Bremhall's men, he thought. They would never come this close with half the men of the holding out practicing with swords. It would be suicide. What, then, had caused Lacy to sing and run without a fight? The question was answered in the next couple of minutes as a large black bear charged out of the trees. Its front paw was mangled, and the injured bear was in an uproar. It would normally have stayed away from all the noise the men were making, but it was in a blind fury. It charged at the men, its front paw injured and causing its gait to wobble awkwardly. They surrounded the thing, working their way toward it, swords at the ready.

Lacy had seen the bear just before Thor had run up beside her. She hadn't even thought about what to do; she did just what her instincts had led her to do. She had jumped on Thor's back and allowed him to take her away. She hadn't even needed to direct Thor. The two had worked like a team. No, it was more than that. Thor had protected her! Marek was right: "If ye get good at riding, yer horse may just save your life someday." Thor had certainly done that today. Lacy glanced over her shoulder and saw Marek and his men closing in on the bear. Incredulous, she pulled back on Thor's mane to slow him, and as she patted him and told him what a wonderful horse he was, she turned him toward the men. Thor was reluctant but finally turned. Lacy watched with fascination and fear. What were the men doing, trying to get themselves killed?

Kenneth got too close too soon and took a paw swipe across his shoulder. The distraction at least allowed the other men to get close enough to get their swords into the bear's tough hide. It was dead in minutes. Galen and Ian hefted Kenneth up between them and headed back to the holding. Lacy coaxed a very reluctant Thor back to where the men surrounded their kill. As soon as she made it to the men, Galen and Ian pushed Kenneth up on Thor's back behind Lacy, and she took him swiftly back to the holding. Jeanette was sent for as Lacy wrapped Kenneth's shoulder to slow the bleeding.

The rest of the men gutted and skinned the big bear, Marek pondering what he had just seen happen between Thor and Lacy as they did so. His thoughts were drawn back to the bear as the men began to discuss why it had attacked.

"What do ye think he did t' his paw?" Ian asked aloud.

Brett was examining it as the others continued to cut the bear into smaller chunks for carrying and distribution. "It looks like he got it caught in a trap. And from what I can see, he had t' work pretty hard t' get it ou'."

"Oh, that would do it, I suppose!"

Galen spoke the thoughts that had found their way into Marek's head, "It could have killed her!"

"Aye, if not for Thor, it might have!" The thought sent a shiver down Marek's spine. "Did ye see how he ran up t' her? The damn horse positioned himself between Lacy and the bear!"

"Aye, it was odd, but then Thor follows her around like a young pup!" Galen pointed out. "I've never seen anythin' like it!"

"Aye, I guess I better find myself another horse!" Marek laughed.

As soon as Kenneth had been taken care of, to Lacy's satisfaction, she headed out to where the men were finishing up with the bear. She slid off Thor's back and walked up to Marek.

"You scared me to death!" they both said in unison.

They stared at each other, Marek trying to figure out what he had done to scare Lacy and Lacy trying to figure out the same thing. Marek recovered first.

"Ye nearly got yerself killed today, Little Warrior!"

"Well, it wasn't actually my fault! How was I supposed to know there was a crazed bear out here!"

"Ye should no' be running ou' here by yerself. Ye'll wait for me t' go with ye next time!"

"No, I won't! You can't keep me sequestered in that hold all the time, waiting for you to protect me! I'm not helpless! And in case you didn't notice, I wasn't hurt . . . unlike one of your men when you decided to take your lives into your own hands and attack that thing! I thought it was going to kill one of you or all of you! What were you all thinking?! At least I had the sense to run!"

A glance around at the men only ticked her off further. They were all smiling at her! The big dopes! Well, all but Marek. He looked stunned!

"What?!" she demanded.

"Ye were worried abou' us?" he asked. "Why?"

"Why?! What do you mean why? It wasn't like hunting a regular bear! That one was injured! It makes it even more dangerous! What if something had happened to you? What would I do without you . . ." She was staring only at Marek then and realized it too late. "All!" She tried to include the others in her tirade, but it just made her feelings for Marek that much more obvious. "Uh, . . . all of you! What would the people at the holding . . . do . . . if something . . . happened to all of you?"

Marek stood there looking into her eyes, a smile spreading across his lips. "Go ahead and take the meat back t' Marta," he told his men. "I'd better escort Lady Lacy back t' the holding." He reached out and took her hand. When Thor tried to nose between them, Lacy turned around and took his reins over to Galen.

"Thor, stay with Galen. He needs help, okay? Good boy!" She patted his nose, kissed his cheek, and turned back to Marek.

Marek took her hand again as they walked toward the holding. "Lacy, I'm sorry we scart ye, but we had t' take on the bear. For starters, it's never wise t' allow a carnivore t' live unchecked so close t' the holding. He might kill someone. And also, we can always use the extra meat and the skin. T' top it off, that bear *was* injured and needed t' be put ou' o' his misery. So we took him down while we could. But we were never in verra much danger. We've done similar things before. However, ye did scare me! I did no' think I could get t' ye fast enough t' help ye. And if Thor hadn't been with ye . . ." He stopped her then and looked into her face, holding her hand in both of his. "The bear would have killed ye, Lacy, and I'd have had t' watch wi'ou' bein' able t' get t' ye!"

122

"You don't know that I'd have been killed. I'm a very fast runner!"

"No matter how well ye're trained or how fast ye ran, I think the bear would have gotten ye before we could have helped."

"Okay, say, the bear would have gotten me. Say, that I had been killed. I could just as easily be killed in the holding while you are out here practicing to keep me safe. I could fall in a well, hit my head and drown or get run over by a truck . . . a startled horse, or get shot by an errant arrow! Lots of things could happen. You can't keep me safe every second of every day and you shouldn't have to try!"

"Well, I've been thinking abou' tha' and I saw somethin' today tha' makes me at least believe tha' I can maybe offer ye a little more protection while I'm no' with ye."

"Oh yeah? Like what?"

"I'm giving Thor t' ye. I was going t' find ye a horse o' yer own, but today Thor did something that a horse would no' normally do. He put himself between ye and tha' bear. He follows ye around like a puppy. He'd rather be wi' you than wi' me. He loves ye and ye seem t' feel the same way about him. So from this moment on, he is yer horse, Little Warrior."

"Marek! I can't take your horse! He's yours!"

"No, Lacy, now he's yers. I only ask ye t' do one thing for me in return."

"What?"

"Always take him with ye when ye go for yer runs . . . please!"

She started to laugh, her hands cupping her face. "I don't know whether to be ecstatic or feel slighted!"

"Why would ye feel slighted?"

"You're giving me a horse to babysit me when you aren't here!"

"Well, I would no' say I'm givin' him t' ye t' babysit ye," Marek countered.

Lacy stared down at the ground and shook her head. "Three weeks ago, I'd have fought you tooth and nail over this. I didn't even like horses! But now, I just want to—" she stopped herself midsentence. Her hands dropped from her face to hold his hands.

"Ye want t' what?" Marek tried to find her eyes, but she kept her head down, staring at the ground in earnest. "Lacy, ye want t' what?" he prodded.

She slowly looked up into his face, but her eyes never got past his lips. She leaned hesitantly forward, stood up on her tiptoes, and kissed him lightly on his lips. "Thank you!" she whispered. "I'll take good care of him."

"Hmmm, do ye think ye could run that thank-you by me one more time? I mean, he *is* the biggest horse in the stable. Surely he's worth two wee kisses!"

Lacy didn't stand up on her tiptoes this time. She smiled shyly and pulled him down to her. She kissed him again, but this time she put all her emotions into it. She started out sweetly, warm and inviting. Marek allowed her to drive the moment, restraining himself, waiting on her. She didn't disappoint him. With every move and touch, she demanded more of him. She felt him shudder down the length of his body before he pulled her so close that she could barely breathe. And then he was kissing her back, his breath warm in her mouth, his tongue seeking hers.

Her fingers laced into his hair at the back of his neck. "Marek . . . ," she whispered between kisses. "We aren't alone anymore! Your men have caught up to us, and in about two or three seconds, a great big nose is going to interrupt us!"

His groan was audible to everyone. Just as she'd said, it was only a second later that Thor stuck his nose right up next to them. He nibbled her cheek and pushed Marek back a few inches with a nudge to his chin.

"Lacy, would ye mind tellin' yer horse tha' I was here first?"

"Galen, would you mind taking Thor back to the holding?" Lacy asked between horse kisses and nuzzles that nearly knocked her off her feet.

"Aye, we'd love t', but he does no' wish t' go wi' ou' his lady!" The men were all laughing and making no effort to leave either with or without Thor.

Lacy did manage to find Marek again by ducking under Thor's head. "Well, you did say you wanted him to help protect me!"

"Yes, but we're going t' have t' train him t' protect ye from people other than myself!"

CHAPTER 10

The Date Is Set

"So this will be the week then?!"

"Aye!"

"Are ye sure she's fully healed?"

"Aye! She said so herself. She's been working out—as she calls it—every day. I've also been workin' wi' her on her fightin' habits."

"Oh?"

"I've been tryin' t' get her t' stop singin' before she attacks. It's a dead giveaway, ye know."

"Aye, I know. I thought ye liked it though! And why would ye be helpin' her wi' somethin' that could tip ye off when ye have t' fight her yerself?!"

"Oh, I can well see when she might be attackin'. It's funny, where she comes from, no one must really challenge her. She does no' seem t' need t' be covert abou' her attacks. She sings as a sort of focusin' point. But she also warns her opponent tha' she is abou' t' attack and they migh' better reconsider! Here, more o' us are trained t' fight an' we do no' see it as a warnin' but more as a telltale sign. I explaint tha' t' her and had her practice it. Sometimes she gets it an' sometimes she sings! What's verra funny is when she keeps quiet, but canno' seem t' focus so her fightin' becomes a bit dysfunctional. I'm no' sure she'll ever get it." He couldn't help but smile as he thought of their sparring practices. The last one had ended with Lacy getting very frustrated. She insisted that she didn't need to sing, but that she wanted to and he could just stuff it if he didn't like it! He wasn't sure what *stuff it* meant, but he was pretty sure it wasn't a very complimentary term.

"When will ye hold it?"

"The last day o' the week."

"Ye seem no' yerself. If I did no' know better, I'd say ye were worried. Do ye think maybe she might win?"

"Oh, aye, she'll win all right."

"What?!"

"Do no' worry yerself, I can beat her—though I dare say she'd put up a good fight—but I'm not goin' t'."

"Why in heaven's name no'?"

"Well, I've been thinkin' abou' it good and hard and the truth is tha' I want her t' *choose* t' stay wi' me. I will no' force her."

"Ah, Marek, ye know she loves ye. The way she looks at ye . . . the way she touches ye . . . it's almost . . . sickening! Take her and live a happy man."

"I do no' want to *take* her. I want her t' be free t' choose. But do no' think I do no' pray every mornin' that she chooses me."

"So why lose too? Just win the match and set her free."

"No, that's like divorcin' her. I'll no' do tha' either. If I do tha' and she does no' choose me, no man will have her even if she does finally choose another. She would always be considered my property. I do no' know if she can get back t' her world or no' and I would no' want t' mess her up socially if she has t' stay. Besides, she might choose me!" He smiled to himself as he remembered their conversation on the way home from the path where Bremhall's men had tried to snatch her. He also remembered the kiss by the pond. Aye, she liked him, she wanted him, but did she love him?

"Marek, will no' losin' t' a wee lass undermine yer authority wi' the men?"

"Hmph, they're free t' challenge me any time they like! I will no' be losin' t' any o' them."

Galen nodded in agreement. "Do ye think tha' Lady Lacy might figure ou' tha' ye've let her win, especially if ye never lose again?"

"Maybe, bu' it canno' be helped. I'll make the fight as believable as I can and hope for the best." Marek stood up from the bale of hay where he had been sitting in the barn while Galen was tending to his horse. Marek had finished with his own big black stallion purchased from a nearby rancher yesterday evening. He hadn't named the black yet. He wanted to bring Lacy down to look at him. Perhaps she might have a good name for him. Actually, he just wanted an excuse to be with her. She spent most of her time either running, with Thor chasing close behind, or working in the little classroom he had found for her.

She had started a morning school for students between the ages of six and eleven. They met every weekday starting at eight in the morning and finishing at eleven thirty. Since none of the children could read or write, she was starting at the beginning. She had told Marek that she wasn't quite sure how to progress with the spelling since the children spoke with such a thick accent. He laughed and assured her that it wasn't the children who spoke with a thick accent, it was her! He thought that it was going to be quite interesting to see how that all turned out. There was some fear in the back of his mind that she would have all the children in the holding talking just like her and Jeanette.

Deciding to go and find her before school started, Marek headed for the main hall. Maybe he could catch her at breakfast. As soon as he entered the hallway, he heard her. She was sitting at the piano running through some scales and small bits of songs, pausing every now and then and playing again. He stepped into the room, and there she was, bent over a paper on the top of the piano, writing something down. She paused, put her pencil in her mouth, and played a little tune. Stopping midway through and pulling the pencil out to write again, she seemed deep in thought, and he hesitated in the doorway watching her.

He noticed she was wearing the newest dress he had sent to her. The others had been picked out by Pauline, but this one he had taken the time to choose himself. It was a coral color, the same as that skin-tight tunic she kept using to run in even though Marek had forbidden her to go out in it. She never listened to him! If she only knew just how very . . . attractive she looked in it . . . No, *attractive* was too tame a word for it. He wasn't even going to think up the type of word that would describe how it made her look! Then again, the color suited her well. It brought out the natural color in her cheeks and gave her a fresh flushed look as if she had been walking briskly through the cool crisp morning air. She took his breath away as he gazed at her.

Drawn to her, the need to touch her almost palpable, he finally got his feet, moving in the direction of the little piano. She must have seen the movement in the corner of her eye because she glanced up just as Marek started toward her. An immediate smile spread across her lips when she saw him. She had allowed her hair to curl naturally this morning, and the sun was caught in it, forming the illusion of a luminous golden halo about her head. The effect hastened his approach. He needed to touch her, even if just to hold her hand. Never in his life had he ever found a woman that could *so* captivate him.

"Lacy, do ye have a moment? I've someone I would like ye t' meet."

"Of course, I was just working on next week's music lesson for my students. A couple of the kids are quite gifted and might be performing during meals before too long. Who is it that you want me to meet?"

Marek took her hand as soon as he was within reach. "Oh, just come wi' me, Little Warrior, he's ou' wi' Thor."

Lacy grabbed an apple from the basket by the door with her free hand, pulled her other hand from Marek's, and moved it up his arm close to the crook of his elbow. Marek laid his free hand on top and laced his fingers through hers. As they exited the main hallway and stepped into the sunshine, a breeze blew over them, filling Marek's senses with Lacy's scent. She smelled of wildflowers after a rain. It nearly undid him. The thought occurred to him that if Lacy did not choose him, he just might die of a broken heart. How could he live even a few hours without her? And what if she returned to her own world somehow?

As bad as it would be if she stayed but did not choose him, it would be worse if she left and he was never to see her again . . . well, maybe. There was always the chance that she would stay and not only refuse Marek, she could also choose someone else. He wondered how he would handle that scenario.

Maybe Galen was right and he should just win the fight and keep her with or without her consent. Damn! He couldn't and wouldn't do that. He wanted her to choose him! He *needed* her to choose him! The need for her was so great that he knew he would do anything for her. If she asked him to go back to her world with her and leave everything behind, he would do it. He'd hate it, but he would do it. How had it come to this? When he first saw her . . . when he watched her fight off two men, . . . he had known that she was the woman for him. But he had maintained some control of the situation then. Now he had no control. When had he lost it? It had been a gradual thing. There was no precise moment when power had left him and been given to her. But it had happened. And there was no going back now.

When there is no way out, what do you do? he wondered to himself. Without really thinking about it, he pulled Lacy's hand from his arm and wrapped it around his waist. He rested his own arm across her shoulders and rubbed her neck with his thumb. He didn't even realize he had done it until she leaned her head into his shoulder.

Lacy didn't know who Marek wanted her to meet, but when he pulled her hand around his waist and rested his arm on her shoulders, she figured it couldn't be too formal of a meeting. Besides, they were meeting in a stable! When he started stroking her neck, she felt her knees go weak. The man commanded her total undivided attention and probably didn't even know it! She had been concentrating on every move he had made since she looked up to see him coming toward her. Oh, how she loved to watch him walk toward her . . . or away from her for that matter, though walking toward her usually meant that he would touch her soon. His practically bare chest displayed muscles that rippled with every movement. She always wanted to touch him now it seemed. She dreamed about it, both asleep and awake! Since the kiss by the pond, she'd been hard-pressed to think of anything else!

As they walked toward the barn, Lacy enjoyed the sensation of having her hand wrapped around his waist. His skin was warm, and the muscles beneath it were firm and lean. She leaned into his shoulder and closed her eyes. She wanted to remember every touch, every movement of his body beside hers. She breathed in deeply so that later when he wasn't with her, she would remember how he smelled. Suddenly it dawned on her that she had indeed crossed that wee thin line. She couldn't put her finger on when or where, but somewhere along the way, she had passed just being attracted to him or just wanting him; she had plunged headlong into loving him.

—

As that revelation dawned on her, so did the realization that she absolutely did not wish to fight him for her right to freedom. She *wanted* to be his lady. On the other hand, she needed him to know that she wasn't being claimed. She was choosing this relationship. It was ludicrous for men to think that they should be able to choose things like this without a woman getting a say in the matter. A woman should always have a say in her own life! If she didn't fight him, she was sure that no woman would ever get the right to choose for herself. She was also pretty sure that no male warrior would ever want a woman that beat him in battle. If she fought and won, she would be setting a precedent for women, but she might lose Marek. If she fought and lost in order to keep Marek, she would get her man but lose an important fight for women. What was she going to do? Unconsciously, she tightened her grip around his waist.

They had just stepped into the barn when Marek felt her pulling him closer. He stopped and looked down into her face. Had it been his imagination? Her eyes were closed, but they fluttered open when he stopped and she looked up into his golden brown eyes. She wondered if he could read every thought in her head. If he could, she hoped he would do just what she wanted and lean down and kiss her like he had done at the pond.

He turned to face her, their eyes locked together. He just stood there gazing into her face. She couldn't move, she couldn't even breathe.

Kiss me, she thought. The apple dropped, and she placed her hand on his chest. It began to wander as if it had a mind of its own. She took her time, touching the muscles she had spent so much time admiring. Finally, her arm found its way up and around his neck. She played with the hair at the nape of his neck, lacing her fingers through it and still he did not move. It was only when her eyes closed and she started to lean her head on his chest that he finally acted. He caught her chin in his hand and held it as he leaned down to grant her wishes. His lips explored hers, pressing and releasing, molding to hers. She moaned as her mouth opened to his, inviting him in. Though she couldn't remember them moving from her chin and shoulder, she felt a thrill rush through her body when his arms wrapped around her back and waist and pulled her closer to him.

Time came to a standstill. Nothing mattered to Lacy but Marek and his touch. She didn't even notice Thor kicking up a fuss in his stall at the lack of attention from his mistress. The apple she had brought to him had fallen a couple of feet out of reach, and Thor meant to remind her of her errand.

She ignored him. Marek was kissing her cheek and working his way down her neck. Lacy was wondering if her legs would keep her standing after her knees melted away like homemade ice cream on the Fourth of July. Even with the melting of her knees, she stood up on her tiptoes and kissed Marek at the base of his neck. Marek moaned softly, sending his warm breath up her neck to her mouth once again. The fervor of their kisses was quickly escalating. So was Thor's annoyance. He managed to kick the back of his stall with such force that he shook the entire wall of the barn. This in turn disturbed the hay stored in the loft above Marek and Lacy. A loose pile near the edge of the loft fell unceremoniously down on their heads.

Marek's laughter started as a low chuckle. He could barely see Lacy through the hay. He reached up and dusted her off as she made efforts to do the same to him. After freeing her of most of the big stuff, he started working at picking out the little stuff.

"I guess I better find that apple and give it to His Highness!"

"Aye, he is feeling a bit unloved."

Lacy lingered there in his arms. She really didn't want to move, but finally, she turned away from him and reached down to find the apple. She had to dig a little through the hay, but she found it. She headed over to Thor and handed him the apple. She patted his nose as he munched.

"You have very poor timing, Thor!"

"Aye, he does!" Marek was right behind her, one arm on either side of her supporting his weight as he leaned into the gate. All Lacy would have to do was turn around, he'd be only about an inch from her face. She resisted the urge as long as she could but finally turned. Before she could turn completely, Galen came running into the barn, sword drawn.

He took in the whole scene, Marek leaning over Lacy, both of them covered in little bits and pieces of hay. They must have looked like they'd had quite a roll together because Galen's face turned a brilliant red.

"Oh, I'm sorry t' have disturbed ye! I heard the horse kick the wall . . . I thought there might be trouble. I'll . . . if ye'll excuse me . . . I'll just . . ." He pointed feebly to the door and headed in that direction, resheathing his sword as he went.

Lacy started to giggle then. "Oh you're in trouble now!"

"I'm in trouble?"

"Oh yeah! Now everyone will think you've been taking advantage of a lady!" Thor had finished his apple and was nuzzling Lacy's ear. "Thor, stop it!"

"Oh, not t' worry, Little Warrior! We can fix tha'." He smiled mischievously down at her. "We just have t' make ye my lady a few days earlier. What are ye doin' this afternoon?"

"Nothing important, but I'd rather watch you squirm a bit first!" she teased back. She reached up behind her and rubbed Thor's cheek, partly to soothe him and partly to push him away from her own cheek.

"If ye'd have opent yer eyes a few minutes ago, ye'd have seen me squirmin' already, Lacy!"

"You didn't feel like you were squirming," she said quietly, not missing for a second the soft way he said her name.

—

"No?"

"No, you felt like you knew exactly what you were doing. No squirming involved at all!" She poked him in the chest for emphasis on each of the last four words.

He caught her hand on the last poke and held it in both of his. "Maybe it was the internal squirming I was feelin' then."

"What internal squirming was that, Marek?" she whispered.

"The kind where I have t' decide just how far I was goin' t' take ye before I could get a good hold on myself and stop. Thankfully, Thor came t' yer rescue, love."

"Did he?" She leaned against his chest.

His arms closed automatically around her. He took a deep breath before he spoke, "Lacy, ye have a class now, do ye no'? I should walk ye back t' the main hall."

"Yes, but, Marek," remembering why they had come out in the first place, Lacy asked, "who was it you wanted me to meet?"

"Oh, slipped my mind! I'd like ye t' meet my new horse!" He led her to the stall where the big black stood munching his breakfast.

"Oh, Marek! He's beautiful! He is a *he*, isn't he?"

"Aye!"

"What's his name?"

"He does no' have one yet. I was waitin' for ye t' maybe help me ou' wi' tha'."

"Me? You want me to help you name him?"

"Aye!"

"I don't know what to name him." But she was smiling at the honor. "I'll think about it. Okay?"

"Aye!"

"Marek, that was"—she gestured to the barn—"that was . . . I . . . mmm . . ." She moaned softly, closing her eyes with the memory.

"Aye, Lacy, I felt the same way." He reached out and pulled a piece of straw from her hair and tucked it behind his ear. Marek took Lacy's hand to walk her back to her classroom. He stopped at the door to the barn. "Lacy."

"Yes?"

"Will ye be ready for yer challenge fight by the last day o' the week?"

Lacy's breath caught in her throat. She answered in a whisper, "Yes."

"Then the last day o' the week, ye will be my lady."

Lacy didn't argue with him.

CHAPTER 11

The Challenge

The last day of the week was only one day away. Lacy had been mulling the whole thing over and over in her head. What was she going to do?

Lacy's mind would not leave her alone. All week, her thoughts kept replaying that morning's events in the barn. Lacy must have relived the moment over ten times again before she found herself standing in front of Jeanette's house. Each time she wanted nothing more than to turn and run to Marek. If she did that now, she knew she would just throw herself into his arms and demand that he make her his lady right then. Clearly Marek was willing! He had suggested as much in the barn. But she needed to think it through just a little bit more slowly. She had waited nearly all week, but finally decided that she needed another woman's input. That's why she was here, standing on Jeanette's doorstep. She needed someone to help her sort it out, to come to a decision about what to do next.

Colter swung the door open before Lacy had the chance to knock. "Ms. Demark!" He had gone back to using her formal name since school had started back up. "What are you doing here? I'm not in trouble, am I?"

She smiled easily at him. "No, Colt, you have been the model citizen and a wonderful student since we started back to school. I'm so proud of you I could just kiss you!"

"Uh no, thank you!" Colter looked horrified. "No offense, Ms. DeMark, you're pretty and all, but I don't let girls kiss me! A guy could get cooties or something! Or worse . . . someone might see!" He peeked out the door as if there might be spies around just waiting for him to do something stupid like that.

"Well, I'll refrain then!"

"I don't care how many times you re . . . re . . . fame . . . I just can't!!"

Lacy just giggled at him. "*Refrain* means that I won't allow my impulses to go unchecked."

"What?"

"I won't kiss you!" Now Lacy was laughing.

"Oh thanks!" Colter smiled and let her in the house.

"Is your mother here?"

"Yeah, just a minute and I'll go get her. I think she's out by the shed."

"Thank you, Colter."

The boy ran out the back door and returned a few minutes later with Jeanette in tow.

"Lacy! It's so good to see you. Would you like some coffee? I have found a way to flavor the cream. We can pretend that we are back home with all the comforts of foofoo coffee!"

"That would be wonderful!"

Colter rolled his eyes. "If you guys are going to sit and talk, can I go to the holding and see if Spencer can play?"

"Okay, but be back before it gets dark!" she hollered at his back. Then she turned back to Lacy. "That's one of the things I like about being here. Colter has friends and he can walk to their house without me worrying about gangs lurking about or cars running him over!"

"Yes, it is a lot more peaceful around here than back home."

Jeanette had set to work, making a couple of cups of coffee and put a plate of cookies on the table. Then she sat down across from Lacy, smiled, and took a sip.

"Well, Lacy, spit it out! What's going on?"

"What? Can't a girl come out to visit her friend without there being a reason?"

"Yes, a girl can, but you have worry written all over that lovely face. Now spit it out. What's wrong? Did you and Marek have another fight?"

"No, as a matter of fact, we didn't have time for a fight with all the electricity flying around between us! All you'd have to do is plug us in somewhere and we'd be able to light the holding for a year!"

Jeanette smiled broadly. "That's wonderful. I told you you'd like him."

"Oh, I like him all right. I want to keep him!"

"Well, judging from the way he looks at you, he feels the same way! I thought I was going to fall over when the two of you came back from that picnic and walked into the main hall holding hands! I knew right then that you were lost to him."

"Yes, but I have a problem. I'm supposed to fight him for my right to freedom tomorrow."

"So? Don't fight!"

"Jeanette, you know as well as I do that women should have the right to choose whether or not they want to be claimed. If I decide not to fight, what are the chances that the law will change?"

"But you've already won! He's agreed to let you challenge him! That's a first right there!"

"He only agreed because he knew I'd fight him anyway!"

"Well, what if you fight him and let him win?"

"I thought about that. But then I doubt any woman would fight if they knew that even a trained warrior woman was no match for a man."

"Good point. Well, you could win and then tell him that you choose to be his!"

"I thought about that too, but then I worried that if he loses to me, he might not want to keep me. What warrior wants a woman that can beat him in combat?"

"Hmm! That's quite the dilemma."

"What am I going to do?"

"Why don't you try being honest with him. Tell him that you don't want to contest his claim to you but that you want women to have the right to choose!"

"I think he'd say something like, 'Tha's no' likely, Little Warrior'." Her accent was perfect, and with the lowered voice to go along, it sent Jeanette into a fit of giggles.

"Well, what are you going to do then?"

Lacy sighed loudly. "I'm going to lose to him! I'll make it look good, but I'm going to lose to him. I can't live without him now! He's always on my mind. I don't want to lose him, Jeanette!"

"Okay, so you lose to him. What about those women you were talking about that won't even try since you lost?"

"I guess I hope to put ideas into their heads. Then maybe I'll be able to fight for their rights from a position as first lady. It may not help, but at least I'll have lots of time to work on it."

"It sounds like you've been thinking this through for a while."

"Try, every waking moment since last week."

"I wish you the best of luck, Lacy. I know you'll be happy with Marek. He's a good man." Jeanette hugged her tightly, then sat back to savor her coffee.

"Speaking of good men, are there any good men in your future?" Lacy asked before her first sip. "Mmm. This is quite good! You should open a coffee shop!"

"Thanks! I'll consider it. But speaking of good men, you remember the groomsman that was here, . . . the one with the dry sense of humor?"

"Yes." Lacy smiled conspiratorially at her.

"We have a date tomorrow night for dinner."

"Tell me all about it!"

Challenge day came too early for Lacy. She pulled herself out of bed sluggishly. She slid into her sweats; Marek was going to love that! Her coral

T-shirt followed. Once she had her hair pulled up in a ponytail, she was ready. Marek had told her to meet him at nine in the morning in the small courtyard behind the holding. She had just enough time for breakfast and a good stretch. Then she'd have to meet him.

As she entered the main hall for breakfast, she saw him sitting at the table closest to the fire. He looked up, smiled at her, stood, and pulled out a chair for her. As his eyes raked over her, Lacy noticed a frown appear on his handsome face.

"Thank you."

"Ye are wearin' those second skins again! I asked ye no' t' wear them!"

"Oh relax, Marek. Look at it this way, in a few minutes you are going to have your arms wrapped around me anyway!"

"Well, tha's no' all. In a few minutes I'm going t' be on top o' ye, lookin' int' yer eyes as ye apologize for insultin' me when we met."

"Do you think?!"

"Aye, I do." He was smiling at her. His warm eyes were sending electric currents shooting through her stomach.

"Marek?"

"Aye?"

"I apologize for insulting you when we first met." She reached out and took his hand. He squeezed it and laced his fingers through hers.

"Apology is accepted."

One of the young boys who worked in the kitchens brought Lacy a plate of food. It was way too much to eat just before a match, and she asked him to please take it to someone else and just bring her a slice of toast and a cup of hot tea. There were others in the hall, and the boy had no trouble finding someone to whom he could deliver it. He wasn't gone long before he returned with her toast and tea.

"Are ye nervous then, Little Warrior?"

"No, why?"

"Ye are no' eatin' much."

"Well, I could eat more, but once we start the challenge, I might just get a little too worked up and throw it all up on you! I thought to spare you as well as myself that experience."

He chuckled. "I thank ye."

They ate in silence then, each thinking about the challenge ahead and planning just how they might orchestrate throwing the match. Marek let go of her hand to greet one of his men. Lacy watched him. He seemed so calm. She was a basket case. It was one thing to go into a match with the intent of winning. It was another thing altogether to plan to throw a match while still trying to make it look good. She finished her toast and stood to leave. Marek stood with her and headed out to the courtyard, trailing behind her a bit.

He was wondering just how he was going to proceed. Look at her, all calm and collected. Here he was as nervous as a woman on her marking night! What was he going to do if she didn't choose him? She did take his hand this morning. He would have to take courage in that. Still, she was ready to fight for her right to be free. Didn't that mean that she hadn't changed her mind? He had given her opportunities to forget the challenge and just let him mark her. She had not taken the bait. Why not, he wondered. She clearly found him attractive, and she liked his company. He had felt her body heat up when he kissed her, so why were they going through with this?

As they entered the courtyard, Marek was shocked at the number of people gathered there! He noticed that a number of his men were in attendance, but the majority of the audience was women! How did they find out? He hadn't even been aware that his men knew! Great, he thought sarcastically, this was just getting better and better. Had Lacy told the women? It didn't seem like something she would do. Well, damn! Might as well get this over with!

Marek and Lacy faced each other in the center of the courtyard. Galen stood and read the rules of the challenge. That didn't take long since there weren't many rules. The first was that the challenge would continue until one of the two had pinned the other to the ground. The "man" on top would be declared the winner and takes the woman. Well, in this case, the one on top either took the woman, or in Lacy's case, gained her freedom.

The two were to shake hands and step to the outer edge of the yard to await the signal to begin. When Marek took Lacy's hand, he pulled her close and whispered in her ear. "Ye do no have t' do this, Little Warrior. Ye can still choose no' t' fight."

Lacy looked first into his golden brown eyes, wanting so much to just call it off, but then she looked around the little square. There were many women there; in some places they were three deep. If she didn't do this, they would never have a chance to choose for themselves. She looked back up at Marek and shook her head. She turned and walked to the edge of the court.

Galen raised the sparring flag. Lacy and Marek assumed battle stances. Marek smiled as Lacy began to hum and then to sing. The flag dropped. They began circling as they closed the distance between each other. Marek waited for her attack. She didn't disappoint him. Her speed had increased tenfold with the healing of her ribs. He had been prepared for her to begin with kicks. He hadn't expected her to attack with her upper body. She was relentless! He withstood blow after blow until he caught her arm and pulled her back into his chest. He held her for a moment. He waited for her to spring the move she had tried on him in the meadow. He had even set up the hold he had on her, leaving his ribs unguarded. Surely she would use the opening to her advantage.

She did not. Lacy wiggled free, sliding under his arms like a fish wiggling out of the fisherman's grip.

What in the heck was he doing? Lacy wondered. He deliberately left his ribs unguarded. He had not struck or kicked back in response to any of her assaults yet! And when he clearly had her in a secure hold, he not only left those ribs unguarded, but he had also allowed her to escape! Marek was not acting like the warrior who had challenged the bear in the meadow or the leader who had trained all those men for combat. What was going on? Was he going easy on her because she was a woman? He must be.

That ticked her off. How was she going to throw the fight successfully if he didn't even try? She attacked again and again Marek reined her in, putting her in a wrestling hold that had her on her knees under him. It would take so little for her to roll and flip him to his back. Blast it! She wondered if she could manage rolling over and making it look like she meant to flip him but was unsuccessful. It's too soon, she thought. She didn't want to insult him. She needed him to fight! Rolling out from under him and standing, she put all her effort into a punch to his stomach. She didn't go for his jaw in case she accidentally knocked him out, but she knew it was going to hurt her because punching Marek in those well-defined stomach muscles was like hitting a wall! She just couldn't think of any other way to get him to respond.

That hit elicited a grunt from the big man. He finally took a swipe at her. He caught her in the shoulder. It rocked her backward a foot. She came at him again. This time he leaned just a little too far forward for good balance; she took advantage of the opening, grabbing his shoulders and leveraging him over her rolling body. Her plan was to under roll, allowing Marek to stop the rotation when he found himself on top. He didn't. He continued the roll, using her momentum against her. As soon as she was on top again, he flopped his legs out straight to stop the roll. He landed with Lacy straddling him, one of her hands on each shoulder.

Galen called the match at that moment, proclaiming Lacy the winner. A cheer went up from the women in the courtyard. Lacy ignored them as if they weren't even there even as they gathered around her patting her back and telling her what a wonderful fighter she was! She didn't hear any of it as she looked down at Marek. The expression on his face was unreadable, his eyes locked on hers. He was controlled while he waited for her to stand up.

She was confused. Marek had thrown the fight! Why had he done that? He had freed her. Did he no longer want her? Was she not to be claimed today? Why had he done that? Hadn't he held her hand at breakfast? Wait, she had instigated that and he had dropped her hand as soon as one of his men came in. But before the match, he had told her she didn't have to fight today. Did that mean that he had planned to let her go all along? He just didn't want to hurt her feelings. He was letting her go with dignity. She stared into his emotionless eyes for one more long agonizing minute then Lacy stood up quickly.

She stepped off Marek, feeling dizzy and sick. She had to get away from here. She pushed through the crowd toward the holding. No sound penetrated the cold dark place she found herself in now. He didn't want her! The realization shook her to her core. Everything was falling apart as fast as her tears fell down her cheeks. She had to get away. She would grab Thor and ride. She wasn't sure where she would ride, but she couldn't stay here!

Marek lay there in the grass of the courtyard looking into Lacy's dark brown eyes. What was the look he saw there? What was she thinking? She looked like she was in shock. Maybe she really hadn't thought she could win. He wondered what she would say to him when she finally spoke. He thought he saw sadness there, but all too soon, she was up and moving. Before he could right himself, she had gotten lost in the crowd.

Galen had been watching the whole thing. He pushed his way through the crowd to where Marek was now standing. "Did it work?" he asked.

"Aye, I think it did."

"Ye did no' look verra convincin' t' me!"

"Oh? Well, she left, I suppose tha' says enough." Marek couldn't believe he'd lost her. She hadn't even spoken to him; she just left. He felt as though the punch she'd aimed at his midsection had pushed all the way through to his heart and delivered a mortal blow. In all his days, he could never remember a feeling so empty and so full of pain all at the same time. He had expected her to say something . . . anything. She hadn't gloated or cheered or . . . anything! What was going on inside her head? He'd give anything to know. Maybe with time, she'd come around.

Galen stared at his laird. The pain in his face was as readable as the stars at midnight. "Go after her, Marek. Tell her how ye feel."

"I've told her on several occasions. It did no' make a difference." He stood looking off in the direction she had gone. Finally, he pulled his attention back to Galen. "I'll be trainin' wi' the men ou' in the field this mornin'. After lunch, I need t' be seein' t' matters among the people."

"Marek—" Galen began.

Marek just held up his hand to stop the protest before it began and turned to head out to the training field.

He walked slowly, alone with his thoughts. Had he missed something when he had kissed her? She had responded, . . . hadn't she? His thoughts lingered on the day at the barn. He'd wanted to take her right then and he'd come close! He should have marked her as his before the challenge! Galen was right! She'd be his now, but that wasn't what he had wanted. Sure that she would choose to remain with him, he had been an arrogant fool. Remembering how her eyes looked when she gazed into his, he couldn't believe that she felt nothing. Maybe he *should* turn around and do what Galen had suggested. Maybe he should go find her and find a way to express his feelings for her. He had shown her how he felt on many occasions, but had he ever said it? He stopped in his tracks. He started to turn but couldn't bring himself to look into her face and see what he had seen today. No, he decided, he had done all he could. Now the choice was hers.

Thor stopped in Jeanette's front yard, and Lacy slid down and patted him affectionately on his neck. She hooked the reins loosely over his neck and turned to make her way to the front door.

"Stay close, Thor!" She didn't bother to tie him up. He never wandered very far from her. They had gone running together on several occasions. Actually, she went running and Thor just trotted along behind her. He was most definitely the biggest and quietest running partner she had ever had! Normally that would have given her a chuckle, but nothing penetrated the fog that surrounded her head right now.

She was so lost in her thoughts that she hadn't even thought about where she would go, and ending up on Jeanette's doorstep surprised her, but not enough to elicit a response on her face. Tears still slipped down her cheeks as she knocked. She tried to wipe them away and put on a pleasant face for Colter, but her eyes wouldn't cooperate.

Usually, Colter opened the door before Lacy even had the chance to knock, but they hadn't been expecting her and there was no school today so perhaps Colter was sleeping a little late. That gave her a little more time to regain her composure. Still, it was taking Jeanette an awfully long time to open the door. Maybe they had been at the challenge this morning. Everyone else had been there, why not Jeanette and Colter. Lacy walked around to the stable. Their horse was still there. And it looked as if he hadn't been fed yet this morning. That was odd. Jeanette was an early riser.

Lacy returned to the front door and knocked more loudly. For a moment or two, she heard nothing, but then there was a distinct crash as if someone had thrown a pitcher against the wall!

"Jeanette? Are you all right? It's Lacy!" She thought sure she heard whispering. She held still and listened intently. "Jeanette, can we talk?" Her voice faltered as the subject matter sprang to mind. There was more scraping and muffled movement. Then there it was; she definitely heard whispering now. Lacy was trying to decide if she should leave or break the door down. It wasn't like Jeanette to neglect the horse and she was always happy to see Lacy, so something was definitely up. Lacy began to sing. Just as she had made her mind up to break down the door, she heard a man shout a rude word and Jeanette began yelling.

"Run, Lacy! Get out of here!"

Her song filled the air as Lacy prepared for battle. She backed up to get a good shot at kicking in the door when it suddenly opened and a large man stepped out and lunged at her. Lacy's foot hit him soundly in his stomach. The man did not fall, unfortunately, but he did begin to cuss. Lacy was not finished with him. She had the full use of her body now and it was a formidable weapon, but even the physical threat had not cleared her mind of Marek and her concentration was in tatters. As it turned out, she didn't have to do anything to the big man; Thor, who had turned to munch on some of Jeanette's lovely flowers not far from the door, kicked him in the head. Lacy smiled up at him.

"Good horse, Thor!"

Before she could catch her breath, another man confronted her. She just smiled weakly, sang strongly, and motioned him with the curling of her index finger to bring it on. Just at that moment she saw Colter slip around the corner of the house. He caught hold of Thor's reins, scrambled up the stirrup like a little monkey, and pointed the horse for the holding. The man standing before her noticed the horse running, but Colter was small enough that Lacy didn't think he had noticed the little guy clinging to the stirrup on the opposite side.

This man took his time approaching her. He didn't lack finesse like the last guy. As the last guy depended on his bulk, this one depended on his skill and intelligence. Add to that the fact that two other good-sized men followed him out the door, and Lacy knew she was in for the fight of her life. She shook her head to clear her thoughts. Jeanette was still in the little house, and Lacy would not allow these men to abuse her. She thought that if she made enough noise, maybe someone back at the main holding would notice and call for help. That was unlikely, she concluded. They were still on the courtyard side of the holding. She could see the holding but no people wandering about it yet. They were probably still standing around talking about that stupid challenge!

Focus, Lacy! she thought to herself. *First things first. Defend yourself and Jeanette and then you can wallow in misery for the duration of your pathetic life!*

All of Lacy's attention had to be focused on the three men before her. They fanned out to surround her. She backed up to keep them within her vision. It didn't work, and she was engaged in the first round before she could even blink. She was forced to fight in a circular motion, taking on the men both in front and behind at the same time. Twice she nearly fell when her song strayed to one that reminded her of Marek and clouded her senses. Too much thinking during the fight was not working well. At one point, her eyes teared up, blinding her long enough for the first man to land a hit to the left side of her face. She retaliated immediately, breaking his nose. She blinked furiously and sang louder.

—

He came back at her with a vengeance but was stopped by one of his fellows.

"Do no' hurt her! He wants her taken wi'ou' hurtin' her!"

"Well, get her then before I break every bone in her body!"

The battle went on for another few minutes or so. All three of the men were bleeding by the time one of them finally got a lucky hit in and knocked Lacy out cold. He had swung just as Lacy had turned to defend herself against his comrade. As she turned, her face was unguarded for the briefest of moments. Lacy saw it coming a moment too late. The man's fist struck just under her jaw on the left side once more. She was out cold in a heartbeat.

"I sure hope ye did no' kill her!"

"Oh, she'll be fine! Just tie her up and get her ont' my horse! Let's go before the wee lad manages t' wiggle free!"

"Where is the wee lad?" one of the other men asked.

"He's locked in his room. He will no' be any trouble for a bit bu' we need t' go!"

The men threw Lacy over one of the horses, loaded up their unconscious companion, and headed quickly away from the little cottage. They were running their horses hard to put as much distance between them and Marek's men as possible before nightfall.

Lacy woke with her head banging against the shoulder of the horse she was slung over stomach down. Even without being jostled around by the horse, her head was throbbing. The horse just made it that much worse. She tried to hold her head away from the horse and got the attention of the man she was riding with.

He slowed his horse and pulled her up into a sitting position in his lap. The new position helped, but her discomfort, she discovered shortly, was not limited to her head or face. She was bound rather tightly by leather straps around her ankles, knees, and wrists. Her wrists were tied behind her back. Her mouth was gagged and her left eye was almost swollen shut. And if that were not enough, her heart ached more than anything. Marek sprang to mind, and tears rolled down her cheeks. On top of that, the man she rode with smelled like he hadn't had a bath in a week! She thought she might throw up at any moment. That would be bad! Then she'd probably choke to death before the man noticed. She decided to fake it. Maybe he'd take the gag off before it really happened.

The choking noises were very easy to understand, even with the gag in her mouth, and the man hurriedly took it off. Lacy continued to cough for a minute until she thought she had it under control.

"I need to stop! I'm going to be sick!"

"Go ahead an' be sick! Just try t' miss the horse!"

"No, really, I need to get down for just a minute, please!"

"We're no' stoppin' before nightfall, so ye migh' as well try t' relax, lady. Oh, an' sorry abou' yer face. Had ye no' fought sa hard, I'd no' have hit ye! But we had t' bring ye or our laird would have taken it ou' o' our hides."

"Why does he want me?"

"I'm sure I do no' know. Ye'll be able t' ask him tha' yerself when ye see him the day after tomorrow."

"Three days? I have to ride with you for three days?"

"Aye, I'm no' so verra happy abou' it myself! Ye're a tough fight, lady . . . an' I use the term *lady* loosely!"

"Thanks! You could just let me go and spare yourself further damage."

"No, I canno' do tha', lady. My laird would dig ou' my 'eart wi' his bare hands! Besides, I doub' ye'll be any more trouble, wha' wi' yer hands and legs tied up good an' tight."

"Your laird sounds totally delightful!" she said sarcastically. "Listen, I promise not to do you any harm if you will untie me and at least let me walk around for a bit. My head is pounding, and I'm feeling rather sick to my stomach."

"I'm sorry, lady, but we canno' do tha'. We are still on Laird McKenzie's land. If he catches up t' us, we would be greatly ou'numbered. I do no' think he would like it much that we took one o' the women from his holdin', even though it was only a woman who fancies herself a warrior!"

That stung nearly badly enough to restart the tears that she had only just managed to control. "Yeah, well, you might want to reconsider when I tell you just who it was you took!"

"Aye? An' who might I have taken, lady?"

"You, sir—and I also use the term loosely—took the woman that Laird McKenzie has claimed. If I were you, I would set the lady free and run home as fast as possible!"

Lacy watched shock register across the man's face. Of course, being claimed was no longer true, but somehow she didn't think meeting this laird of Bremhall was going to be in her best interests.

"Ye lie, lady! It was a nice try, though it's unbecomin' a woman t' lie!"

"You will soon discover that I don't lie. In the words of Captain Hook, 'the truth is much more fun!'"

"Aye? Who is this Captain Hook?"

"A fictitious character from the Peter Pan stories. That line was from a movie entitled *Hook*."

"Movie?"

"Never mind! The point is, I'm not lying. But you go ahead and find out for yourself! Since you will not allow me time to walk around or rest on the ground, would you mind greatly if I leaned back on you to sleep for a bit? It won't be for long, my head is going to explode at any moment now anyway."

"Suit yerself. I would ask ye t' please lean t' my left side. Yer last kick has left my right side a bit tender."

"Sorry about that. By the way, what did you do to Jeanette and Colter? Are they all right?"

"Aye, the wee lad was blocked in his room and the lady was tied to a kitchen chair. Do no' worry yerself though, the boy will work himself free before long."

"Oh aye," Lacy mimicked the man, "I'm sure he will!" She felt some hope now because the boy in question had raced off on Thor even as they had fought. She was sure that even with the fast pace with which they were now traveling, Marek would easily catch up to them. It was only a matter of time.

She leaned back on the man. Whew! He smelled of a week of sweat! It was almost too much for Lacy with her head already throbbing and nausea just below the surface. But she opted for a chance at unconsciousness to alleviate the pain.

"Donnie! Hold up a bit, will ye?" Lacy had drifted off to sleep fairly quickly, but when the man she was riding with hollered at one of his men, she flinched at the pain that shot through her head. "Sorry, lass! Try t' go back t' sleep."

The other man, Donnie, must have slowed because soon, she heard his horse come alongside and the two men began to discuss their options. The others must have slowed their horses too because as she listened to the conversation, she could count two other voices besides the man with whom she rode. The last she had seen, the man that Thor had kicked was still out and hanging over a horse, belly down. She wondered if Thor had killed him. He'd been out a long time. Her answer came before long.

Donnie was the first to speak. "Do ye think we've put enough distance between us and McKenzie?"

The man Lacy rode with answered, "No, I do no' think so. We bought some time by goin' through the hills rather than takin' the road bu' we will no' know for sure until we reach the river. We may have another problem though. Our laird may have left ou' an important wee detail! Accordin' t' the lady, she has been claimed by Marek himself. If that is so, we can expect company sooner than we thought. Our best hope is tha' the lad is slow t' escape."

"Is she marked?"

Lacy had heard something about marking before, but she had no idea what it was or how it was done.

"I do no' know!"

"Maybe ye better look."

That made her nervous. There was no way she was going to let these brutes look for some mark!

"I'll have her show us when she wakes up."

Hmmm, she thought, someone was going to have to show *her* first!

"It will no' matter much since her horse fled back to the holdin'!" another voice spoke now. "As soon as they see it wi' ou' the lady, they'll come lookin' for her."

"Aye, but we may have a little time while they look."

"We better no' count on it. We best make haste. Is Derk all righ'? He should have awakened by now I would think!"

"I think he is all right. He's go' a hard haed!"

"I have no' seen a horse defend its master . . . or mistress before! Good thin' it ran off t' the holdin' I'd have hated t' fight a horse *and* the lady!"

"Aye! Were ye payin' attention t' the way the lady fights? Did ye no' see anythin' familiar abou' it?" Lacy thought that this voice came from the one called Donnie.

There was a moment of silence as the others thought back to the fight. Lacy waited to hear what they were going to say. She wanted to open her eyes and look around at the men, but she thought they might be more likely to continue the conversation if they thought she was sound asleep. She was hoping they would hurry because as aromatic as her backrest was, the others riding so closely quadrupled the effect; and Lacy thought that if she didn't get fresh air soon, she'd die of secondhand stink! Her discomfort was interrupted by the continued conversation.

"Aye! Ye're right! It was verra familiar! She fought just like him! Ye do no' think they're related, do ye?"

"No, no' related, she does no' look a thing like him. But I would bet my life tha' they come from the same place. She talks like him."

"Aye, tha' she does."

"Do ye suppose we're borrowin' more trouble by bringin' her t' him?"

"What else can we do? Our families are there."

"We best be careful wha' we say in her presence. She might tell him."

Lacy yawned then and dared to enter the conversation. "Why would I tell him anything? I don't want to leave McKenzie holding. Whoever this man is, you don't like him either, so why not pick a different laird?"

The men began laughing at that, but they didn't bother to explain anything. They just picked up their pace and ignored her again. Lacy wondered about the man who talked and fought like her. That was curious. Was he also from Riverton? She guessed it could happen. But surely not! How would he have gotten through that maze without falling to his death since Colter and she had caved in all the floors as they crashed through? Then again, Jeanette had made it through without caving in the floors. It could be that this man had gone through more carefully before Lacy and Colter and the floors had held. Still, it was a long shot that anyone had come from Riverton.

—

The men had also said that she fought like him. But then, she had been sparring with Marek. Could it be that one of Marek's men had left his holding and joined Bremhall's? No, that couldn't be it. It had to be someone from Riverton because even if someone did leave Marek's holding, he would not rise to the position of laird of Bremhall and it was unlikely that he would have picked up her accent. To take this one step further, if he fought like Lacy and came from Riverton, he had to be an ADD! But why had he been given the position of laird?! She wished she had the answers. Then she could plan a bit before she met this bully.

Colter was having a difficult time climbing on top of Thor while the horse ran at full speed toward the holding. He was hanging on with one hand on the saddle, one hand holding the reins and both feet crammed into one stirrup. It was all he could do just to keep Thor headed in the right direction. He was so short that he couldn't see over Thor's back to see what was happening back at the cottage. All he knew was that he had to get to Marek. Lacy was good, but there were four men there. He was pretty sure she could take them since one was already down. But he didn't have the old assurance he used to have at school. Colter had watched the men train for battle a few times in the last month. The men around here knew how to fight! She wouldn't have the advantage of being the only one trained, and every one of them outweighed her by a good deal.

Thor ran straight into the main gates, and Colter jumped off so fast that Thor had not had time to stop. He didn't land well. He twisted one ankle and rolled about three feet but jumped up and limped into the main hall. He was yelling at the top of his lungs all the way. Marta ran out of the kitchen where she had been supervising the cleanup after breakfast and beginning the cooking for lunch.

"What in heaven's name are ye yellin' abou, lad?"

"It's Lacy and Mama, where is Marek?"

"Well, he's ou' wi' the men. What's the matter wi' yer mama and Lady Lacy?"

"Men! There are men!" Colter yelled over his shoulder as he limped hurriedly out the door. He would have hopped back on Thor, but the darn horse was missing! Colter would have to run. He gritted his teeth, thinking about what Lacy would do and sang his ABCs, the only song he could think of, all the way out the holding gate and straight to the fields. One thing that Colter was good at was belting out a song, and he sang for all he was worth as he put the pain of his ankle behind him and forced himself to run!

He was winded and hurting badly by the time he reached the field, but he kept up the singing. As he ran down the hill, he saw the men sparring with each other. There were around fifty of them, and he was beginning to fret

145

that he wouldn't be able to find Marek fast enough when all of the sudden he saw him!

Marek and Brett were in the middle of a heated practice, neither wishing to allow the other to win the match when Marek heard the song. He put up his hand in a sign to halt the match and turned in the direction from which it came. He recognized Colter's singing immediately. How many times had the hold listened in while Lacy and Colter sang in the main hall? He knew that voice as well as he knew Lacy's. And he could also hear the panic in it as he broke through the crowd of men and saw Colter running crazily across the field toward them.

Confusion descended upon him as he hurried toward the lad. What was he doing? Marek was shouting questions to the boy before Colter got within fifteen feet of him.

"Colter, what's wrong? What are ye doin' here?"

His song stopped abruptly as he struggled to catch his breath and answer questions. "Lacy . . . came . . . to visit!" he blurted between gasps for breath. "But the men . . . were there . . . and . . . she's . . . fighting them. They blocked me in my room . . . and they tied up my mama! You gotta come now!"

Marek turned to call his men, but they were already by his side. He started barking orders over his shoulder as he took off running toward the holding. Damn! He wished he'd have had training on the other side of the holding! Now he had to run through the holding to get to the other side where Jeanette lived.

"Galen, gather some men and meet me at Jeanette's cottage. Bring the horses! Brent, bring in our people and close the holdin' gates after us! Make sure ye set up extra guards and be ready for anythin'!"

It didn't take Marek more than ten minutes to reach Jeanette's cottage at a dead run. He could see the telltale signs of battle and knew that Lacy had given them a run for their money. There was blood near the door, and two of Jeanette's lovely flowerpots had been overturned, the freshly watered soil dark in contrast to the dryer ground. Marek threw the door open without knocking, sword in hand, ready to run through anyone in the room who did not belong. All he saw was Jeanette, gagged and tied to a chair in the kitchen. Her eyes were wide with panic, and she began squirming anew at the sight of him.

In two steps he was kneeling before her, pulling the gag out of her mouth.

"Get me out of this! Colter is locked in the bedroom!"

"No, he's no'! He came t' find me." Marek was cutting through the rope as he spoke. "Where is Lacy?"

"They took her! There were four of them! One of them might be dead, but the other three took her on together. She fought well from what I could hear, but they overpowered her! They rode off only about thirty minutes ago!"

"Who were they?"

"Bremhall's men! They said their laird sent them for the beautiful singing female warrior!"

"They had been here about an hour when Lacy showed up. They had been trying to get Colter to go after her, but he wouldn't! Then Lacy knocked on the door! The men held us both quiet, but Lacy banged on the door loudly and called out to me telling me that it was her. When she figured out that Colter and I were in trouble, she started to sing! Then they knew for sure that it was her. They blocked Colter in the bedroom and went out to get her. The first guy fell in about fifteen seconds, but the others fought her all at the same time!"

Marek's face was pale despite his race for Jeanette's cottage. He paced the floor as he waited for his men to catch up with the horses. He didn't have to wait long, all things considered, but it was about thirty minutes and those minutes dragged by in agony for Marek.

As soon as his men got within a few yards, Marek was running toward them. He mounted his big black horse quickly and gracefully. He told his men what had happened as he started off toward Bremhall's lands.

"Four o' Bremhall's men have taken Lady Lacy. They have abou' an hour's lead on us. I think we can catch them if we hurry. We need t' take her back before they reach the safety o' their own lands," he yelled over his back, already in pursuit.

"Why would Bremhall risk comin' t' yer holdin' and stealin' yer lady?" Galen yelled to Marek as their horses raced down the road.

"I can answer tha'," yelled Ian. "Bremhall is no longer the laird o' his own holdin'. There is another man in control there. He took the hold by force! He's the one tha' wants Lady Lacy!"

"Why does he want Lady Lacy . . . aside from the obvious? T' risk war over a beautiful woman is no' verra wise," Brett asked.

Marek spoke up then. "I think the laird of Bremhall is from the same place as Lacy and Jeanette. I think he knows her."

"What?" All of Marek's men responded at the same time except Ian and Kenneth who had been in on the interrogation of Bremhall's men two weeks ago.

"Aye, Lacy told me tha' there is a thing called a gun where she's from. It throws a verra fast and verra deadly piece o' metal ou' o' a long pipe. If it's aimed at ye, it can kill ye and ye'll never even see it comin'! The men we caught before told us tha' the new laird has such a thing. He killed Bremhall wi' it and took over the holdin'. If we canno' get Lady Lacy back before they get to Bremhall's land, we'll have t' face tha' thing in a couple o' days. Bu' the way I see it, we're goin' t' have t' face it sooner or later anyway. It does no' seem tha' this man is goin' to leave us or Lady Lacy alone until we do."

CHAPTER 12

Camping Is Not All It's Cracked Up To Be

That night, Lacy's captors camped beside a small river. The man she had been riding with untied her long enough for her to take care of personal business after she swore she would not try to escape, but he refused to leave her presence and would not look away from her. He did allow her to step behind bushes, but she was told to keep her head where he could see it or he'd come behind the bushes after her.

As soon as she finished, he took her to the river to get a drink and clean up a bit. But he stood right next to her, watching her every move. She was sure she could take him. After all, it had taken all three of the men to subdue her, but their hearts hadn't seemed to be in it. Lacy knew that the laird of Bremhall holding had forced them to take her. He must be leveraging them somehow. They had been saying that the laird had their families. For the sake of the families, she had decided to go along with them. She would do what she could to help them.

Lacy took a short inventory of her appearance. She noted that her favorite shirt had a tear in the sleeve, but she thought she could mend it. She was dirty and rumpled, but for the most part, her clothes were still in good shape. She was thankful for that anyway. She washed her face gingerly and combed her hair out with her fingers, giving up on getting it tied into a ponytail again.

Marek would be coming after her, she knew, whether or not he still wanted her. It was only a matter of time. He wouldn't stand for anyone being taken by force from his holding. When he got here, she would have to move quickly to save these men. Marek would be ready to take his revenge. But once she explained what was going on, she would ask Marek to help. The ADD, and Lacy was convinced that's what he was, that had taken over Bremhall holding had to be stopped. The thing that kept nagging at her was that if an ADD was missing from Riverton, why hadn't anyone noticed? It should have made the news! ADDs just didn't go missing without notice! At least not in Riverton.

Standing and turning back to her captor, Lacy let him know she was ready to return to camp. He retied her hands behind her back and pushed her lightly in the right direction.

"Sir, I understand that your laird is holding your families until you return. I also heard you say that he fights like me. If that is so, I know what kind of fighter you are dealing with. I know his strengths and his weaknesses. I would like to help you get rid of him."

"Righ'! How could a wisp o' a woman like ye take a giant like him ou'!"

"Well, it did take three of you to take me down. That ought to count for something!"

"True, bu' we were tryin' no' t' hurt ye and even so, I still do no' think ye would be o' much help. My job is t' take ye to him and tha's what I'm goin' t' do."

"But that doesn't solve your problem!"

"An' what would ye have us do, lady? He has our children and our wives. He has taken over our lands. We have nothin', and he has made it abundantly clear that rebellion will be met wi' death."

"Then do nothing. Deliver me to his man and I will handle him! But untie me and trust me not to run. I will not try to escape. And when Marek comes, allow me to talk to him. I think we could talk him into helping."

"Laird McKenzie will no' catch up t' us. We have taken a route he is no' familiar wi'. An' if he did somehow find us, he will be too busy tryin' t' kill us t' listen."

"Trust me."

"I do no' think tha' would be wise. Too much rides on yer arrivin' at Bremhall holdin' in two days. I'm sorry, lady, bu' there are a lo' o' lives at stake. They're worth more than one woman."

"Well, trust me or not, I'm going willingly. But you need to do me a little favor . . . please!"

"An' wha' might tha' be?"

"Take a bath and have your men do the same! You're killing me! At this rate, I'll be dead before we arrive at Bremhall!!"

He laughed loudly. "Aye, we can do tha' for ye!"

Marek was frantic. They were not on the road! He and his men should have caught up to them by now. It was late and they had been riding by moonlight for more than two hours. The horses were spent and they needed to rest, but it was all Marek could do to call a halt to their pursuit for the night. Damn! Had he just turned and gone after her as Galen suggested, she'd have been home safe right now and maybe, just maybe in his arms. Perhaps that was too much to ask for, but he knew he loved her and once he got her back, he was not letting her out of the holding without him again! And he would get her back! He had to! He needed to tell her how he felt and beg her to reconsider his offer to make her his own.

"Set up camp, men! We'll catch them first thin' in the mornin'." Marek's thoughts drifted back to *that* morning in the barn. Only days before, he had held her and kissed her. And she had kissed him back! He shivered at the thought of her possibly hurt or being mistreated. He'd kill them! He'd enjoy it! He argued with himself about how to approach her. Should he be forceful? Or would she respond better to a softer approach? She had to love him, he could feel it, but would she ever admit it? He should have settled this earlier. No laird would ever take a marked woman! That was unheard of in the history of their land. But she was not marked yet; Bremhall's laird could still claim her and mark her for himself. If he marked her before Marek got there . . .

He tried not to think about it. He could do nothing about it tonight. His horse could go no farther without some rest though Marek doubted he himself could rest. He paced the small meadow beside the road as his men started a small fire and bedded down for the night. They had not had time for packing provisions although Brett had managed to grab a small bag of jerky as he raced through his house, yelling to his wife to watch the kids closely until his return. He pulled out the bag and passed it around in the firelight now. Marek declined and continued to pace. He told them he would take first watch, and his men drifted off to sleep.

Around two in the morning, Marek roused Galen to take the next shift and lay down in the grass to try to nod off for a while. It took him some time to relax enough to even rest, but exhaustion won out and sleep finally overtook him. He dreamed of Lacy.

In the dream, she had agreed to take his mark, but the ceremony had been interrupted by aliens. They came at him with long tubes, shooting fire and death at him and his men. One of the aliens caught Lacy. She was fighting and singing and then the song stopped. When he could pause in his fighting, he looked to where she had been fighting. He was stunned to see her kissing the alien. Even more amazing was that she seemed to be enjoying it! Then she transformed into one of them! Marek was yelling "NO!" and running toward her when his body began to shake. He opened his eyes and sat up in a cold sweat. Galen was kneeling beside him, shaking him awake.

"Are ye all right, Marek?" Galen asked quietly.

"Aye!"

"Ye were talkin' in yer sleep! Well, ye were saying no over and over again! And ye have no' lain still since ye lay down in the first place."

"Aye. Thanks! I'll take over for ye! I do no' think I wish t' go back t' sleep."

"Oh no, ye've only been asleep for an hour. Ye need t' sleep, Marek. Lady Lacy needs ye t' be rested."

Marek could see the logic in this, but he was quite sure that sleep would elude him. Still, he lay back down and closed his eyes. He did manage to sleep finally. And to his great relief, he did not dream again.

—

Lacy slept badly. The men refused to untie her arms and had also tied her ankles together. Getting comfortable with her hands tied behind her back was not happening and made sleeping next to impossible. She lay down on a blanket that had been put out for her. One of the men took a little pity on her and threw another blanket over her, but it didn't help much with the hard ground under her. She thought perhaps she'd change her mind about helping them. Camping was never her strong suit, and when she did camp, she had always had a sleeping bag and pillow. And she had never been tied up for it either! The barbarians!

She was relieved beyond belief when the sun came up. She had managed to doze a bit through the night, but most of the night had been just highly uncomfortable and cold! She was so ticked at them that she decided that she would just lie there even when the sun came up though her first instinct had been to wake everyone up right then and demand that they leave. Instead, she held her tongue, hoping that they would sleep long enough for Marek to catch up with them. She was certain that he would be up before the sun and be on his way after her. If she could stall, she would be untied and in his arms before breakfast . . . she hoped. In his arms . . . hmmm . . . well, maybe that wouldn't happen, but at least she would be with him and his men . . . and untied for sure! That thought was not much consolation, and another tear escaped her pretty brown eyes.

Marek *did* have his men up and ready to go before the sun came up. They were riding hard by the time the sun crested the first hill. But they did not catch up that day. They didn't see anyone. Marek's mind was working overtime. Where had they missed them? They must have taken a different route. It didn't matter, Marek decided. He and his men were going to have to take on the laird of Bremhall sooner or later. It might as well be sooner. They would sneak into the holding somehow and find her. He would get her out first, then he would make sure that the laird of Bremhall never bothered Lacy or his holding ever again.

Lacy stalled to the best of her ability, but to no avail. The men woke up with the sun and packed up in less than ten minutes. She was unsympathetically pulled from her "bed," allowed a few very brief minutes for personal matters, and set roughly upon a horse. They were off at a run in no time. Around noon, she caught a glimpse of blond fur running up behind them. It was not long before she heard the hoof beats. The men saw it too. It was a great blond horse with a saddle but no rider. Lacy was ecstatic! It was Thor. He'd followed. If he was here, perhaps so was Marek not far behind!

The man Lacy was riding with pulled up a moment to look at the horse, disbelief in his eyes. "The thing is like a damn bloodhound!" he bellowed.

"Thor! Come here, baby!" Lacy called to him.

"Take cover, Marek's men could be righ' behind it!"

The men scattered into the trees. Before long, none of them were visible from the narrow path they had been following. Thor followed the man who had Lacy. The man secured Lacy to a tree and crept off into the foliage. Thor approached her and nuzzled her cheek.

"Hi, Thor! Have you been running all this time? You poor thing! I hope you stopped to rest along the way. Is Marek behind you?" She looked into the horse's big brown eye. She peeked through the leaves, straining to see the path. Where was Marek? Was he not following Thor? That was a stupid thought. It's not like horses *were* bloodhounds! Why would he follow Thor when he thought he knew the direction they had gone? And yet, she thought, here stood Thor! Then it occurred to her that if Thor could follow *her*, couldn't he follow Marek?

"I sure wish you could understand me. It would sure be nice if you could go get Marek."

Thor dropped his head down to grab some sweet grass that was growing by the tree. Lacy would love to have reached out to touch his beautiful mane, but the ropes securing her to the tree would not allow it. She decided to give her foolish thoughts a try. What did she have to lose?

"Thor!" His head sprang up with his mouth full of grass. "Go get Marek! Go! Thor!" The great horse just nuzzled her cheek again. *Ah well*, she thought, *it was worth the try.*

"Lady!" her captor called to her. "Is it safe t' come untie ye wi' tha' horse standin' so close!"

"Yes, it's safe, so long as you don't threaten me. If I start singing, he'll go nuts. So you might want to be gentle with me from now on!" She wasn't sure if the singing was what did it, but she did know that if they threatened her, Thor would react.

"Aye? Well, ye mi' want t' know tha' if yer horse attacks one o' us again, we'll just pu' it down with a swift cut t' his throat! So ye mi' just want t' keep yer singin' t' yerself."

"Touche!" Lacy responded in almost the only word in French that she remembered from high school.

The man untied her from the tree, tied her hands once again behind her back, and put her back on his horse. He then swung up into the saddle behind her and they were off again.

"Sir, what is your name, please."

"My name is Sonder, milady."

"That's an unusual name. I like it."

"Thank ye, lady. It was my father's name and his father's before him."

"Well, Sonder, it seems you have eluded Marek for the time being. But he will catch you sooner or later. I suggest we come up with a plan to save you and your men."

"Aye, we have a plan. We ride for all we're worth t' beat him to the holdin' and let Laird Bremhall worry abou' him."

"Oh, he'll find you before you get there. How could he not? You are both heading in the same direction, aren't you?"

"Ultimately, yes, but we have taken a route much less travelt. Actually, only Bremhall's men know this route. Marek's men will no' take it because they do no' know abou' the tunnel."

"Tunnel?"

"Aye, we only just completed it last month. It goes straight through the bluffs. We no longer have t' go around."

"How in the world did you accomplish that? How did you move all that earth?"

"Well, we did no' actually have to move much. We found a cave and it took us almost completely through. We only had t' dig the last fifty feet or so."

Lacy swallowed hard. She was thinking about the tunnel. "How long is the tunnel, Sonder?" she asked in nearly a whisper.

"Oh, it will only take us abou' two hours t' navigate. It cuts off abou' a day's rough ride up and over."

"Well, resign yourself to the up and over because I'm not going in a tunnel!"

"Oh aye, ye will be goin' in the tunnel, lady. Ye have no choice."

"I don't do tunnels, Sonder. I can't go in there!"

"No sense in getting all worked up abou' it now, lady. We will no' get there until tonight, and we will no' enter until the mornin'. Ye might as well no' borrow trouble."

"I'm not going in, Sonder! I won't! I will fight you with everything I have!"

Sonder chuckled over that, wondering just how she would fight when she was all trussed up like a Christmas goose. "Are ye scart o' the dark then, lady?"

"No, I'm not afraid of the dark! I just don't like caves or tunnels."

"Ye're a warrior and ye're scart of caves and tunnels?"

"Yes, and spiders while we're at it! Yes, I . . . am . . . afraid . . . of caves and tunnels! That is how I came to be in your land! I'm from a different dimension or something! I fell through the floor of a mine shaft and ended up here! I walked for two or three days in total blackness towing a small child behind me!" she was yelling at him now and Thor was getting restless. "I vowed I would never go in another cave or tunnel . . . with the exception of one!"

"And what is the one, lady?"

"The one I would have to go through to get back home! But . . . I've been told that I can't get back. I've been told that the cave I came through is like a one-way gate . . . I can't get back!"

Lacy felt nauseated. She hadn't voiced the possibility of not returning in all the time she had been here, partly because she found that she at first was attracted to Marek and finally was in love with him. But now that he had let her go, she realized that home was the only place for her. There was no one here for her without him. And she couldn't look at him every day and not want him. So she'd have to try to get home. Then another thought occurred to her. What if caves were a porthole for some people and not others? What if she entered the cave and came out in still another place? It would be bad enough to be without Marek. Ending up having to start all over in yet another dimension would be torturous. She couldn't go in that hole! Even if it wasn't a porthole, she could not stand two hours in the blackness! Heck, she couldn't stand even ten minutes in that kind of hell again!

"Sonder, please, if you have any decency in you, don't make me go in that tunnel!"

"Do no' worry, lady, I will no' let anything happen to ye. I'll hold tigh' to ye the whole way."

Lacy's mind began to race. She had to get out of these ties! She had to get away! She would continue to head toward the Bremhall holding and take care of the impostor when she got there, but she would not go in that tunnel!

Marek and his men made the river and crossed with no sign of Bremhall's men. They raced toward the bluffs, hoping to get there before nightfall. Sonder and his men crossed about a mile up river from where Marek's men would have crossed. Sonder sent one of the men to see if Marek had crossed yet. When his man caught up with them again, he confirmed that they had indeed crossed. Sonder and his men continued on toward the tunnel. They made it to the entrance just at dusk and set up camp.

"Marek is ahead of us," Sonder told Lacy. "Bu' we will still make the holdin' before him. We will make it t' Bremhall holdin' a full day before yer Marek."

Lacy did not respond. She was too busy working on loosening her bindings. She needn't have bothered; Sonder took them off her to allow her some personal time. As was the routine, he would not take his eyes off her, allowing her to go behind bushes but keep her head in view. She had planned to call Thor, jump on him, and take off. But her captors were not stupid. They held the horse with a sword to his throat until Lacy was once again tied up. Any loosening of the straps she had accomplished earlier in the day was worthless now as Sonder retied the straps tightly once again.

The night went much like the previous one save for the fact that Sonder rolled his saddle blanket up and gave it to her for a pillow. But even with this small act of kindness, she couldn't sleep. She knew the tunnel was coming, and she wasn't sure her nerves could stand the tension. Morning came all too soon.

"Please, Sonder, don't do this to me! I promise to come to Bremhall holding. Just set me on Thor and tell me how to get there and I'll come, but don't make me go in that hole!"

"I canno' do tha', lady. He'd kill my kids."

"Your kids? He'd kill your kids?"

"Aye, tha's what he said."

"And you believe him?"

"I canno' take tha' chance. Ye do see, do ye no'?"

Lacy sighed in resignation. "Yes, I wouldn't be able to take the chance either." She looked around at the trees and sky above her. "Okay, Sonder, I'll go willingly. But when we come out, I want to be in the same place and time as you. So just . . . don't let go of me. Actually, would you mind too much tying me to you? That way, where I go, you go. Would you mind, please?!"

"Aye, I'll do tha' for ye. And I will no' let go o' ye. No' for a second. Bu' ye must promise me somethin' too."

"What?"

"If ye get scart in there, ye may sing, bu' ye may no' hurt me!"

She laughed then. "It's a deal."

Sonder tied Lacy's arms around himself. Then the men lit lanterns that had been left at the entrance to the tunnel and started down into the blackness. It was a huge opening, large enough to accommodate men on horses. Lacy noticed that it did help to be on a horse with Sonder holding on to her. She was able to keep her eyes closed and pretend she was just riding at night. She also noted that Sonder had taken a bath in the river for her and smelled quite nice now. Thank goodness!

As the first hour dragged by, she decided to play a little game and pretend that Sonder was Marek. That helped a lot though Sonder, wiry but not built quite like Marek, pushed her imagination to its limits. She replayed the morning she had spent with Marek in the barn once more in her mind. Wow, she really missed him!

The second hour had her rethinking the question she had meant to discuss with Jeanette, hoping that it was not a moot point in light of her recent capture. What should she do about Marek? Should she tell him that she wanted him? Could she bear to hear the truth if he really didn't want her? It didn't matter, she decided. She couldn't live without him so she would have to confront him and hear him out, just in case things weren't as they seemed. She had nothing to lose but a little dignity. She could live without her dignity for a while, but she couldn't live at all without that man!

The questions kept flitting through her head. She tried on every scenario she could think of. Then she tried on every possibility of how Marek would react. She had not come to any conclusions when she noticed that she could see light through her eyelids. They had made it outside!

"The men and I thank ye for the beautiful songs, lady," Sonder said when he noticed her eyes flutter open. "Yer singin' is quite lovely."

"Oh, you're welcome. Now how far is it to Bremhall holding?"

"Oh, no' far. We'll be there for the noon meal."

"When will Marek's men get there?"

"Well, if they're ridin' as hard as I think they are, they could get there by late night or early mornin'. I doubt he'll stop t' sleep, bein' so close."

Marek and his men did make it by early morning. They dismounted and tied their horses far enough from the holding not to be heard and began making their way noiselessly toward the walls surrounding it.

"How are we goin' t' get in wi'ou' bein' seen or heard?" Galen was asking as they stood under cover of trees looking toward the outer wall and gates of the holding.

"I'm no' so sure just yet. I think we might need t' walk the perimeter and see if we can find a weak point," Marek answered.

"Oh, no need for tha'," came Kenneth's voice as he noisily dragged something big and bulky into their midst. It was a Bremhall warrior. "I found him snoopin' abou' no' six yards from here!"

"Shhh!" the captured man scolded them. "I've come t' help ye get in and help the lady. My name is Sonder Bremhall."

Lacy was escorted into a small suite as soon as they made it to Bremhall holding. The suite included a sitting room with a fireplace and a bedroom off to the side, also complete with a small fireplace. Each of the rooms had windows that overlooked the holding two stories below. A bath was prepared, and Lacy had to admit that she greatly appreciated the lovely rose-scented soap that had been provided along with the hot water.

Too bad she didn't have her blow-dryer with her. Her hair was going to be very curly. Actually, that wasn't as bad as having to allow it to dry on its own. It would take forever! Lacy put on the lovely gown that had been left out for her. She hadn't really wanted to feel indebted to the laird of this holding, but she needed to wash out her sweats and shirt. The bath water was plenty dirty after her bath, but she used it anyway to rinse out her "second skins" as Marek so lovingly called them. The plan was to take care of this bully as quickly as

—

possible and make her exit back to . . . well, back to Marek. She would tell him she loved him and if he didn't want her, she was going back to the cave. But first she needed to dethrone this wannabe dictator. Of course, fighting in this dress was going to be difficult, but she was hoping that she would only have to take down one man. That seemed a likely scenerio since none of the Bremhall men seemed to like him.

The noon meal was served to her after she had finished bathing. And maids bustled in and out, taking with them the soap, water, and bathtub. Well, actually, they dumped the bath water out the window. Then several of them carried the bathtub out the door. She sure missed her own bathtub back home . . . just plug, fill, bathe, and drain!

Her meal was set in front of her on a small table to the left of the fireplace, and Lacy was left alone to eat. Walking quickly to the door after everyone had left, Lacy tried to open it. It was locked. She then looked out the windows. There was a ledge not far from one of the windows, but if she missed it, it would be a long hard fall. Also, there was too much activity below. Everyone would be able to see her. She would have to wait for darkness. She guessed that was okay because the infamous laird of Bremhall holding had not shown up yet. As a matter of fact, the evening meal was served and he still hadn't shown.

The maids flitted in and out, preparing her bed and removing her dinner dishes. She asked one of them if the laird was ever going to show, but the young woman only shrugged and left without so much as a word. Wow, this guy must be quite a pain in the neck if maids are not allowed to talk to guests . . . uh, prisoners at all! Or maybe because Lacy talked like the man, she was being cold-shouldered. She guessed she couldn't blame them really. A fire had been prepared, and Lacy sat on a nearby chair and watched the flames lick the wood. It was around eight when she checked her sweats and her coral shirt. They were dry, and she changed from the dress to her own clothes. She was thankful for the time that allowed her clothes to dry because she was going to need to be able to fight.

Lacy sat back down and waited. She wasn't sure how long she sat there, but it had to be well after midnight by the time she thought to get up and go to bed. He must be toying with her, getting her into a nervous and vulnerable state before he graced her with his presence. She had to admit that it was working. But she wasn't going to wait for him any longer. She was going to get up out of this chair and climb out that window. It would at least have been nice to sleep in a real bed. She sighed as she took a last glance at it before she turned to the window. Lacy was stopped in her tracks when the door suddenly opened.

A large man stepped in the door. Lacy's eyes flew open in shock! Of all the people in the world, she would never have expected to see the man whose face she now stared into here in this place. "John! John Finley?"

Sonder urged Marek to hurry. "Ye haven't much time! The laird of Bremhall will be attending her at any moment!"

"Attending her?"

"Aye! We kept him busy most o' the day wi' anythin' we could think of. It was no easy task. He was verra anxious to see the lady! Follow me and I'll get ye t' her room. O' course, it will have t' be from the ou'side. I can no' risk anyone seein' ye. If anyone knew it was me takin' ye in and we failed . . . well, someone would talk."

"Yer own people would sell ye ou' even though yer tryin' t' help them?"

"No' on purpose. Bu' he'd find someone's family to threaten. If they knew somethin', they'd tell t' save their wives, sons, or daughters. Would you no' talk t' save the lady?"

"So why are ye helpin' us then?"

"Because yer lady talked me into it. She fights like our laird. She talks like our laird. She said she knew what kind of person we were dealin' wi' and that she could take care of it, bu' I'm no' so certain. The lady nearly took ou' three o' us, bu' the man she's facin' now bested five men at once. Then he pulled somethin' ou' o' his belt, a metal thing wi' a long tube on it. He pointed the tube at Laird Bremhall, there was a loud bang, and the next thing we knew, our laird was dead."

"And ye left my lady wi' this man?" Marek looked murderous. "How many bullets do ye think he has left?"

"How many what?"

"Bullets! Lacy told me all abou' guns. Tha's what it was, a gun. It runs on bullets. It only holds so many and if he does no' have any refills, he'll run ou' sooner or later. I suppose he did no' tell ye tha', did he?"

"It will run ou'?"

"Aye, and when it does, the thing will no' work again! Well, unless he finds a way to make the bullets here. Has he been workin' on tha'?"

"I do no' know. Bu' I'm pretty sure tha' if he was, someone would have told me. I'm the rightful heir t' Bremhall. He's holdin' my family t' keep me in line. I see them once a week. My men and I had decided t' rush him and try t' take the thing away from him. Bu' we do no' have the details all worked ou' yet. We were no' sure just what the thing could do. Bu' ye say tha' it can only kill so many before it runs ou' o' . . ."

"Bullets."

"Aye, maybe our plan is workable after all! Can a bullet kill more than one man?"

"No' unless it makes it through one man and into another. Lacy told me tha' happens once in a while, bu' it's no' likely."

Marek saw hope rise in the other man's eyes.

———

"Well, get me t' Lacy and maybe we can all come up wi' a plan where no one gets killed. Well, except this laird o' yers." Marek motioned for Sonder to lead the way and then asked, "Ye did no' hurt my lady, did ye?"

Sonder stopped, turned, and looked Marek in the eye. "Well, she was no' fightin' like a lady, laird. She seriously bruised my ribs! And tha' horse o' hers kicked Derk in the head. The man is recoverin' thankfully, bu' he was ou' for most o' the day!"

"Ye hurt my lady?" Marek's face had turned red and his fist wrapped around Sonder's leather straps. He lifted him off the ground and shoved him up against a tree. Sonder started to resist but then reminded himself that if Marek had taken *his* woman, he'd have done the same thing. He chose instead to take his medicine and then plead for Marek's help. He hoped that Marek wouldn't kill him. If the two holdings could not get rid of this one man and his gun, things would be changing for both holdings, not just Sonder's.

"She's all righ'! Bu' I had to render her unconscious t' take her. She fights like a warrior! We tried t' take her wi'ou' injury, bu' she was beatin' the fight ou' o' all o' us! So when her guard was down for a brief second, I hit her in the jaw." Marek curled his free fist up into a ball to punch Sonder senseless, but Galen stopped him.

"We need him and you've sparred wi' Lady Lacy. Ye know she would have given it her all. The man is lucky t' be standin' at all! And he did say they were tryin' t' keep from hurtin' her."

Marek didn't lower his fist right away. "Did ye break her jaw?"

"No, she talked and sang all the way here!"

"Why did she have to sing?" Marek had started to lower his fist when Sonder mentioned singing; he raised it again. Marek knew that she would sing if threatened or thinking deeply . . . which was it?

"Mostly, she sang when we went through the tunnel. She does no' like tunnels bu' she willingly went t' save our families. She is a verra brave woman."

Marek put the man down. "Ye took her through a tunnel?"

"Marek, I'll tell ye all abou' the tunnel later, bu' righ' now we have t' get t' her! He could be wi' her now!"

Marek stepped to the side again and motioned for Sonder to take the lead again, "Okay, lead the way."

Sonder led them through a back gate that he was supposed to have been guarding. They soundlessly made their way through the holding, ducking behind barrels and crates. They were obviously on the market street where the surrounding farmers sold their harvests. It was very late, and everything was closed up and dark. Sonder pointed up to a window just above a small-covered farmer's booth. The roof of the booth would allow Marek to get pretty close to the window. There was a ledge running just about up to the window. He thought he could climb up on the roof of the booth and then walk along the ledge. At the edge of the ledge, he could lean across and peek into the window. It would be tricky getting her out, but he would do it.

It didn't take him long to reach her window. He leaned over and peeked in cautiously. She was alone, sitting by the fire. She looked as though she had just had a bath; some strands of her hair were still damp. She was wearing her second skins though a pretty dress had been provided. It was pink, with puffy sleeves and lacy cuffs. The front was low cut with the same lace trimming the edges. Marek was pleased that she had chosen not to wear Bremhall's dress. Even without it, she took his breath away. Gone was the warrior he had battled three days ago. Here sat a lady whose beauty could make him forget where they were and what he was here for. Galen whistled from somewhere down below and pulled Marek back to his senses. When he looked back at her, she was standing, looking wistfully at the bed. She started to turn toward the window just as Marek began to call softly to her, but he was stopped abruptly when the door to her room opened suddenly.

Marek ducked quickly out of sight and listened. He heard her call out the man's name. She knew him! She was surprised, but she definitely knew him!

"Singer!" John called back warmly.

Lacy was up and hugging him before she knew what she was doing.

He laughed as he hugged her back. "I knew it was you as soon as those two screw-ups told me that the warrior woman they had come across with the child had sung before she attacked! You took two of my horses! Then you left the men alive. That was not a smart move, Lacy! They came back and told me everything."

Marek stole a look through the window then and his dream came back to him in vivid detail. She was hugging him! What was she doing?! He was the enemy!

"John, what in the hell are you doing here?!" Marek suddenly heard Lacy shout. As he peeked over the sill again, he was glad to see that she had pulled out of his arms and was now pacing the room.

"I should ask you the same thing!"

"I am not talking about *how* you got here! I'm talking about what you are doing to these people—threatening children and kidnapping women! And how did you get here anyway? The last thing I heard, you were going to Detroit to teach at a high school!"

"Yeah, well, the interview must not have gone as well as I thought it did. They decided not to hire me. So I had decided to try for a position in Riverton. I thought you and I could pick up where we left off."

"Where we left off? I didn't know we had started anything." Lacy giggled nervously.

"Oh, but we did, singer. Remember the hickey I gave you on the mat the day I taught you how to take down an opponent twice your size?"

"Yes, I remember that I was pretty upset with you and didn't speak to you for almost a week!"

"Yes, but we both knew you liked it. As a matter of fact, if you think about it, I should get first marking rights!" John started to laugh. "Can you believe the luck? I followed some punks into a mine shaft and got lost! They had been dealing drugs outside of one of the biggest high schools in Riverton. I figured if I could catch them and stop them, the principal would have to hire a hero! I was almost on them when I thought I saw them enter this shed. It obviously wasn't a shed. It was a mine shaft! I heard talking coming from a hole with a ladder leading into it. I followed the sound.

"I found the sound, which turned out to be a babbling underground brook and bats! I was stuck in that bat-infested shaft for about two days. Nearly killed myself when I lost my light and hit my head on a low ceiling. I was out for a while, I think, since my body temperature had dropped considerably by the time I awoke. Then when I finally find my way out, I'm here! They know nothing of guns and I am suddenly all powerful! It's a dream come true. But it gets better! You show up here too! Singer, this is our chance!"

"Our chance for what, John?"

"We can be king and queen!"

That statement shook her to her core. The man was an egomaniac! Before she could respond to that, another thought entered her mind. "What did you just say about a gun?"

"I had my gun on me when I went through that mine shaft! Since no one here has ever heard of a gun, they believe that I can kill at will forever. They will never challenge me! I can rule! It's like a dream come true! But it would be so much better if you agreed to be my queen! Singer, they have never learned to fight like you and I have been trained to do!"

"No, but then we have never been trained to fight the way they do! They fight to kill, John. We were taught to fight to defend without taking lives. Don't you remember that?"

"Singer, it will never come to it again. I only had to kill one man to subdue them. They are so afraid of the gun they will never challenge me again! So what do you think? Would you like to be my lady?"

"Well, John, that might be a little awkward. I have been claimed by Marek McKenzie. He is the laird of McKenzie holding. I don't think he would appreciate your taking his woman. Claiming is sacred around here. Did you not know?"

Marek was dumbfounded. He hadn't expected her to use this defense. He supposed she was just buying time to think. He needed to get in there, but he waited to discover what John's answer would be.

John smiled down at Lacy as he spoke. "Singer, you don't need to worry about that. I could shoot the man if he challenges me for you. Of course, I probably wouldn't have to resort to that. I'm sure I could take him in a fight. All you have to do is tell me you want me. I've waited for this moment for so long, love."

As John stared into her eyes, her expression gave away nothing. She wasn't singing, however, so that must be a good sign, he thought.

Marek peeked through the window to see her face. She was now facing the window and saw him but looked away quickly to keep from drawing attention to him from John. She wasn't quick enough, and John started to turn. She suddenly reached up and wrapped her arms around John to be able to make visual contact with Marek while she distracted John. She was making frantic motions to Marek, trying to talk to him with her eyes. Marek had no idea what she was trying to tell him, but he did not like seeing her with John's arms wrapped around her. Finally, in exasperation, Lacy pointed to John and then made a gun out of her hand. When Marek still didn't understand, Lacy pulled up John's coat so Marek could see the gun stuffed into his belt at his back where he always carried it. John felt the maneuver and assumed Lacy was responding to his proposition. He moaned in pleasure.

Lacy motioned Marek to go away again in panic. Marek saw the panic but didn't budge. She waved him away again just when John started kissing her neck. She squeaked in surprise, eliciting a chuckle from John and an audible hiss from Marek. She started to sing but caught herself. Marek had drummed it into her head that singing gave away too much information to an enemy. At this minute, John was a substantial enemy, being highly familiar with her singing habit.

Fortunately, John had not heard the hiss through his own chuckle. Unfortunately, he took the squeak as permission to continue and pulled her face up to kiss her on the mouth. Her eyes never left Marek. She motioned him to go again. But he shook his head. His eyes were hard as steel. Thinking to step through the window and beat the snot out of the big man, Marek grabbed hold of the sill and swung his leg over the edge. He didn't make it. He was angry and had put a little too much energy into the swing; his momentum carried him from the ledge across to the roof of another vendor, but his feet were still in the air when he landed on his back. The roof had a slight incline toward the back, and Marek began to roll down toward the front.

He grabbed for any kind of purchase he could find, but the edge came too soon and Marek fell eight feet to the ground. The fall knocked the wind out of him, and he was trying to catch his breath when he opened his eyes and stared up at a sword pointed right at his face. They were surrounded.

"Listen," Sonder tried to reason with the leader of the men. "Do no' do this! We have t' work t'gether t' get rid o' this man. Work with us, Michael!"

"Right! I'm no' goin' t' work wi' ye when the man has our families in this holdin'! What's t' stop him from shootin' them all?!"

"He can no' shoot them all!" Marek had found his breath.

"Aye?"

"Aye!"

"I am still unwillin' t' risk even one o' them. So get up and let's go." The man looked back at Sonder. "If ye promise t'go on home, Sonder, I'll let ye go. I'd no like t' see anythin' happen t' yer family."

"I can no' run and hide! We have t' take back what belongs t' us!"

Michael would not agree. He could not. He was a young man and had only been married a few weeks when John had come into their lives. He felt his duty was to keep his bride safe no matter the cost. He would not risk her. John had threatened to kill the entire family of any man who dared to challenge him. Michael finally looked Sonder in the eyes and replied, "I will no' risk it and I will no' risk yer family either. Ye are free t' go, Sonder. Do what ye will, but think o' yer family before ye act."

Marek stood then, and he and his men were taken at sword point to the laird of Bremhall. He was kicking himself all the way up to the second-story room. How had he been so stupid?! He had trusted Sonder and the man had proven himself a trustworthy man, but he had failed to plan for the probability that there would be men in the holding who would not support them. Then there was that ridiculous leap for the windowsill. If he hadn't been so distracted by that . . . that . . . brute kissing Lacy, he'd have made it! Well, he'd wait for his moment. Then he'd take care of the laird of Bremhall!

CHAPTER 13

Trapdoors and New Friends

Lacy had seen Marek's attempt to get in the window. Her first instinct was to punch John in his egomaniacal, chauvinistic overgrown head and run to the window. But the more she thought about it, the more sure she was that the best way to help Marek was to bring no attention to him. Of course, with all the noise he had just made outside, he probably managed to wake up everyone in the holding.

The only oblivious person in the area had to be John. He was still moaning with pleasure as he continued to kiss her neck. Lacy had had enough. She pulled her arms down from around his neck and gently pushed away from his chest. John wasn't ready to break the kiss and pulled tightly against her. She put one hand on each side of his face and gently pushed him back.

"John, slow down, please. You are moving so fast. Let's . . . um . . . get to know each other again. It's been a while since I last saw you. Tell me about yourself."

"We can talk later, singer. We have all the time in the world." He tried to pull her back into his embrace again.

Lacy asked him to stop again as she was pulling his arms from around her waist. She smiled tentatively up at him. "I need a little time, John, to think about the proposition you just offered."

"Well, you started this with that unsolicited hug."

"Yes, I did, didn't I!" She giggled nervously. "Forgive me! I don't know what got into me. I was just so excited to see someone I knew. I really miss home. Don't you?"

"No! I have everything I could possibly want here. And now I have you too!"

"What if I decide that I don't wish to stay at Bremhall holding? McKenzie holding is my home now."

"That's okay, singer. I can give you McKenzie holding too."

"John, I don't want McKenzie holding. I just like living there."

"Well, you probably can't have it both ways, dear. McKenzie is not going to allow the laird of Bremhall to live in his holding now, is he? Especially if

Laird McKenzie has claimed you as I've been told. You don't have feelings for this guy, do you, Lacy?"

There was a knock at the door, giving Lacy an excuse not to answer. John looked exasperated with the interruption but called for their entrance anyway. The door was pushed abruptly open, and Lacy was shocked to see Marek stumble into the room. There was a song just begging to burst from her lips, but Marek recognized her intention even before she did. He glared at her, willing her to stay silent. She shut her mouth tightly, but her body looked taut and ready to pounce. Marek's eyes warned her to relax.

Easier said than done, she thought. If need be, she would fight in a moment's notice. She would have liked to kick some booty right then, but Marek's gaze had not left her eyes. His message was clear: *Wait for it!*

She would! But she wouldn't like it.

John tore them from their visual conversation, demanding to know what was going on, his anger at the interruption of his reunion with Lacy flavoring his demands. His irritation only increased as the rest of Marek's men were paraded into the room. Lacy's face visibly fell at the sight of them.

"Laird, we found these men sneakin' around below." He shoved Marek forward again as he continued. "This one was climbin' around ou'side the lady's window before he fell."

John looked at Marek and then back at Lacy. She tried to put on a blank expression, but it didn't fool anyone; and truth be told, it pleased Marek though it didn't help their cause much at all.

"Singer, who is this man?"

"Well, he's . . ." She figured there was no point in lying to him; he'd find out soon enough. "He's the laird of McKenzie holding. This is Marek McKenzie."

"Ah, the man who you say has claimed you."

Marek's eyebrow perked up at that. He was thrilled that she had told him that little tidbit . . . though again it didn't help their cause much.

"Yes."

"Has he marked you yet?" John asked her, not that it mattered much since he wouldn't have honored that local tradition anyway.

"Well . . ." Lacy looked hesitantly at Marek. Shoot! She didn't even know what *marking* really meant. No one had ever bothered to answer her questions about it.

"No, she is no' officially marked, the ceremony is set for three days from now at McKenzie holding," Marek volunteered. "Ye are no' invited! Lacy, we need t' be goin'."

"No, Marek, I can't leave yet." She saw his startled look but continued on. "I have unfinished business here."

A large mischievous smile spread over John's face. "You aren't leaving anyway." He stepped menacingly closer to Marek. "You are my prisoner. You made it so easy for me to take over McKenzie holding." He looked back at Lacy. "See, singer, you get to live at your precious holding after all! And I didn't even have to shoot anyone! Though I still might. We'll see!"

Lacy could almost see demons dancing behind John's evil stare as he turned to her. It sent goose bumps up and down her body. Getting out of this was going to take a considerable amount of cleverness. Her mind raced through several possibilities. She could fight now and try to take John down before his guards could respond. She was pretty sure that Marek and his men would follow her lead and fight too.

"My holdin' will fight ye all the way. Ye will never get past my gates!" Marek stood to look John straight in the eyes as he spoke. The two men were nearly of the same height. Lacy thought that if testosterone levels increased any more in this room without some kind of outlet, body parts would be the only thing left in the room to find.

John reached behind his back and pulled out his gun. He stroked it like a favored pet and then pointed it at Marek's head. "Perhaps I would have more luck if I throw your head over the gate first!"

"No!" Lacy responded a little louder than she had intended. She hurried to reason with the warped and severely twisted mind that had taken over the man she used to think of as a friend. "John, I don't think throwing the head of a well-loved laird over the gate of his holding will make the conquest any easier. It would be better to shoot him in front of his gates. Then the people would realize your true superiority!"

Every eye from Marek's ranks stared incredulously at Lacy. She tried to ignore them as she worked her plan through her mind. She had to get John alone. She didn't think he would shoot her—she hoped he wouldn't anyway. She was going to have to trick him into a false sense of security. She felt a cold rivet of sweat trickle down her spine. Marek wasn't going to like what she was about to do. Frankly, she didn't like what she was about to do. She hoped it would work.

Lacy reached out and put her hand on John's arm. He turned his attention from his target and looked at her. She turned him toward her, placed a hand on his gun to lower it. She stepped into his arms. She reached behind his neck with one hand and drew him down to her. She kissed him soundly on the lips. For Marek's benefit, she reached behind her own back in plain view of Marek and crossed her fingers. She sure hoped crossed fingers meant the same thing here as it did back home. If not, he'd just have to suffer for a bit while the plan played out.

John and Marek were both taken off guard, one man lost in a hopeless fantasy of Lacy's making, the other in a rage also of Lacy's making. When Lacy pulled away from his lips, she leaned close to his ears. "John, doesn't this place have a dungeon?"

What in the heck was she up to? Marek wondered. A dungeon? And what did the crossed fingers mean? He didn't have long to ponder these questions.

Having had his plans delayed slightly by Singer, John instead punched Marek in the stomach. The blow was sudden and fierce. Marek dropped to his knees. Lacy started to move toward him, panic in her eyes, but Marek's glare stopped her. Almost imperceptively, he shook his head at her, staying her steps. He wanted to pound the blond man into the pavement. And what kind of game was Lacy playing? She had told the man that she chose to live at McKenzie holding and that she was claimed by Marek. She would have run to him just then, he was sure of it. So why was she now kissing the enemy right in front of him? At this rate, Marek was sure that he would never figure women out. He wasn't sure which was worse—losing Lacy to this insane moron or waiting for her to put him in a dungeon.

"Yes, there is a dungeon. But I'd rather just shoot him." John was looking at Marek again.

"Don't be silly, John. Why waste the bullet? Come on, show me the dungeon and we'll lock him in together."

John's free hand was caressing Lacy's arm. He finally pulled her in to his side and nodded at her. "Okay, we can take them all down to the dungeon."

"Uh, John, could we leave the rest of them here with the guards for a bit and just you and I take Laird McKenzie down alone?" She leaned into him and whispered something in his ear.

Marek couldn't hear her, but he watched a very lustful smile spread across John's face. His hand began to wander lower and lower on her back. It was all Marek could do not to kick the snot out of the guy. Then John was kissing her again. He was making a production out of it. Marek happened to look down at Lacy's hand, still stashed behind her back. She was crossing her fingers again! What in the world did that mean? He thought she might be trying to tell him something, but he had no idea what.

John began to chuckle in anticipation of the trip down to the dungeon. He broke the kiss and told one of his men to tie Marek's hands behind his back. Then he directed the men to follow him and bring the prisoners.

This order worried Lacy. Maybe he hadn't taken the bait! She looked provocatively up at John. He smiled that lazy, arrogant smile that made Lacy want to spit in his face. She hoped her face did not reflect her feelings. When John took her hand and squeezed it, she supposed she had been successful.

"Let's go, gentlemen, I don't want to keep this lovely lady waiting. She has fantasies to fulfill!"

He led them down the hall and down the same set of stairs that Lacy had been brought up on her arrival. When they reached the main landing, they took a hard left and walked down a narrow empty hallway. It was cold even though it was lit with torches every few feet. Lacy shivered and John took it as a cue to draw her closer to him. Was that a growl she heard from Marek who was hiking along behind them? She smiled to herself. He cared! It made him uncomfortable for her to be in John's arms. As pleasing as that thought was, if they got out of this, she was going to have some explaining to do to get him to listen to her. She would make him listen. She had to!

They had reached the entrance to the dungeons. John pulled the latch open and retrieved a torch from the outside wall. He motioned for Marek to go ahead of them. When his men tried to follow with the other captives in tow, John stopped them. The lust-filled grin was back on his face.

"Gentlemen, please wait here until I call for you to bring these men down. Allow us a little alone time please." He glanced down at Lacy and then amended his order, "Oh, and if anyone comes up these stairs without me . . . kill them!"

"John, don't you think that the two of us could take him if he gave us any trouble?" Lacy asked him coyly.

"Singer, I have no doubt that we could take him, but I'm not stupid. Your loyalties are still in question, my dear, although it pleases me that you have not begun to sing."

"Well, I haven't perceived any danger to myself. Am I wrong? I could come up with a fighting song if you think I should." She toyed with him, circling her finger slowly over his chest.

"It is true that I would love to hear you sing, but I would rather it not be a fighting song. You have such a lovely voice, don't you think, Laird McKenzie?" He turned his attentions on their captive as they stepped off the final stair. John pushed Marek farther down the dark hallway. He lit a couple of torches on the way and finally stopped in front of one of the cells. "Marek, do you know what we're going to do now?"

"I'm sure ye are goin' t' tell me."

"Yes, it seems that my singer here has had some very vivid fantasies about dungeons. I am going to fulfill all those fantasies right now." He pointed the gun at Marek and leaned down to plant a wet kiss on Lacy. He was surprised by her song instead. The moment of confusion was all Lacy needed. Her leg flew at his gun hand, sending it sailing harmlessly through the air. John recovered quickly and readied for her attack. They had practiced this so many times together in training. He had taught her how to take down a man his size, but she had never managed to take him down. He had always known just how she would attack and had only been tricked by her once during their testing. But even then, he had won and he would win now.

168

It was a pity, he thought, that instead of having her complete cooperation in their relationship he would now have to force her to choose him. Of course, he would make her an offer she could not possibly refuse. He would keep her pathetic warrior alive and in exchange she would be his queen. Okay, it sounded a little melodramatic, and John lacked the appropriate black handlebar mustache, but he didn't care much. He just wanted Lacy, and he was most certain that once she got used to the idea, she'd learn to love him. If she didn't, . . . well, . . . he still had some bullets left!

He circled to the left and Lacy countered. John had wanted to get the two of them in view so he could watch his enemies. At least Marek's hands were tied. Well, they were for the moment anyway. John watched with exasperation as Lacy reached into her pocket and produced one of the dinner knives from her meal earlier in the evening. Marek turned his back just long enough to retrieve it. He was already working on the ties, but the knife was not very sharp and John was sure it would take him a minute or two to work it through the leather straps that held him. Just the same, he thought he better subdue Lacy quickly. He hadn't even formulated a real plan of attack when she surprised him. She attacked with a blunt forward assault, one fist to the left side of his face and the other to the right. He had never seen her use this approach in all that training they had been through. Where in the heck had she learned that? As he tried to reason out what had just happened, she threw her head forward, using it as a weapon against his nose.

Lacy was a blur of movement. John had been so surprised by her choice of attack that she had done some real damage on her first attempt. She had opted not to use any of the moves that John had taught her. Instead, she employed only moves learned from Marek's teaching. She was unable to stop the singing, but she worked hard to keep John off balance. Unfortunately, John had a few new moves himself and Lacy soon found herself in the fight of her life.

Blood oozed from John's nose and the corner of his mouth, but Lacy was also bleeding from a scrape received when the bare skin on her left arm hit and slid across the stone flooring. She rolled and jumped to her feet just in time to catch a fist to her jaw.

"Chits! The jaw again! Great, at this rate my face will never look normal!" she thought out loud. The fact that she didn't pass out with the blow was greatly due to quick reflexes on her part. The blow was glancing, but still hurt. She began to sing more loudly, legs flying to John's face. He saw it coming and ducked to the side. The hall was narrow enough that he dodged into a doorjamb and groaned with the impact. But he didn't go down. He lunged toward Lacy, but he caught his forward foot on something and sprawled toward the floor. He recognized Marek's foot as the offending object just before he hit. Unfortunately, the man was large enough that he still managed to push Lacy hard against the wall on his way down.

169

John's large body hit the floor just as Marek pulled free of his bindings. He flipped the big man over and landed a solid punch to his face. John's fist came at Marek, but Marek arched back and the hit missed by centimeters. Marek pulled the man to his feet in one fluid move that would have impressed Lacy had she been able to see anything but stars. He pummeled John then with blows to the stomach and head. John was probably unconscious about three blows before Marek stopped, but Marek wouldn't let his body sink to the ground. All the rage and worry from the last three days had to run its course. Finally, he dragged John's sagging unconscious body over to the cell that had been meant for Marek and threw it in. He slammed the door shut and ran to Lacy.

Lacy was leaning breathlessly against the wall, the knock in the head still reverberating through her skull. At least she wasn't sick! So perhaps she didn't have a concussion, she thought . . . or was that the right symptom? It was a little hard to think at the moment. Maybe that was a sign of concussion. No, she was thinking. She was sure of it.

There was a man leaning over her. Which one was it? She couldn't see in the dim light at first, but then his golden brown eyes came slowly into view. They were worried and he was talking to her. It took her a moment to understand. She thought she was recovering when the words finally registered meaning.

"Lacy, sweetheart! Are ye all right, honey?"

Nope, she wasn't recovering, she was dreaming. Marek wouldn't be using sweet terms of endearment after all the crap she had put him through in the last hour. Surely he'd be yelling at her. She felt him pick her up off the floor, cradling her in his arms.

"I'm sorry I was no' faster. I should no' have tripped him." He sat down on a nearby bench and stroked her hair. "Lacy, talk t' me, love."

Lacy's mind cleared. She sat up . . . a little too quickly. Dizziness kept her sitting for a moment as she waited for it to dissipate.

"Take yer time, love. Are ye all right?"

She didn't answer him; she just looked at his handsome face, grabbed it between her hands, and began kissing him over and over again with tears running down her cheeks. "You came for me! You didn't like him touching me!" She managed to get out between kisses. Lacy whispered his name, kissed his whiskery chin, then whispered it again. She was moving so fast from one part of his face to another that Marek had to take her face in both of his hands to take aim himself. He held her still and kissed her until she stopped squirming and relaxed into him. He let go of her face then and wrapped his arms around her waist.

"Of course I did no' like him touching ye, Little Warrior. What did ye expect?"

She smiled at him, then her face got serious. She was facing toward the cell where Marek had thrown John's limp, beaten body. She saw him stagger out, and before Marek could turn to see what she was looking at, she was up and running, a song on her lips. She sailed through the air, throwing her feet up at the last minute to catch him in the abdomen. He saw it coming and deflected her before she could do any damage. He caught her around her ribs and began to squeeze the air out of her, but Lacy was familiar with this move. She threw all her weight into swinging her legs up and over his shoulder while at the same time slipping from under his grasp. He was too slow to tighten, and she slid out, her legs extended just above his shoulders. John, being still a little dizzy from Marek's punches, found himself struggling to maintain his balance. When Lacy's weight shifted suddenly over his left shoulder, he staggered and fell backward. Unable to stop his descent, he fell fast and hard. His head hit awkwardly on a bench outside the cell. It broke his neck instantly. Lacy landed with her upper body on top of him and her legs sprawled out on the floor over his left shoulder.

"John?" Lacy jumped up and felt for a pulse. She already knew he was dead, but she had to check. "Ah, John, look where your greed has left you! You stupid, stupid man!" Her tears fell freely for the sparring mate she used to know . . . not the evil man he had become.

"Are ye hurt? Did he hurt ye anywhere?" Marek was by her side and frisking her in the dim light, inspecting every inch of her. She grabbed his hands, and he pulled her into his embrace.

"I'm fine! How are you?"

"Fine bu' is yer haed all right? Ye took quite a blow!"

Lacy was barely listening. "I'm fine. Really!"

He scooped her up again, apologizing for not having locked the cell before he ran to her. He sat down again, holding her in his lap. He took her face in his hands and smoothed her hair back as he inspected her face for new injuries.

"Marek." He wasn't listening to her, concern etched in his face. "Marek!" she said again to get his attention as she took his hands and held them. "There's something I have to say to you. It's important and I need to tell you now!"

"Aye? Ye can tell me anything, Little Warrior."

"It's about the challenge." She took a deep uneven breath. "Marek, I realized that I love you, so I tried . . . but I don't know what happened during the challenge." Her thoughts were all tangled up in knots. She was talking fast, trying to get everything out before she lost her nerve. "You didn't fight . . . I thought you changed . . . You don't . . . I'm not what . . . You don't want me anymore?" She couldn't believe that was true, but she had to know. She needed to hear him say it. He had said that he didn't like John touching her, but maybe it was just that John was an evil man. Maybe he would do the same for any woman in the same situation. But he had kissed her and he was still holding her.

"Slow down, Lacy. I can no' understand what ye're tryin' t' say. Where did ye get the idea that I did no' want ye anymore?"

"Well, Marek, . . . I thought . . . the challenge . . . you . . . you let me win."

"No, ye won fair and square!"

"No, I didn't! You let me win and we both know it!"

"Why would ye say such a thing?"

"Because I went into that challenge with the intent to let *you* win! I didn't want to fight you. I . . . wanted . . ." She sighed. She looked into those incredibly sweet eyes. She might as well bite the bullet. If she couldn't voice her own feelings, how could she expect Marek to guess them? She took a leap of faith, hoping beyond hope that she was and had been reading his affection correctly. "I wanted you! Marek, I still want you."

His smile was so wide that it took up almost his whole face. "But, Lacy, tha's why I let ye win! I wanted ye t' *choose* me. It was no longer enough just t' have ye. I wanted ye t' want me too! So I gave ye the choice. But then ye broke my heart. Ye did no' say anythin', ye just left. Why?"

"Because I thought you had changed your mind about me and were allowing me a graceful way out!" A sob stuck in Lacy's throat at the memory. Tears formed and splashed down her cheeks. "I thought you didn't want me anymore! So I got Thor and ran to Jeanette's house!"

"Lacy, how could ye not know how I felt abou' ye after the picnic . . . after the barn? For heaven's sake, I nearly threw ye over my shoulder and took ye straight t' my room then!"

"Well, I thought I knew what you wanted, but then you let me win. I couldn't figure out why you would do that unless you had changed your mind."

"What a mess we made ou' of everythin'!" Marek hugged her tightly. "Galen told me t' go after ye after the challenge bu' I was . . . I should have gone after ye. I will no' make tha' mistake again, love. I will always come after ye. Ye're mine and I'll no' let ye ou' o' my sight again."

"Well, I don't think you're going to have the chance because we're sort of trapped in here. I hadn't anticipated that John would order his men to kill us if we came up without him. We have more fighting ahead of us, Marek." She might have panicked under any other circumstances, but she was in Marek's arms. Whatever happened now, it would happen with him beside her. She was comforted by the thought. Peace wrapped itself around her, and she leaned into his chest. Her forehead rested against his neck.

Marek's arm rested around her shoulder, and his hand cupped her jaw, his thumb stroking her cheek as a plan formulated in his mind. "Aye, bu' I do no' think we need to fight on their terms."

"What are you planning?"

He kissed her quickly on the forehead and stood, pulling her to her feet to lead her deeper into the dungeon. She pulled him back briefly. "Oh, no you don't! I'm not settling for any kisses on the forehead! We might not get another chance at this for a while, so if you have some kissing to do, get it right, Huge Warrior!" She pulled him down into a deep kiss that left them both wanting more and quite breathless.

"Lacy, do no' start somethin' that we can no' finish . . . unless ye really do have fantasies abou' dungeons!" He smiled mischievously.

The look on her face told the story if her curt answer hadn't. "No, I definitely do not!"

"Well then, follow me." He retrieved a torch, took her hand again, and led her down the dark corridor. When they came to the last two cells, Marek opened the one on the right and began inspecting the walls. He was looking for something, but Lacy had no idea what.

Looking just as intently around the room, Lacy finally gave up trying to discover what he was searching for. "Marek, what are we looking for?"

"Our way ou'!"

"Okay, honey, did John get in a punch that I missed? Are you okay?"

"I'm fine. Ye see, when the two holdin's were built, we were all one family. My father's father had a sister. She claimed one o' the Bremhalls from three valleys over."

"Wait! She *claimed* him? She had the right to claim a man?"

"Aye! It was her righ' as an heir t' the land here."

"Marek, I thought women didn't have the right to claim a man."

"Oh well, usually they do no', but if the lady has land and does no' have a father or older brother t' fight for her in the event the man who claims her is no' a good match, the woman is allowed t' claim her own mate. But did ye no' want t' know wha' I'm lookin' for?"

"Oh yes, sorry."

"Anyway, both holdin's were built by the same family. So we hired the same builder. He was verra clever. He designed escape routes ou' o' the dungeons in the case that either holdin' was ever invaded by another clan." Marek continued to scrutinize the walls.

"Marek, won't Bremhall's men be expecting you to try to escape that way?"

"Well, I do no' think so since the only ones who would know o' the escape route would be a laird and his mate. T' keep the passage a secret, no one is told abou' the secret unless they are told by a laird when he turns the hold over t' his successor. My father told me and now I have told my mate." He smiled back at her. "Since tha' maniac killed the rightful laird of Bremhall, I doubt seriously tha' the old laird told the new 'laird' where it was. The rightful laird had no' taken a mate yet, so no one bu' him would know abou' it. The only problem is tha' the two escape routes are in different places. So I'm no' sure where this one is. But I know wha' t' look for."

He finished scouring the cell they were in with no sign of the secret door. He led Lacy to the cell across the hall and began looking again. The sun was just coming up outside and shone brightly through a small window in the outside wall. The light angled down at just the right place and illuminated what looked like an error in the masonry. One of the bricks had been put in the wall at an odd angle.

"There it is!" Marek pointed to the aberrant brick. He leaned down and pushed the brick in. A panel opened. The two of them slipped through the opening and started down a dark tunnel. The panel closed behind them, and they were left in darkness except for the torch that Marek held.

"Great! Marek, I don't like tunnels!" Lacy complained. Her fingers dug into Marek's hand.

"It will no' be too long." He pulled her in close to him. He liked how she fit so snugly under his arm. She wrapped her arm around him with something like a death grip. She sang lightly as they walked.

"Lacy, ye are a puzzle t' me."

"Am I?"

"Aye, ye took on tha' great man wi'ou' blinkin' but ye are afraid of a wee tunnel."

"Well, one of the 'wee' tunnels I went through recently took me right out of my comfortable life and dropped me in a foreign land. And just to put icing on the cake, it dropped me in a place without hot and cold running water!"

"I'll build ye a bath, but I'm goin' t' have t' think about how t' produce hot and cold running water."

"You are sweet, Marek, but it isn't as important as it was in the beginning."

"No?"

"No. Well, most of the time anyway."

"Wha' is important t' ye, Little Warrior."

"What's important to me, Marek, is you."

"I like t' hear tha'." He leaned down to kiss her, but she interrupted him.

"You are very important to me, Marek, but I'm not stopping inside this place even for a kiss from you! I don't like it and I can't wait to get out!" She was humming again.

"When we get ou' o' here, I want ye t' wait where I tell ye. I've got t' go after my men."

"No! I'm going with you. You aren't going to leave me anywhere. I'm not losing you again!"

"Lacy, first of all, ye did no' lose me. I was right behind ye the whole way! And secondly, ye will no' argue wi' me. Ye will let me protect ye."

"Then you will protect me from right in front of me because I will not stay here and wait for you. I'm going with you."

"Lacy, ye are my lady and ye will do as I tell ye t' do."

It was clear to Lacy that she was getting nowhere with this argument. She wasn't budging and neither was he. "Fine! Have it your way! But if you don't come back by the time I finish singing . . . let's say . . . two songs, I'm coming after you!" Of course, she had no intention of allowing him to go by himself; she just wouldn't admit that she could sing those songs in less than two minutes.

Marek was no dummy. He knew exactly what she was up to. "Lacy, ye will no' follow me! If it takes me until nightfall, ye will wait!" She tightened her grip on him as if to say in answer, "Just try to pry me off you." "Ye will wait, or I'll tie ye t' a tree!"

"You can try! Besides, you just told me in the dungeon that you weren't going to let me out of your sight again. So how can you leave me alone?!"

He rolled his eyes at his impossible, beautiful woman. It seemed clear that he wasn't going to get his way without wasting a lot of time. At least he knew she could hold her own in a battle. Maybe just having her there would help with the psychological battle. After all, the Bremhall men already knew she was a force to contend with. He sighed as he looked down at her. "Okay, ye can go, but ye will stay behind me at all times!"

"Deal! Thank you. I didn't want to stay by myself."

"Lacy, since I am makin' this concession, will ye do me a favor after we get home again."

"If I can, I will."

"Good! Please get rid o' those second skins! Ye are my lady, save the scenery for me!"

She smiled. "Does this mean you and your men will be wearing shirts?"

Marek just growled.

The conversation had at least distracted Lacy as they made their way through the tunnel. It hadn't taken long at all to reach the door to the outside. Marek unlatched it and pulled it open. As soon as the door opened and they stepped into the early morning sun, Marek turned to her and pulled her close. He lifted her chin then leaned down to brush his lips against hers. He thought to make it a quick kiss, having been denied the same in the tunnel, but Lacy was not in the mood for a quickie. She took full advantage of the moment. Her lips pressed warmly to his. She had him alone for the moment and she wouldn't have him to herself again for several days, so she didn't want to waste the moment. She wrapped her arms around his neck and pulled herself up into his embrace. She shivered when his arms wrapped tightly around her and he participated in the kiss with enthusiasm. A slight breeze blew his long dark hair across her cheek. She sighed in response, her kiss demanding more. Her body began to respond without Lacy thinking about what it was up to. Her hands were exploring his shoulders and his back. She kissed his neck and nipped at his shoulders.

175

Marek was surprised by Lacy's boldness, but he didn't miss a beat. He responded to her kisses in like manner. When she nearly climbed right up his body, he wrapped his arms around her and pulled her closer. He stroked her back and thrilled to the shivers he sent through her. Marek was totally lost in the aggressiveness of his lady. She was kissing him down his neck, but he just about lost it when she nipped his shoulders. The woman could make him forget he had a mission . . . almost. Reluctantly, he released her waist, running his hands up the sides of her body and down her arms, seeking her hands. She moaned in response and followed that just as quickly with a groan of disappointment as she realized he was not continuing the progression but bringing them back to reality. He chuckled at her disappointment.

"Later, love. Right now we have t' go get my men."

Lacy pulled back and looked into those lovely golden brown eyes, desire still lingering there. She loved that look, but he was right. She nodded her head and stepped back a little.

"Later then. Let's go get them."

The entrance was overgrown with shrubs. The only way out was to crawl under them. Marek led the way, all the while thinking that having a shirt right now would be a good thing since the bushes were so thick. Lacy wiggled under the bushes right behind him. Once they made it out the other side, Lacy inspected his various scratches.

"That shirt idea is looking better, don't you think?" she teased.

"What, and deny ye yer entertainment?" came his retort.

"My entertainment?" Lacy's eyebrows raised in question.

"Ye did say ye liked t' watch me walk across the holdin'. How could I deny ye tha' simple pleasure?"

"You make a fine point. I would miss that!" She was quiet for a bit while they snaked their way around the holding. "Marek?"

"Aye?"

"Can I ask you a question?"

"Ye can ask me anythin', Little Warrior."

"It's something I have wished to know almost since the first time I saw you."

"Go ahead and ask." Marek's curiosity was piqued.

"Do you have a big white X on your chest and back?" She was giggling.

"A what?" He couldn't help turning to look back at her. When he turned, she slapped her hand over her mouth, trying desperately to get control. But the thought of a big white X on his chest left from the lack of sun on those places where the leather straps hugged his perfect upper body was more than Lacy could stand. Laughter erupted from the beautiful warrior. As Marek moved his straps around to check for the dreaded white X, Lacy doubled over with laughter.

"Lacy, though I greatly enjoy seein' yer face lit up wi' laughter, ye must keep in mind tha' we are just ou'side the holdin'. It would do us no good t' be found righ' now. Do ye no' agree?" Though she was ribbing him unmercifully, there was no irritation in Marek's voice. He was serious though, and Lacy tried to sober her thoughts.

"Yes, I'm sorry." She tried to get herself under control. She tried . . . and she failed. When the giggles wouldn't subside, Marek finally took a very quick two steps, hauled her up tight against him, and captured her lips in a kiss that completely wiped every thought from her mind once again. Wow, he was good at that. She could already feel the heat spreading throughout her body when he suddenly stopped kissing her, let go of her waist, took her hand, and continued to lead her through the trees and underbrush toward the gate in the holding wall.

She followed him in a daze. Little jolts of electricity shot randomly through her body as her mind wandered through the replays of Marek's embraces and kisses. She let her eyes feast on the big man in front of her in the early morning light. His strong body rippled with strength. His large calloused hand engulfed her small soft one. Sadly, her reverie was short-lived. Too soon, they found themselves staking out the small gate where Sonder had originally snuck Marek and his men into the holding the first time. Who would be guarding the gate this morning? And, Marek wondered, what had happened to Sonder? He hadn't seen him since Marek and his men had been taken into custody.

Suddenly, the guard came into view. He was pacing back and forth in front of the gate. There were no people coming or going from the holding yet due to the early hour. He was probably pacing to stay awake in the last few hours of his watch.

"How are we going to get past him?" Lacy whispered to Marek.

"I do no' know yet. We'll have t' watch for an opportunity. Maybe he'll turn his back t' us for a moment and I will be able t' sneak up on him from behind." They watched a few minutes more, but the guard never turned his back on the outside of the holding. He always turned toward the wilderness.

Frustration edged onto Marek's face. Lacy noticed and then got an idea. True, it was an old trick, but maybe these guys hadn't seen it yet. She stepped out of their hiding place, hearing Marek hiss his disapproval, stretched provocatively and began a slow methodical saunter toward the now stunned gate guard.

Even in her sweats and T-shirt, Lacy was clearly all woman. The guard was soaking up the catlike approach. His response was obvious and immediate. Marek watched from the bushes. Saints have mercy, he thought. The woman radiated femininity! The guard hadn't even had a chance. His eyes locked on the sway of her hips, then they slowly made their way up to her face, lingering on several parts of her anatomy first. Marek was thinking of ways to kill the man even as he watched Lacy toy with him.

—

When she finally reached the guard, he stood frozen before her. She reached up and ran her fingers through his hair, ruffled it, and turned to enter the gate. The guard hadn't even managed to get his wits about him to request her name or her business in the holding! He just turned and watched her walk down through the marketplace. His eyes were very obviously locked on her sexy backside, and Marek took offense as he snuck up behind him and knocked him out cold.

When he caught up to Lacy, there was ice in his voice. "Ye will get rid o' those skins! I will no' have men lookin' at my lady like tha'. Do ye understand, Lacy?"

"What, no 'great job, sweetheart'? I got us in, didn't I?"

"Aye, and ye will no' do it tha' way again!"

"Okay, next time, you do the sexy walk and ruffling of hair and I'll sneak up on the man and knock him out."

"Do no' sass me, Lacy! Ye're mine and I will protect ye, but ye need t' help me ou' a bit! So do no' provoke men, please!"

"I like that!" she told him in a husky voice.

"Ye like wha'?"

"I like when you call me yours."

"Changin' the subject will get ye nowhere, love. Now let's go retrieve my men!" Then looking down at his lady he continued, "And steal ye a dress t' wear!"

They ran into Sonder . . . literally . . . as they rounded a corner outside the holding's main hall. This time, Sonder had amassed a group of about fifteen men.

"Lady Lacy! Marek! How did ye two get ou'?"

"I'll tell ye all abou' it later, right now I need t' get my men ou' o' trouble!"

"Tha's just where we were goin'! I thought we were goin' t' have t' rescue you and yer lady from the monster!"

"Well, the monster is no longer a threat t' anyone. He's dead. I'll tell ye how the lady and I escaped the dungeon once this whole mess is cleared up."

Sonder nodded in agreement. "I do no' think we will have t' fight at all, once everyone hears tha' the monster is dead. But just the same, let me talk t' them before ye let them see ye."

"Good enough!" agreed Marek.

As it turned out, the guards were relieved to see Sonder and once he explained just what had happened in the dungeon, the guards sent down one of their own to check the story out. When he returned with the happy news that their enemy was indeed dead, the men dispersed to their homes and left Marek and his men with Sonder. If they wondered how Marek and Lacy had gotten past them, they didn't voice the question. Perhaps they were too tired to think clearly. In any case, Marek took a few moments to lead Sonder down to the last cell on the left and showed him the passage.

—

"Marek, would you and yer men like t' stay for a couple o' days. Ye could stay in the guest rooms and catch a little sleep before ye have t' make tha' trip back home."

"Tha' would be nice. We can no' stay more than a day, but we could surely use the sleep. Oh and, Sonder, . . . could ye spare a dress for my lady! I confess I'm no' so happy wi' her choice o' clothes of late."

"Aye, there's already one in her room."

"Oh, and just one more thing, Sonder, if ye would be so kind."

"Anything, cousin!"

"Would ye have yer maid take the clothes she's wearing and burn them. Do no' tell her wha's goin' t' happen t' them, just let her think they're goin' t' be washed again."

Sonder laughed out loud. "Are ye no' scart she will be angry when she finds ou' wha' ye've done?"

"Oh, she will be angry for a while, but the second skins will be *forever* gone!"

"Can she no' get more where she got those?"

"Ah, no. The trip t' tha' market is too difficult t' navigate!"

"Sometime ye'll have t' enlighten me on just where John and Lady Lacy came from."

"Well, why don' ye bring yer family over for the harvest fest in the fall? It's been too long since our two holdin's behaved like family. Then we will have time t' talk and I'll tell ye all I know abou' it."

"Tha' sounds wonderful! Right now, I need t' get ye settled and retrieve my wife and family. I hope ye rest well, cousin."

"And you also, cousin!" Marek slapped his new friend and rediscovered relative on the shoulder in camaraderie as they reached the top of the stairs. There were feelings still to heal between the two holdings, much time had passed with little to no contact, and John had not helped matters when he sent out his raiding parties, but now the healing could begin and it was a fine start. Marek and Sonder would be good friends!

CHAPTER 14

Promises

The trip home had been uneventful except for Lacy's anger over the loss of her sweats and her favorite coral T-shirt. Despite the lovely blue dress that had been provided, despite the fact that when she looked in the mirror after putting it on, she was quite pleased and couldn't wait to see what Marek thought; and despite the fact that Marek had stood speechless as he admired the incredible beauty before him . . . despite all that, Lacy couldn't get past the thought that Marek had taken something of her past life from her. And she had precious little of that life left to begin with.

She knew Marek had orchestrated the laundry "mishap." Sonder had tried to apologize for the clumsiness of his maid when she knocked the laundry basket over and the sweats and T-shirt had inadvertently toppled into the fire. Yeah, like she believed that! They had gone up in flames too quickly for the maid to retrieve them. Though he apologized profusely, Lacy refused to accept it, declaring that he didn't owe her the apology . . . Marek did! Did they actually expect her to believe that cock and bull story?

Stomping around the campsites, ignoring Marek's attempts at lightening the mood, Lacy had struck fear into every face she looked into. Even finding that Thor had followed her into Bremhall holding and had been rounded up by Sonder's men and cared for until their departure had not helped Lacy's mood. After all, she didn't go around burning up Marek's clothes. Why would he do that to hers?

Marek had put up with her stomping, growling, and glaring all the way back to his holding, but now he'd had enough. His men were beginning to growl at him too! They missed Lacy's smile and sweet-tempered attitude. This new angry side was . . . well . . . it was just miserable! She hadn't sung anything the entire trip! Galen had complained the loudest, insisting that Marek do something to put the song back in the woman!

This was their second morning back home, and Lacy had been avoiding everyone! She had even skipped dinner last night. Marek was going to take the

---

time to straighten out this problem right now! The marking ceremony had been scheduled for that evening, but he wasn't sure that Lacy would cooperate in the mood she was in. He wouldn't let her stew over this any longer. He marched purposefully into the main hall where breakfast was being served.

"Has Lady Lacy been down t' eat yet?" he asked the cook.

"No, I have no' seen her yet. Would ye like yer breakfast now?"

"No, I'll be down with my lady shortly, we'll eat together. Thank ye, Marta."

"Ye're welcome, my laird."

He took the stairs two at a time up to Lacy's room. He knocked once and then entered without waiting for her reply. She was sitting up in bed with her knees pulled up to her chest. Her arms were wrapped around her knees, and her head had been resting on them until Marek burst into the room. Now she was looking at him and struggling to get the covers up far enough to cover her to her chin.

"Marek! What are you doing? You didn't even wait for me to answer the door before you came barging in here! It's bad enough that I'm still in bed, but you could have walked in on me when I was dressing . . . What are you thinking?"

He strode back and forth across her room as he began talking. "I'm thinkin' I've had enough o' the sulking over a pair o' pants and a shirt! Lacy, we will talk abou' this and get it straightened ou' now." He dropped a brown-paper-wrapped package tied with a string that he had been carrying with him down on the foot of her bed.

"I'm listening! Go ahead and talk!" she raised her voice slightly.

"Okay, I will! I had yer second skins burned, Lacy! It was me, no' Galen, no' Sonder, no' any o' the other men, so quit takin' it ou' on them! Ye've got them all worked up and now they're takin' it ou' on each other!! If ye need t' take it ou' on someone, take it ou' on me!" He had significantly raised his voice. "At least then I only get it from one side, . . . not twelve sides!"

"Fine! I will!" She threw the nearest thing she had at him; it was her pillow. Marek caught it easily and crossed the room, slamming the pillow down on the bed beside her. She jumped even though it was only a pillow and not a baseball bat or something more substantial! "Marek, I don't have another set of clothes for working out! They were comfortable! They stretched any direction I needed them to stretch! I told you that! Why do you have to have your way all the time? This was a little thing! Why couldn't I wear my sweats when I run? Who was I hurting?"

Marek sat down on the bed beside her. "Lacy, ye did no' see what I saw. Every time ye put those things on t' go run, every man in the holdin' stopped work t' turn and watch ye."

She tilted her head to the side and squinted her eyes at him. "So you are jealous?"

181

"No, . . . yes, a bit . . . bu' tha's no' it."

She smiled a little at his admission. "So what *is* it?"

Marek took her hand and pulled it to his lips. He kissed it tenderly, sighed, and scooted closer to her. He hesitated. What he really wanted to do was kiss her lips. The bruises from the last few days were still evident on her face, the underside of her jaw just a little swollen, and still she was the most beautiful woman he had ever encountered. If he didn't mark her soon . . .

"The truth, Lacy, is tha' I want ye all t' myself. I'm unwillin' t' . . . I do no' want anyone lookin' at ye like the men did when ye ran in yer sweats. It made me crazy, love. So I guess it is jealousy though I never though' I would succumb t' it. I'm sorry I burned yer sweats . . . well, no I'm no' sorry I burned them, but I am sorry I made ye sad and angry. If I could replace them, ye have t' know I would . . . I'd hate it, but I would, just t' see ye smile again." Even as he said it, he hoped he would never have to back up those words! "Please, do no' stay angry wi' me, Lacy. A man will do stupid things when the woman he loves is around."

Lacy's ears perked up. "The woman he loves?"

"Aye, Lacy, I love ye. I've known it since the day I kissed ye at the pond. When ye were fightin' me so hard to keep from learnin' t' ride a horse. Then the next thing I knew ye were kissin' the horse! I *knew* it then . . . but it started even before that, when ye fought so hard to save Colter even though ye were injured yerself. And when ye sang that beautiful love song and ye looked like ye had a specific love in mind as ye sang. I should have known it then, but it took me a bit longer."

"That is the sweetest thing anyone has ever said to me." Tears filled her eyes and spilled down her cheeks. She chuckled nervously. "I did, you know!"

"Ye did what, love?"

"I had a specific love in my head when I sang that song in the main hall . . . that morning just before our picnic."

"Aye?"

"Yes, I was thinking of you." She leaned forward, putting her forehead on his chest. Her legs were still pulled up in front of her, making the move awkward, but she needed to be close to him.

Marek lifted her head, wiped the tears from her lovely face, and pulled her onto his lap. Lacy was wearing the cotton nightgown that had been given to her on the first night she had arrived. There wasn't much material between her and Marek, and she found herself scrambling to pull the blankets around her. Marek smiled at her and pulled on the string wrapped around the small package he had brought with him. The paper fell away, and he pulled out a crisp white shirt. He slid out of his leather straps and pulled the shirt on slowly, watching her face all the while.

He buttoned the first button as he watched Lacy's eyes dance with amusement. He buttoned the second button as her eyes filled with tears once again.

"Now, ye can no' start that again! I just had it pressed. Ye'll get it all wet!" He continued to button the rest of the shirt, then tucked it in as best he could with Lacy still sitting on his lap. Then Lacy pulled his leather straps up over the shirt.

"Stand up and let me look at you." Lacy turned him around as she inspected every inch of him. "Hmm! Clearly, I was wrong, Marek."

"What were ye wrong abou', sweetheart?"

"You look just as incredible in a shirt as you do out of it, only now instead of just watching your muscles flex and relax, I'm thinking about taking the shirt off . . . I'm not sure that is better, it sort of makes it worse!"

"Oh, aye?!"

"Oh, aye!" She brushed her hands against his chest and slid them up around his neck and back down again. "It feels good, but not as good as your skin." She began unbuttoning the shirt. She got to the third button before Marek was kissing her hard. He moaned when her hands slid under the shirt and over his shoulder. Their open mouths locked together, as electric sensations pulsed through their bodies. Lacy couldn't seem to gain any semblance of control and pushed forward closer into his embrace. Marek stepped back to steady their balance, but the bed was right behind him and he fell onto the soft mattress, pulling Lacy down on top of him. He could feel the soft curves of her waist through the light nightgown and barely controlled the urge to explore further.

Lacy pulled away and sat up on him, one leg on either side of his muscled body. Her hands rested on his chest, and her eyes never strayed from his gaze.

"Marek . . . ," she whispered.

She didn't have to say anything else; he could see it in her eyes, the desire and the need. It was the same for him. He rolled her onto the bed and wrapped himself around her. His leg pinned both of hers to the bed, and his arms pulled her close. He kissed her tenderly at first, engaging her mouth in a play that sent her senses soaring. His hand caressed her cheek, her neck, and the hollow at the base of her neck. She moaned in pleasure, arching her back to press into him.

She finished unbuttoning the shirt and was shaking with anticipation as she pulled it from his leathers. Now her hands explored his stomach and chest, massaging, memorizing every indentation. His hands found hers, and he rolled back onto his side, breathing raggedly and holding tight to her wandering hands. He wanted to let go and let her finish her explorations, but now wasn't the time. It took all of Marek's self-discipline to hold tight to her hands. Placing both of her wrists in his left hand, he pulled Lacy into his side with his right arm. He had let it get out of hand, he knew. And truthfully, he didn't regret any part of it

—

except pulling away from her. He took a deep breath as he stared at her face. She looked confused and tried to pull her hands loose. He held them securely.

"Marek sweetheart, why did you stop? What's wrong? Did I do something wrong?"

"No, love, ye did nothing wrong. But we need t' wait t' finish these explorations until after tonight."

"Why? You claimed me! Why do we have to wait?"

"I have claimed ye, but I have no' marked ye. There's an order t' things, love. And a man can no' call himself a man if he would take a woman he has no' marked. Once ye wear my mark, then ye will be mine t' have, no' before. Though I must say ye made it damned difficult t' stick t' my morals. Do ye no' have anything like this in yer world, love?"

"Yes, we do. We call it marriage. When a man loves a woman and a woman loves him back, they go to a church and a pastor unites them as husband and wife before God and witnesses. That's where they make their commitment. The couple exchange rings to symbolize their love. It's supposed to last forever, but sometimes it doesn't. Marek, we will last forever, won't we?"

"Sometimes it does no' last here either, bu' once ye are mine and ye are marked, we are bound forever, love. I'll never let ye go. I'll be here when ye are sick, hungry, tired, and even if ye get fat and ugly . . . though I hope ye don't. I promise t' take care of ye from this night forward. Ye can count on tha'."

"Marek, you already are taking care of me, but now I will be here for you too. I promise to never let you go. I'll stay by you when you are sick, hungry, tired, and even if ye get fat and ugly too . . . though I also hope you don't! I promise to listen to you and do as you ask . . . so long as you have a good reason." She paused to smile at him. "I love you, Marek McKenzie." She leaned in to kiss him but was interrupted.

"Lacy love, do no' kiss me now," he whispered. "I still have no' recovered from the last kiss and we have t' wait just a little longer."

"I'll never make it!" she grumbled.

"Aye, ye will. I'm goin' down t' request our breakfast. Get dressed and I'll have it on the table when ye get there." And with that he was out the door.

CHAPTER 15

The Marking Ceremony

Jeanette had been fussing over Lacy the entire afternoon. She had insisted that Lacy have a nice hot bath and had brought scented soap and spent an inordinate amount of time on her hair, first blow-drying it, then arranging it so that most of it sat on top of her head with tendrils left loose to curl attractively around her face. Jeanette turned out to be a master with the limited makeup that Lacy had with her. The bruises left on her face were nearly imperceptible. A beautiful gown was brought in for her. It was coral in color with the left side sleeveless and dropping just under her arm, the other side swept up in soft folds over the right shoulder and draped down her back in a waterfall of coral to the waist. It was a floor-length gown that fit Lacy like a glove and seemed to float as she walked. *Stunning* was the word that Jeanette used to describe Lacy when they had finally finished.

Lacy stood before a mirror to survey the effect of Jeanette's work. Her eyes widened as she took in her appearance. "Wow! Jeanette, you do wonderful work! But Marek isn't going to like this at all!"

"What? What do you mean he won't like it!? You're beautiful!"

"Well, that's the point! If he thought my sweats were bad—"

"You are not making any sense, Lacy! You look much lovelier in this than in those sweats!"

"Yes but, Jeanette, you've hidden all my flaws! You've made me look like a goddess! Marek is going to have a cow! You've missed your calling, woman! You should be in cosmetology, not medicine!"

Jeanette's smile spread across her face and erupted into a very contagious laugh. Lacy joined her until Jeanette suddenly stopped her. "Stop laughing, Lacy, I don't want you to start crying next and ruin my makeup job!"

"Why would I cry?"

"I don't know, that's just the way it works. If you laugh too hard, the next thing you know someone's crying!"

She looked so serious that Lacy decided to listen to her. She wanted to ask her about the marking ceremony anyway. To date, no one had answered any of her questions about it. She still didn't know exactly what was going to happen. Everyone just kept saying the same thing. "Well, when you get there, you will have an identical mark placed on you as Marek has on him."

Well, that really narrowed it down! Every time she asked them to explain, they had been interrupted. She was getting so flustered about it that she was ready to strip Marek down to find out just how he was marked! That thought brought a blush to her cheeks as she mentally reviewed every inch of his body that she already knew by heart . . . and imagined the parts she hadn't met yet.

Jeanette was looking straight at Lacy who had been about to ask her something but had stalled before the first word had gotten past her lips. Lacy suddenly looked a little pale, then she turned and looked at the dress in the mirror again and a look of surprised understanding crossed her face. She zeroed in on her left bare shoulder.

"Jeanette! Great stars above us! I'm going to get a mark tonight!"

"Well yeah!" she responded, but it sounded more like she was saying, "Well duh!"

"Jeanette! They are going to tattoo me, aren't they?!"

"Yes, Lacy, what did you think they were going to do?"

"I don't know, I guess I really hadn't thought about it. I have been thinking of it as more like a wedding ceremony! Not a tattooing party!" Her eyes were huge, and her hands were shaking. "Jeanette, I don't want a tattoo! Teachers don't have tattoos! Military wives . . . they have tattoos! Biker's wives . . . yeah, I can see that . . . but a teacher?! Great stars above us!" Lacy sat heavily on the bed, the reality of the situation just beginning to dawn on her.

"You said that before!" Jeanette noticed that Lacy had a little touch of sweat on her brow, and she was wringing her well-manicured hands together. "Lacy, every married woman in this holding has the mark of her husband on her shoulder, just below the collarbone. It's in the same place as her husband's mark. The boys get them as soon as their talent is discovered. It includes their official holding color, a turquoise blue in this case, their family symbol, or crest, and a personal mark indicating the person's trade, or talent . . . something like that. They choose their own personal mark. When they claim a wife, she is marked with their mark. In our world, we exchange rings . . . but you could never tell to whom a woman belongs just by her ring. Here, if another man saw your mark, he would not only know that you are married and unavailable, he would also know to whom you belong."

"But, Jeanette, I have not seen these women's marks . . . so what is the point? They are always hidden beneath their tunics. So technically, a man could accidentally claim a woman, not knowing she was marked! And if she chose not to tell him, he could . . . he might . . . transgress quite a ways into another man's territory before he realized that she was not available. Oh, and what if a woman's man dies and she wants to remarry? How would they change the tattoo?"

"First of all, any man who would touch or kiss a woman would check her for a mark first. And if he was stupid enough not to check, once he finally found it, he would stop whatever he was doing at that point and evacuate the area! It is not something that these people take lightly, Lacy. Once Marek marks you, no one, and I mean no one, will ever do anything to undermine that mark. If they did, they would be killed by your husband quite quickly!"

"But, Jeanette, Marek didn't check my shoulder before he claimed me!"

"Well, actually, I'm quite sure he did, but you were probably asleep. Did you ever fall asleep around him before you met me?"

The look on Lacy's face answered the question before she could verbally respond. Jeanette continued quickly so Lacy wouldn't be able to stew on that thought long.

"Now to answer your next question, if a woman's husband dies and she is claimed by another man, the first mark is not changed or removed, the second husband's mark is applied beside the first. Once a mark is placed on a woman, it is there forever. In this way, her dead husband is remembered respectfully."

"Well, what if a woman is claimed by a man who is abusive and beats his woman? Can she leave him?"

"If it is proven that a man is beating his woman, the laird of the holding will kill that man, releasing the woman from the hold of her mark. These people do not beat their wives or their children because judgment is swift."

"What if a wife beats her husband?"

"Have you noticed the size of these men? They are allowed to tie a woman up and leave her there until she cools down!" Jeanette chuckled at that. "Why are you so worried about this, Lacy? Marek is a very good man. You will not have any of these problems!"

"You'll laugh."

"I will not laugh."

"Yeah, you will, but I guess that's okay because it really is silly."

"Okay, hit me with this hysterical tidbit!"

"I don't want a tattoo!"

"I gathered as much! But why?"

"I heard . . . don't they . . . well, don't they do this in front of everyone?"

"Yes, but everyone doesn't stay the whole time. It takes a while. So everyone will be there for the first part of the ceremony and for the first needle prick. They will probably cheer when the needle first touches you but then they begin the wedding party while you are getting marked. Then when the marksman—I love that—the marksman," she paused, giggled, and then continued. "Anyway, when the marksman finishes your tattoo, everyone will reassemble for the finish of the ceremony and you will be pronounced as Marek's lady. It's very romantic!"

"Yeah, romantic . . . everyone parties while I'm in pain!"

"Lacy, will you relax! It's a smallish tattoo and it will only take a couple of hours to accomplish. Marek has the best marksman hired for the occasion. He'll be fast and efficient!"

"Two hours?! It will take two whole hours? Never mind . . . it's not the pain I'm worried about. Listen, Jeanette, I had stitches where Colter bit me. They took only about forty-five minutes and I passed out within the first ten seconds! As soon as I saw the needle, I got woozy and as soon as the doctor stuck me, I dropped like a rock! I can't do this! There has to be another way! Marek will be so embarrassed if I can't do this! Imagine, a warrior woman who can't stand the sight of a needle!"

It was almost time for the ceremony and Jeanette had walked over to the door to open it for the two of them to make their way downstairs, but she left it open and returned to sit on the bed beside Lacy. She put her arm around her friend and squeezed her a bit.

"Lacy, don't sweat it! I used to be a nurse, remember? I worked the emergency room a couple of times when they were short of people. I watched more guys drop at the sight of a needle than you can imagine! They handle getting their leg nearly ripped off in an accident just fine, but pull out the needle to shoot them with pain medicine and their lights were out in a heartbeat. If you think being a warrior saves anyone from being squeamish about needles, you're dead wrong. I would be willing to bet that there are a lot of men here who didn't make it through their own marking ceremonies completely conscious! Besides, if you keel over, Marek will be there to catch you." She smiled triumphantly.

"Gee, thanks!" Lacy rolled her eyes at Jeanette. "As if it would make any difference at all who caught me when I would be completely unconscious! And then he'll know what a true wuss I am! He'll probably change his mind altogether right then and there!"

"Who will change his mind?" Marek walked unannounced into the little room. He stopped dead in his tracks when he looked at Lacy.

Jeanette saw the look in his eyes and made a hasty retreat. "I'll see you downstairs! Congratulations, you two!"

"What?" Lacy demanded when he just stood there staring at her. During the discussion, she had forgotten how lovely Jeanette had made her look. She looked up at Marek, noticing that he was not wearing the freshly pressed white shirt that he had been wearing the last time she saw him at breakfast. His tan skin and golden brown eyes begged her to touch him. His hair was pulled back into a neat ponytail, and he was wearing a new pair of leathers. Her eyes lingered on the two-by-two-inch tattoo just below the place where his collarbone met his shoulder. She stood and walked toward him, not looking into his eyes but focusing instead on the intricacies of the tattoo. She ran her fingers over it. Slowly, her eyes followed the muscles of his shoulder up his neck, past his strong fine jaw to his lips. They lingered there for a moment and finally sought out his eyes. There was a look there that Lacy could not quite identify. He looked like someone had landed a solid hit to his stomach and he was having difficulty breathing.

"Marek, why are you looking at me like that? Are you all right?"

"Lacy . . ." His voice was a whisper. He cleared his throat nervously. Then he reached up to hold her face in his hand and stroke her chin with his thumb. "Lacy," he said more clearly. "Ye are the most beautiful woman I have ever seen. Every time I think ye could ge' no more lovely, ye manage, somehow, t' do jus' tha'."

"Oh well, you'll have to thank Jeanette for that. She can work miracles! I told her she should go into cosmetology but . . . she . . ." Lacy noticed that Marek wasn't listening. He was staring at her lips. He looked caught in the grip of some great dilemma. "Where is your shirt?"

"I can no' wear it during the ceremony." He answered absently, still staring at her lips. Suddenly, he seemed to pull himself together just a little, but enough to ask her again, "Who will change his mind and abou' wha'?"

"What?" Lacy had gotten lost in the closeness of his lips and the feel of his thumb, which was till stroking her chin lightly and making her legs wobble.

"Ye were tellin' Jeanette that someone would change his mind righ' then and there. Who were ye talking abou'?" When Marek restated the question, he meant it only as a diversion from the need to take her in his arms and kiss her until they were both beyond control. He figured that would have only taken one touch, so he had found a way to distract himself. But when he saw the flush rise in Lacy's face, he knew he had asked a question that was much more important than he had originally thought.

He pressed her, "Lacy, answer me please."

She started to back up, but his arms wrapped quickly around her waist and held her there. Lacy watched as the desire left his eyes and was replaced with determination.

"You!" she said in resignation. He might as well know the truth now rather than in a few minutes in front of an entire crowd.

"I will change my mind abou' what?"

"About marking me!" She raised her voice just a bit, irritation at herself finding its way into the verbalization of the truth.

"No' likely!" He smiled. "But why would ye think I would change my mind abou' markin' ye?"

"You are either going to laugh at me or yell at me, and either one is not going to make me feel better!"

189

He kissed the top of her forehead reassuringly. "I will no' laugh and I will no' yell, so tell me what is troublin' ye, sweetheart."

Lacy looked down then and rested her forehead on his chest. "Marek, when I said that I wanted you, I didn't know what *marking* meant. Jeanette just explained to me that I am to get your tattoo tonight."

He lifted her face up to look into her eyes. "Ye mean, ye did no' understand wha' was goin' t' happen tonight?"

"Well, no . . . I mean, I should have figured it out, but I didn't and everyone was sort of too busy to explain it fully. But I understand now and I can't do this, Marek!"

"Why can ye no' do this, Little Warrior?"

"I bought something for you today. I used the money that some of the people paid me for teaching their children." She pushed away from his arms and turned toward her dresser. She opened a drawer and pulled out a little woven sack with a drawstring. She turned around to bring it back over to him, but he had followed her and she found herself still only inches away from him. She opened the little drawstring to retrieve the gift, but Marek's hand folded over hers.

"Lacy, ye are tryin' to avoid tellin' me. Please tell me why can ye no' do this."

She sighed. "Well, I . . . don't you want to see what I got you?"

"I want t' know wha's botherin' ye! Tell me! I can no' help ye unless ye tell me!"

"I'm . . . Marek, you know I love you, right?"

"Aye!"

"You know I would never leave you . . . you know that, right?"

"Aye! Lacy, get on wi' it please."

She wasn't looking at his face again. She had buried her head in his chest, and Marek wasn't sure whether or not to allow her to hide or make her face him. In the end, he let her stay where she was. And then he waited for her to work up her nerve. She was getting there, he knew, but damn if she wasn't taking her sweet time.

"Okay, Marek, I can't do this tattoo thing!" she blurted out quickly. "There, I said it. I can't do it! It involves needles and I have an aversion to needles. I'd just embarrass you. Everyone would be looking at us and I would pass out, or throw up or something and embarrass you and me! I can't do it, Marek, . . . I mean, maybe I could do this if only you and I were there and maybe if I had some time to get used to the idea, but this is . . . well . . . couldn't we just go with rings? I . . . what a wuss! You think I'm a wuss, don't you?! I don't know why you wouldn't because I think I'm a wuss!"

He didn't say anything for a minute, and Lacy finally worked up the nerve to look up at him. He was smiling down at her.

"Why are you smiling? Marek! This is serious! I can't go out there! If I thought Galen was bad when I was afraid of Thor . . . just think of how bad it will be when your tough little warrior passes out before the needle has even gotten close to her skin! Stop smiling!" She hit his chest lightly to get his attention. He just caught her hand and began to laugh loudly.

"Marek! I knew you'd laugh!" Her face got red, and the scowl she directed at him should have stopped his levity toute de suite! It didn't! Tears welled up in anger and threatened to roll down her cheeks. That was finally what got Marek to sober up!

"Lacy sweetheart, I'm not laughing at you, love! I'm laughin' in relief! I thought ye could no' go through with it because ye did some horrible thing or were in love with someone else too . . . or . . . well, I was no' sure, but I was so relieved when yer reason was only fear of a needle!"

"ONLY?! ONLY FEAR of a needle?! Well, it's not really fear, exactly . . . it's that I can't seem to . . . it makes me feel queasy and then the room starts to spin and then I black out! I can't help it and it happens all the time! I finally stopped giving blood because I couldn't do it without making a fool of myself! Now you want me to do that in front of the entire holding? I won't do it!"

"Giving blood?! Never mind, save tha' explanation for another time." Marek furrowed his brows in thought. "Ye will do it, Lacy. But I think I can help ye do it with dignity. Would tha' help, love?"

"What did you have in mind?"

"Let me handle the details. Jus' give me abou' ten minutes before ye come down, aye?"

"Marek, . . . what are you going to do? I . . ." Lacy paused.

Worry lined the lovely face before him. Marek leaned down and kissed her sweetly on the lips and then whispered in her ear. "Trust me, Little Warrior." He smoothed out the worry lines between her eyes with his thumb and turned to go.

"Marek?" she called before he had taken two steps.

He turned to look back at her. "Aye?"

"Don't you want to see what I got you?"

He smiled and came quickly back to her. "Aye, I would!" He took the pouch from her and opened it. He turned it upside down over his palm and watched a golden ring drop from it. It was made of several strands of gold interwoven into an endless pattern with no starting point and no ending point. The craftsmanship was exquisite. He turned it around and around, looking for the seam that was not perceptible.

"The ring has no beginning and no end. Like our love, Marek. It seems as though I have always loved you and I always will. You have your mark already, so I'm giving you this token to remember the day." She took the ring from his hand and slid it on his left ring finger. This time, Lacy stood up on her tiptoes and kissed him. It was a light sweet kiss that if Marek could have made last forever, he would have.

She pulled back from the kiss and came down from her tiptoes. She smiled up into his handsome face and said, "I trust you, Marek. You won't let me pass out in front of your people."

He smiled at her and turned and left, calling over his shoulder as he went, "Ten minutes, sweetheart. Come down in ten minutes."

Jeanette came up to the room as soon as she saw Marek come downstairs. She hurried into the room. "Well, what happened? Did you tell him?"

"Yes," Lacy beamed. "He said he was going to fix it so I could keep my dignity. I'm wondering if that means he is going to switch from needles to markers!"

Ten minutes flew by. Jeanette went down to make sure everything was ready and smiled up the stairs at Lacy when it was time. Lacy started down. Every eye was raised to see her as she walked nervously down the stairs. Marek stood beside a beautifully covered, very well padded table. There were flowers in vases on the floor at the corners of the table, and there was a tall chair sitting at one end with a stool in front of it. There was also a sheer curtain draped around the back of the table and ribbons hung at the corners and curled in corals, yellows, and shades of orange from the ceiling to the floor. In the center of the front opening of the little curtained room was a table with a little glass duck pond displayed on it. It was the one she had seen on her first day in the holding, only now there were two ducks with their necks entwined, swimming in the middle of the pond. The effect was so beautiful that tears sprang to Lacy's eyes. As she made her way past Jeanette, she heard her whisper, "Stop crying, you'll mess up your makeup."

Even having already seen Lacy, Marek noted that his knees wobbled when she hit that last step and turned to smile at him. The room was silent except for a soft melody coming from the piano in the corner. Lacy noticed that it was one of her students playing the sweet melody. She smiled at the little girl as she watched her concentrate on each note of the music. She approached Marek and took his hand as soon as she was close enough. She thought that if he didn't wrap an arm around her right now, she just might melt into the floor. She shook with nerves.

Marek saw the nerves surfacing in her face and felt the trembling in her hands. He pulled her to his side and wrapped a solid arm around her waist. When the music stopped, he faced the audience.

"From this day on, I claim Lacy DeMark as my lady. She will become, with the finish of the markin' ceremony, Lady Lacy McKenzie. I promise befor' these witnesses tha' I will take care o' her every need, shelter her, and defend her."

Then he turned to Lacy. "Lacy, I love ye. I love the way ye defend the helpless and fight for wha's righ' even when the odds are no' in yer favor. I love ye when ye laugh and when ye cry. I love the way ye are so tough and then so soft all a' the same time. I can no' imagine a life wi' ou' ye in it." When he finished, he took her face in both hands and leaned down to kiss her. If she hadn't known how he felt after his declaration, she would have known by his kiss, his lips pressed tenderly on hers, warm and inviting. He opened his mouth just a little and nipped at her lips in a promise of things to come later.

Lacy caught herself before she let a moan of pleasure escape. But the tightening of her hands on his waist let him know that he was hitting his mark. He pulled back and smiled down at her.

"Is it my turn?" Lacy whispered up to him.

"Aye, if ye wish. But if ye're nervous, it's no' necessary."

Lacy smiled at Marek and took a deep breath. "Marek, I love you too. I love the way you love your holding and take your responsibilities seriously. I love the way you can take on a wounded bear and shrug off the danger . . . though I hope you don't do that again soon. I love that you would give up your wonderful horse just because I fell in love with him. I love that you would throw a challenge to give the woman you love the choice to choose you or not." There was a noticeable murmur among the people after that admission. "And, Marek, more than you will ever know, I love that you came after me when I was in trouble even though you were unsure of my love for you. I am so honored to be your lady."

Now it was Lacy's turn to initiate the kiss. She stood up on her tiptoes, but she needn't have bothered because Marek wrapped his arms around her waist and pulled her up to his level. Her arms were already wrapping around his neck as their lips met once again. For just a minute or so, they forgot where they were. They forgot the ceremony and they forgot their audience as they focused only on each other. But it didn't last long because the crowd broke out into a loud cheer accompanied by applause and the start of a joyous song played on the piano.

Marek let Lacy slide back down to her feet, but she had barely touched the floor when he reached down and swept her off her feet to carry her to the beautiful table behind them. He could feel her body tense when she realized where he was taking her.

"Trust me, sweetheart."

"I do," she responded and immediately relaxed into his arms.

Marek set her down on the table but told her to wait a minute before she leaned back. Then he sat down on the chair at the head of the table and helped Lacy settle herself mostly on the table with only her upper body leaning back in his lap. He leaned down over her as if to get in one more kiss before the marksman began his work. The crowd hooted and clapped.

Lacy was surprised when Marek whispered in her ear instead, "Lacy love, relax yer body completely now. Then look at me while the marksman works.

Keep your hands in my hand, and if ye feel ye're goin' to pass ou', do no' worry. No one will be able t' see yer face, but the marksman and me and neither o' us will be tellin' anyone anything."

"Marek, does every woman stretch ou' on a table for this part?"

"Aye."

"Does every man sit with his woman in his lap?"

"No, love, tha' part is new as of today, but do no' worry abou' it. I'm thinkin' tha' it will no' be the last time it's done! Since a man has t' stay close anyway for the marksman to copy his mark, it seems this might jus' be a verra nice way t' spend the time!" He did kiss her then. After he sat back up, the marksman took his place in front of them. He set out his tools and readied his needle.

"Lacy, look at me, love."

She did as Marek asked, concentrating on his golden brown eyes. She could get lost in those eyes. His fingers tightened on hers in a reassuring squeeze. For one brief moment, Lacy thought she was going to make it through this whole thing without a hitch . . . and then she felt the needle. She was out like a candle in a draft, but Marek held her head facing his middle so no one could see her unconscious face.

It is truly amazing how quickly a tattoo can be applied if you are unconscious during the process. Lacy didn't regain full and continuous consciousness until the marksman had completely finished. She had come to a few times during the event, and each time she looked into Marek's warm eyes, only to feel another prick and be out yet again.

Each time she awoke, she noted that the party had gotten a little rowdier during her nap. Marek would squeeze her hand in reassurance and smile at her just before she'd pass out again. Marek wondered to himself about just how many times a person could pass out in one two-hour period. He caught Jeanette's eye once and motioned her over. She wandered over, and Marek suggested that she take a look at Lacy just to make sure she was doing all right. Jeanette took her vitals and smiled to Marek, letting him know that Lacy was just fine.

When the marksman finally finished and packed up his tools, he shook Marek's hand. Marek pulled him close enough to be able to talk to him above the noise of the party going on around them. "Remember, no' a word abou' the lady's inability to stay awake through ou' the process."

"I have no idea wha' ye're talkin' about, laird!" the man replied.

Marek smiled broadly. "Thank ye, sir!"

"Ye are so welcome, sir! I think I might go get a bite t' eat and a bit o' drink before yer men finish it off."

"Enjoy yerself!"

Marek lifted Lacy up a bit and leaned over her. "Ye need t' wake up, love. It's all finished. Ye need t' greet yer people. Lacy honey, are ye awake?"

She groaned a bit but finally pulled one hand from his grip and reached up to brush the hair from his face. "Hi! Sorry, I couldn't . . . I'm such a wuss!"

"Ye were jus' fine, love. No one knows yer a wuss but me and the marksman and neither o' us will tell a soul. Actually, I rather like tha' ye are no' as tough as ye seem. I like yer soft spots!"

"Mmm, well, you my love are partial." She sat up and swung her legs over the edge of the table.

"Lacy, take yer time. After all tha' we did t' keep yer secret, I would hate for ye t' stand up too fast and keel over now."

"Yeah, me too!" She waited for a moment, taking time to look down at her new mark. It matched Marek's exactly. She started to touch it, but decided against it because it was a little sore and she was afraid she might get queasy again.

As the people began to notice that the marking had finished, they began to gather around the front of the marking table once again. Galen brought her and Marek each a glass of wine and the toasts began. After many well wishes, drinks, and cheers, the people parted to allow Marek and Lacy to approach the banquet table. Marta had saved a plate of food for each of them and had set a small table for them to sit and eat. They sat side by side looking out over the dance floor in the great hall.

Dancing had begun while the marking took place, had paused for the toasts, and was now picking up again. Lacy thought the whole affair was quite lovely. There were flowers and ribbons, and tooling laced through the chandeliers and draped from one to the other. A brilliant sunset lit up the windows, and candles were being lit to compensate for the loss of natural light. It gave the hall a merry and very romantic feel. Lacy reached over, took Marek's hand, and laced her fingers through his.

"It's lovely, Marek."

He leaned over and kissed her warmly. "Aye, it is!"

The party went on into the wee hours, but around one in the morning, Lacy and Marek said their farewells and headed for the stairs. When they reached them, he scooped her up in his arms and carried her up to his room. He managed to turn the handle while still holding her. He was kissing her as they crossed the threshold.

Lacy was so lost in the kiss that she hardly noticed where they were until Marek sat down on the bed with Lacy on his lap. He pulled the pins from her hair and watched as each lock was released to fall to her shoulders. Her beauty took his breath away. He caressed her cheek and felt a jolt through his body when she sighed in contentment.

Her brown eyes moved over his face, noticing everything about it. They came to rest on his lips. She brushed her fingertips over his lower lip. Marek responded by nipping her index finger. He held it gently between his teeth, closed his lips over it, and smirked playfully at Lacy. She giggled back at him, pulled her finger free, and leaned closer to claim his lips with her own.

At last they were alone, they belonged to each other, and Thor was waaaay down in his stall, unable to interrupt! Lacy giggled in delight as Marek pulled her back onto the bed with him. When he pulled her tightly into his arms and kicked off his shoes, she began to sing!

—

9 781450 038553